# A TIME TO LOVE

## TRACY HIGLEY

# FREE NOVELLA

I'd love to give you a free novella!

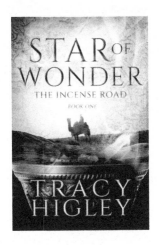

A MAGE, A SOLDIER, AND A PRINCESS,

ON AN EPIC QUEST ACROSS THE SANDS OF ARABIA.

FOLLOWING A STAR, IN SEARCH OF A KING.

Get a FREE ebook when you join "The Caravan" – my affectionate name for those of you traveling through the pages of history and fiction with me.

You'll also receive discounts on books, updates on new releases, and fun history tidbits along the way!

To claim your free book, visit this link:

https://BookHip.com/MCRMCST

## Previously, in *A Time to Seek* and *A Time to Weep*...

Sahara Aldridge, a young Egyptologist in 1922, is working in Egypt alongside Howard Carter, searching for the tomb of Pharaoh Tutankhamun. Sahara's parents, also Egyptologists, were believed to have been lost at sea near Venice when she was fifteen years old, but she has been provided with an education and opportunities by Lord Carnarvon, who also provides the funds for the dig.

Sahara discovers she is able to travel in time, an ability inherited from her parents. She also discovers her parents are still alive, stranded somewhere in time with a younger sister Sahara has never met, because that sister was born in the past. Her parents cannot return to their own time without leaving their second daughter behind, since she cannot travel to her own future.

After an adventure in the ancient Egypt of Tutankhamun's time, Sahara begins to trust fellow time-traveler Jack Moretti, despite his being the nephew of Giada Moretti, whom she suspects caused her parents to flee. She is beginning to learn the rules of time travel, including the inability to go back in time to within eighty years of where you've already been, and the fact that while most time travelers are only Observers, some carry a special ability to change the past, and are called Revisionists.

When the tomb of Tutankhamun is opened, Sahara is shocked to find a message from her father, instructing her to meet her family in ancient Rome, on the day of Emperor Nero's death. To have left her this message, one of them must also be a Revisionist.

Rather than meet them in Rome, however, Sahara wants to find them in Venice, just before they disappeared, and try to prevent their getting stranded in the past. Jack warns her that changing her own past this way can have devastating consequences on her mind. Before she can decide her next action, she realizes Giada is still hunting her, and has sent someone to question Jack about her, and about her family. She decides to go to Rome.

She and Jack travel to Rome and are swept up in the political chaos surrounding Nero, as their attraction to each other mounts. They fight to reach the rendezvous with Sahara's parents in time. Renae, Alexander, and their daughter Persia are also in Rome, making their way to meet Sahara, but after getting into trouble with political dissidents, are forced to escape. Sahara catches only a glimpse of the three of them, before they time-travel elsewhere. In that glimpse, however, Sahara realizes her sister has the ability to stop time, apparently for everyone but the two of them.

In several flashbacks, the history of Giada Moretti and Sahara's parents begins to unfold. The three first met during their initiation into the secret society Tempus Vigilia, when they are sent back to the assassination of Julius Caesar. Thus begins a friendship through college, as they continue to jump back in time together. Both Renae and Giada are clearly in love with Alexander. In one of their college trips, while working on the digsite of Seti I, the tomb discovered by "The Great Belzoni," the three jump back in time to 1155 BC for another adventure. During their escape, Alexander hides a jeweled necklace as a joke, saying Giada can find it later, after they return to their own time—something they all know is impossible. However, when they return to their own time, Alexander is at first missing, and Giada indeed finds the necklace. It becomes clear that Alexander is a Revisionist, able to change the past.

Safely back in the Rome of 1922, Sahara and Jack encounter Reuben, the man sent by Giada to inquire after Jack. It is revealed that Giada has been unscrupulously using Revisionists over many years, ever since that first college find of the necklace, to grow rich. She is clearly searching for Sahara, her parents, and even her sister, to exploit them for her own benefit.

Furious at this information, Sahara announces that she will confront Giada herself.

Jack is forced to admit the secret he's still been keeping: that he is actually a traveler from the year 2002, come back in time to 1922 to meet Sahara. The betrayal devastates Sahara, who pushes Jack away, even as she is beginning to love him.

With no more information about where to intersect her parents in the past, she decides again to go to Venice, to try to find them in the nineteenth century, where they went to meet Belzoni. Despite her mistrust and anger, Jack insists on joining her, as they head to Venice to continue the search.

# PROLOGUE

We are here again, you and I.

At the start of this, the final stretch of our journey through the past.

Not all memories are good. But then, as I have learned, not all memories are true, either.

One must unearth the treasures of memory, out of the sands of time. Sift away the inconsequential. Brush off the gritty, clinging falseness.

But even then—even then, there is deciphering, interpreting, assigning meaning.

And in all these actions, we have no guarantee that we do not err.

So yes, the past. Fragmentary and illusive, perhaps unknowable as it truly happened.

And the future, also unknowable.

For a woman who craves answers, *unknowable* presents a problem.

But perhaps the problem is, in itself, a type of answer. To come face-to-face with one's own insufficiency. To realize that

1

the Story being told—both my own and the greater Story in which every person plays a role—are not of my own making. Are not of my own *knowing.*

Can there be freedom in this?

Yes.

I have seen too much of the history of the world, of the people of the world, of the drama of the world, to believe in randomness or meaninglessness.

Even in this, my story, you will see. All the threads weave together. All the broken fragments fit. All the story-bits have a purpose. Even if we cannot always know.

But I am getting ahead of myself.

First, we must finish the story.

# CHAPTER ONE

*V*enice, City of Water.

Jack and I surveyed the interior of the Santa Lucia Train Station, a squat building built like a tunnel, with most of the crowds moving to our right.

I pointed to the east. "City is that way, I believe."

Jack nodded and followed, uncharacteristically silent.

But after his revelation last night, our usual banter would have been ill-timed.

*The year 2002. That's where I came from.*

Jack's announcement, given over coffee as though nothing more than a bit of interesting backstory, rocked me.

But that number—*2002*—it lodged in my mind like a pebble. A constant, painful pressure I was trying to ignore.

Better to focus on our goal here. Find traces of my parents in the early 1800s, when they'd come to Venice for "the Great Belzoni." Giovanni Battista Belzoni, circus strongman and discoverer of Egyptian tombs, was somehow connected to their disappearance, though I'd yet to figure out how.

Our arrival in Venice coincided with the arrival of rain, and in a repeat of our entrance into Rome a few days ago, we stored our luggage and emerged from the station into a gray mist.

Across a paved lot, the Grande Canal snaked in both directions, a greenish highway through the tiny city. A lineup of *vaporetti* idled in the canal, waiting to ferry passengers across. On the other side, clusters of gondolas docked in front of the green-patina dome of a church. To our left, a footbridge spanned the waterway. The city smelled of water and fish, not unpleasant.

"Shall we grab a taxi?" Jack searched along the canal.

I squinted up at him. "For having Italian roots, you don't know much about Venice. No automobiles allowed. The Grande Canal winds through the city, with lots of smaller canals intersecting. That's their road system." I pointed to a *vaporetto*. "There's our taxi."

Minutes later, we mingled with a dozen other travelers across the canal in Santa Croce, one of Venice's six districts.

"I'm assuming you'll want to buy a map?" Jack's half-smile seemed an attempt at camaraderie.

I scanned the close-fitting streets. "We need more than a map. A guidebook, if we're going to figure out how and where to search for my family, more than a hundred years in the past."

We soon stumbled across a tourist shop selling guides, then ducked into a tiny cafe nearby, book in hand.

I skirted tables to an iron-legged one in the back and started skimming the contents of our purchase.

Jack joined me minutes later with a tray of Italian chocolate brioche and two steaming cappuccinos.

I breathed in the scent of coffee and flashed him a look of gratitude. I'd eaten little in the past two days, and Jack knew my fondness for pastry.

"Well?" He sank into a chair beside me, too close. "Figure anything out yet?"

"It's been three minutes."

"Right. What's taking so long?"

I sighed and looked away. Perhaps we *would* resume our

light-hearted relationship, despite the eighty-year age difference and the impossibility of anything serious between us.

If Jack wanted casual, what else was there?

"I guess hunger slowed me down." I reached for the brioche and took a hearty bite. But the flaky layers tasted like dust.

Jack let me study the guidebook in silence, though his hand on the tabletop strayed uncomfortably close to mine on several occasions.

By the time I drained my cup of cappuccino and reduced the brioche to crumbs, I had a plan.

"Here." I pointed to the map in the guidebook's flyleaf. "The next district over, San Polo."

Jack leaned over the book, his head brushing my cheek.

I pulled back and tapped a tiny square. "Where it says *Campo dei Frari*, that's where we're headed. To the *Archivio di Stato di Venezia*."

"My Italian's pretty rudimentary, but I guess that's the State Archives?"

"Right. The book says they established it in 1815. It's our best shot of finding records of my family here during that time. And of Giovanni Belzoni."

"So do we ride a gondola over there, or what?"

"We're not tourists, Jack. We're researchers."

"Got it. So no gondola at all?"

"We'll see." I wiped my mouth with a napkin and stood. "But the State Archives are about a half-kilometer away. I think we can walk it."

"Fine, but if you think I came all the way to Venice to skip seeing the sights…"

"Understood. But first, we research."

Using the map in the front of the book, it took only twenty minutes to navigate to the *Campo dei Frari*.

Jack kept to my heels the entire time, giving me a chance to think, to reorient myself to the new reality.

I had seen my parents. And my sister. Truly *seen* them. They lived. Persia existed.

And then I lost them once again, watched them disappear in a strange, time-frozen moment I did not understand, when my sister and I locked eyes and then were snatched apart.

And my parents... even from that briefest of glances, I could see they had aged. So it would seem the same seventeen years had passed for them. I hadn't intersected them somewhere in their past. But of course, Persia's existence and her age told me that.

I tried once more to push away the other overwhelming new piece of information.

Jack. From the Philadelphia of 2002, not 1922.

Perhaps in another fifty years, as a hunched-back woman in her eighties, I could peek in on baby Jack in his nursery. But that would be the closest we could come to a life together.

All the more reason this Venetian search for my parents *must* yield results. I clung to this slim chance to find them, before Jack returned to his own time and left me utterly alone.

The *Archivio di Stato* began as a Franciscan monastery, according to the book, and the pinkish stone and three-sided courtyard lined with stone arches did not disappoint. We passed under various sculptures of winged angels, long-bearded saints, and monks with kind faces and extended hands. Hopefully, those inside would be as welcoming.

I approached a spectacled woman typing at a front desk.

She continued her key-pounding for a few moments, then widened her eyes to peer over her glasses without lifting her head.

"*Ciao.*" I tried for a friendly smile. "I—we—were hoping to examine some archives from the early 1800s. I'm looking for records of my family whom I believed—"

"*Parli Italiano?*"

"No. No, I'm sorry. English only." Well, also Arabic, but that seemed of little help.

She sighed, a deep and affected huff of frustration, then pushed away from her desk, held up a finger and disappeared into a windowless office to our right.

Moments later she reemerged, a diminutive man trailing. "Signor De Luca," she said, then reclaimed her seat to resume attacking the typewriter keys.

He squinted, rubbed at a full mustache, and tilted his head. "Yes? You need?"

I tried again. "I'm looking for records of my family. I believed they lived here in the early 1800s."

"Ah, yes, of course." He held out a hand, heavy with rings. "Your application form?"

I glanced at Jack and bit my lip. "We don't have an application. We came—unexpectedly."

"No application?"

"No."

Jack nudged around me. "We're on our honeymoon in your wonderful city, actually." He gave the man a conspiratorial grin. "And my bride's just discovered she has Venetian ancestors." He wrapped an arm around me. "It would be the highlight of our trip to have a few minutes to search them out."

Signor De Luca's pencil-thin eyebrows lifted into tiny points of horror. "'Search them out'? But no, no, this is not possible. You must make request, fill out form, wait in Study Room for archivist to bring you records."

Despite my best intentions, my eyes welled with tears. Another delay, when I was perhaps so close. I dared hope that even by the end of today, I would walk nineteenth century canals of Venice with my parents and sister.

The man's glance flicked to me. A note of surprise crossed his face.

"Oh, but *signora,* you must not cry." His hands fluttered at his chest. "No, we cannot have the tears."

I breathed and blinked, but only succeeded in spilling the tears down my cheeks.

Beside me, Jack shook his head. "I'm so sorry, darling. I know how much it meant to you—"

"Come, come. *Prego.*" De Luca extended a hand. "Today is

quiet. You wait in the Study Room. Tell Allesandro what you need."

Jack's arm, still around my waist, hugged me to him and then released.

We trotted after the man into the Study Room, passing under an enormous doorway into a cavernous and silent corridor of a room, the ribbed-vault ceiling in the Gothic style looming far above. Massive stone columns lined the center, with rickety wooden tables pushed against both sides.

"Allesandro!" Our guide waved a younger man over. "You must help *signora* find her family."

Allesandro glanced between us. "She has no application?"

De Luca beamed a beneficent smile over me and winked at Jack. "Today we do this for love, eh?"

I clutched his hand. "*Gracias, Signor. Gracias.*"

He disappeared, and I gave Allesandro all the information I had, while he scribbled with a blunt pencil in a palm-sized note-book. My "ancestors," I told him, Renae and Alexander Aldridge, were most likely residing in Venice around 1814, with a daughter born to them at the time, whose name I believed to be Persia.

He held out the notebook for me to check his spelling, which was surprisingly accurate.

"I know it's not much to work with. They may have been associated with Giovanni Battista Belzoni."

Allesandro's lips parted. "The Great Belzoni?"

"Yes! You know of him?"

"But of course." He bowed. "You will wait. I will find them."

Jack and I wandered the Study Room while we waited, examining the architecture and the more general public records in shelves along the walls.

Toward the back of our tour, Jack intertwined his fingers into mine.

He shrugged at my expression. "Just playing the part of honeymooners. Wouldn't want them to get suspicious."

I kept my hand in his. So help me, he was making it difficult to keep my distance.

Minutes ticked into an hour, and still no Allesandro.

When he finally reentered the Study Room, he wore the expression of a doctor bringing bad news to a waiting family.

He crossed to where we stood beside one of the scratched wooden tables, then shook his head.

"Nothing, *signora*. I have found nothing of these Aldridges. No birth records, no death records. All of last century I searched." He tut-tutted as though the missing information were an errant child. "Perhaps records have gone astray." He lifted sad eyes. "Or perhaps they were never here."

I inhaled against my last chance slipping away. What did I know of their time here? Only my mother's journal page, found crumpled in the back of a drawer by my friend, Eve. A page which mentioned traveling to see Belzoni, but not having *seen* him. Perhaps whatever happened to rip them from my life happened before they ever reached Venice.

"And Belzoni?" I glanced toward the door of the Study Room. I would love to search those records myself. "You know when he was here?"

"Yes, yes. Only a short time, after he came here from Padua. In 1814, then leaving in 1815 for Egypt, to begin his stupendous work there."

*Stupendous.* Or "destructive," as my mother had called it.

Allesandro circled the two of us and extended a hand toward the doorway, a clear signal. "You have my hardest effort, *signora*, searching for your family in all the years around Belzoni's time here in Venice. But I have nothing."

Jack pressed a hand against the small of my back to guide me toward the exit.

I arched away from his hand and held my ground. One could always ask more questions.

"What about other writings? Not just birth and death records, but perhaps academic works? Might there be mention—"

9

But Allesandro was smiling and shaking his head. "Ah, *signora,* that would take perhaps weeks of research. And with no application..."

"Right."

Too bad I couldn't travel back to a few months ago and send this guy an application. Though I suspected without the credentials of a university behind me, even an application would yield little.

"Come on, Sahara." Jack's words were quiet. Kind. "Let's leave this man to his work."

Another closed door.

This time, I held the tears at bay. Crying was as pointless a reaction as adding a few drops of water to the city's canals.

# CHAPTER TWO

*December 12, 1922*
*Venice, Italy*

$\mathcal{I}$ hadn't the heart for tourism, but Jack insisted we see the major landmarks of Venice before heading back to the Valley of the Kings, and I was too soul-weary to object. Even though by now I assumed Howard was back from his supply-gathering trip to Cairo and ready to re-open the tomb and begin the work.

Jack confiscated the guidebook, and soon had us crossing canals over iron-latticed bridges, wandering tiny cobblestoned alleys, and gazing into shop windows filled with riotous colors of turquoise and apricot, berry-red and honey-gold, in dizzying displays of candies, jewelry, and masks.

I took in the sights with a silent numbness, unable to think past the dead end of research we'd hit in the State Archives. I felt adrift, like one of the thousand little boats bobbing in the canals, but loosed from my mooring, with no place to connect.

"It says here there are four hundred bridges in this little town." Jack expertly stepped around a puddle while focusing on the book. "And two thousand alleys."

"Hmm. Do you think my parents will leave me another clue somewhere?"

Jack stopped and turned a determined expression on me. "No talk of parents yet. We're going to see a few sights, have a nice morning, then sit down for some sandwiches at a cafe, and I promise we will figure it out. You need a break."

"But if they weren't ever here in—"

"Sahara." His fingers interlaced mine again. "You need a break."

I blew out a breath and eyed a nearby pastry shop. "Fine."

The not-to-be-missed sights of Venice turned out to include the famed Rialto Bridge, its ashy-white stone spanning the Grande Canal and offering swoon-worthy views down the canal. Pastel buildings lined either side, decaying elegantly into the greenish water. A hint of music floated to us from the outdoor seating of restaurants, and gondolas ferried tourists back and forth under our feet. An incredibly romantic spot.

The perfect place for Jack's fictional honeymoon, in fact.

"You okay?" Jack studied my face. "You seem a bit flushed."

"Just tired."

"Let's take a *vaporetti* to St. Mark's Square, rather than walk."

We descended from the bridge, waited minutes for the next water-taxi, and then curved around the San Marco district to its far side, to the most famous square of Venice.

Jack directed me from the *vaporetti* at the first San Marco stop, before we'd reached the actual square, but already the famous Campanile, the brick-and-white bell tower, loomed above us.

We finally breached the line of shops at the back of the piazza, to the opulent gold of the Byzantine St. Mark's Basilica across the square, with the lacy columns of the Doge's Palace to its right.

Jack exhaled in surprise. "I've seen so many pictures, and in movies, of course, but..." His words were a whisper, more to himself than to me.

"Pictures and... movies?"

"Sorry, photographs. And... talking pictures? We call them 'movies.'"

I broke from him and descended the steps. No more talk of the future for me.

Thus far, I'd diligently avoided all conversation about the year 2002, or any years between his time and mine. Jack told me yesterday, in all his previous trips to the past, the people he'd encountered felt unreal to him, like characters in a book. In thinking of *myself* as part of Jack's past, a creepy sense of my own unreality wormed through me. Nothing more than a fiction, an actress unaware of the part she played, or even of the existence of the story.

Not to mention, *we call them movies.* Another reminder that Jack's "we" did not include me.

A tour of the Basilica ensued, then a tour of the Doge's Palace —soon to be made a museum—and then we emerged to a flock of pigeons descending to the tawny stones of the piazza, like a cloud of feathery smoke. "More pigeons here than people," Jack informed me, still glued to the guidebook.

"Great. How about coffee? Is there coffee here?"

Jack eyed me sideways. "Someone's a little grouchy."

"Coffee."

"Right." He pointed across the square. "There's a famous cafe at that corner, I think. The Caffé Florian—been here since the early 1700s. The book says Casanova hung out there."

"Fantastic."

We crossed the square, Jack traded a few coins for a news-paper—*The New York Times,* I noted—and we entered the warm ambiance of the Caffé Florian.

I sank into a red-velvet couch with a grateful sigh and surveyed the gold-scrollwork mirrors and art pieces by famed Venetians.

An odd chill passed across my body, raising the hair on my arms. Something like a memory. But not a memory that was my own. Strange.

While we waited for coffee and sandwiches, and Jack perused

the paper, I idly watched couples at tables, some all darting eyes and guidebooks and cameras, and others with the casual repose of locals.

"So, what is happening in New York?"

Jack lowered the paper, enough for me to see his eyes and his furrowed brow.

I straightened. "What is it?"

New York seemed a world away from the soft music and warm lights of the cafe. What could be so concerning?

"It's not New York." He folded a sharp crease down the center of the paper, then turned it for me to read the headline at the top—*Egyptian Treasures Threatened by Flood—Rain Clouds Cause Panic Among Archaeologists at Open Tomb of Tutunk-Hamen.*

"What? No!" I grabbed the paper.

Ignoring the horrible spelling of the boy-king's name in the headline, I skimmed through the article, then returned to the top and read it again.

Apparently, priceless antiquities would be destroyed by tomorrow morning, if a flood raged through the Valley, and the water entered the tomb.

"'*If*,' it says." I jabbed a finger at the sentence. "*If* a flood comes. Floods are rare in the Valley." I laid the paper on the table and rubbed my forehead. "But the newspapers wouldn't report such a thing, if it weren't imminent, right?"

"They—"

"Oh, wait." I glanced into his eyes. "You're not actually a reporter, are you? So you wouldn't know."

The words emerged more hostile and sarcastic than I intended, but I didn't pull them back.

He blinked once and looked away, mouth turned downward.

The arrival of the pastrami sandwiches and strong coffee saved us, and I took a quick gulp, burning my mouth.

"We need to get back there. I need to help."

The clipped statement didn't do justice to the heaviness in my chest. I was failing everywhere—in finding my family connection and building my future as part of the dig team.

Jack bit into his sandwich and chewed slowly. "There's no way you can get back to Luxor before tomorrow morning. Not in 1922, anyway."

I held up a flat hand. *Don't tell me more.* Was it possible to reach Egypt from northern Italy in less than a day in 2002? Perhaps by aeroplane, but only a military man would have access to that kind of transportation. Was Jack in the U.S. Army?

Jack shrugged. "I think we resume our trip as planned. You'll help in whatever way possible when we get back."

I drummed my fingers against the tabletop. "I suppose that's all I can do."

"So, let's talk about your parents."

*Yes, let's ignore my jab about all your lies.*

"You asked me this morning if I thought your parents would leave another clue for you somewhere. I'd say *yes*, it seems likely. But can you think of where—or when—it might be?"

I studied an art canvas across the wall, the robin's egg blue and olive green blurring before my unfocused eyes. "Why Belzoni? Perhaps that's the question to ask. Why did they come here to Venice, or intend to come here, to meet him?"

"What was it she said? Your mother, the journal?"

*"We hope, of course, to intercept Belzoni before his impressive, yet destructive, work begins. Though Alexander is still fighting me on whether we will try to change Belzoni's methods or subvert him entirely."*

I ignored the flash of sympathy in Jack's eyes at my recitation. Was it pitiable that I'd memorized each word? The words were all I had.

"So they wanted to somehow stop Belzoni from what he was about to do. Why?"

I shrugged. "I can only guess they wanted to stop his discoveries in Egypt."

"Or perhaps one in particular? You said he discovered Seti I, right? The tomb where we spent the night together?" A little smirk accompanied the words.

Why did he have to add "together"? It flavored the whole

disaster of that night with a tinge of romance. He was always doing that—trying to make our relationship into more than it could be.

"Yes. Seti is Belzoni's most famous discovery."

"Could your parents have wanted to keep the Seti tomb a secret?"

"I don't know. There is also my father's message in Tut-ankh-amun's tomb, warning me about Giada Moretti. So they knew your aunt was a danger to them, and maybe to me. Did they discover her targeting them *after* they came to Venice? Or was the threat part of the reason they came?"

I flexed my shoulders at the unanswerable questions. They seemed to be multiplying rather than yielding answers. I peered at Jack. Were there still more answers inside of him? Answers he was unwilling to give?

"What about the things that red-haired man in Rome—Rueben—said about Giada? About her history of stealing from the past?"

Jack raked a hand through his hair. "I haven't stopped thinking about that. I feel like a fool, really. I've lived most of my life on privileges paid for with that money, never questioning her business practices."

"She wasn't born into money, then?"

"Ha! Far from it! My grandparents were poor, and my parents struggled to pay bills, even before my mother's depression and my father's downward spiral into drinking. No, Giada prided herself on being a self-made woman. She made her first big find in her mid-twenties."

"But Reuben said she was in college when it started."

"Yes, true, I heard those stories. But she found something that ended up in a museum—nothing she cashed in for herself."

"What did she find?"

Jack rubbed at his jawline and studied the table. "There were so many stories when I was growing up. They were like her version of a bedtime story—entertaining me with all her discoveries and the colorful characters from history to whom they belonged. But the earliest of them?" He closed his eyes.

I waited, letting the memories surface.

"I can think of one story, that seems to have been during her college years. She was on a dig, I believe, with a university. But she ended up in the ancient past. Egypt. And got embroiled in some kind of conspiracy."

I sat up. "What kind of conspiracy?" Juicy ancient stories were easy to remember and to place in a specific time period.

His forehead crinkled in concentration. "Something about a harem? That's not much, I know—"

"The Harem Conspiracy!" I slapped the table.

Jack started laughing. Quietly at first, then drawing the attention of the afternoon crowd now filling the cafe.

"What?" I felt myself blushing.

"Of course, there was a 'harem conspiracy.' And of course you know exactly what I'm talking about. Only Sahara Aldridge could take two simple words and pinpoint a date out of them, three thousand years in the past."

"Don't be ridiculous, Jack. There are at least a hundred other scholars who could do the same."

He shook his head. "Okay, then. You are one in a hundred. So who were these harem women, and what were they conspiring about?"

But my mind raced ahead. "You said she got embroiled in it? So that would place her there, at the time of the attack..."

"What attack? But yes, she was involved. In fact, now that you mention it, that story had some kind of grisly murder in it. She liked those tales." He grimaced, as if only now seeing the oddity of growing up on such "bedtime stories."

"Ramesses III—"

"Yes! Yes, Ramesses! I always thought that was a cool name, that's why I chose it when I was—trying to hide from you—in Egypt."

*When you were lying to me, you mean.*

"So what did this Ramesses guy do?"

I waved away the question. "Long story, not important right now. The important thing is, if it was the Harem Conspiracy and Ramesses III when Giada got her start in looting, then we know when and where."

"Does Belzoni connect, though? Did he discover the Ramesses III tomb?"

"No." I sat backward. "That tomb's been stripped since antiquity. And I don't think he worked there."

We fell silent. Another dead end?

The cafe continued to fill, the conversation building to a loud hum. Did we look like a couple having an argument, both of us in our own thoughts, eyes averted from each other?

"But you said she was on a digsite in this story?"

Jack nodded. "Yes, she was there with her school, I think. And then went back in time to Ramesses."

"She wouldn't have been on a dig at KV11—Ramesses III's tomb—I don't think. The wall paintings in Ramesses' tomb are still being studied, but nothing to dig there. Can you remember anything about the digsite, the work there?"

He returned to eyes closed, and I returned to waiting.

"I feel like I asked her about the mummy—I was very interested in mummies in my boyhood—and she told me it wasn't there. That it was found somewhere else, decapitated..." His eyes widened.

I nodded, smiling. "If you're about to ask if it could have been found in the royal cache at TT320, the answer is most likely *yes*."

"Okay, I need a recap on that history lesson."

"Back in 1075 BC, they moved a bunch of mummies and grave goods to what we now call the Royal Cache, numbered as TT320, to hide them from looters. It didn't work forever, since that's the cache a couple of brothers looted for years, starting around 1870, until they were caught."

"Right. The guys who found it after their goat fell down a shaft. But if a ton of mummies were moved to that cache, how does it help us?"

"Well, not a ton. About fifty. But you've got one extra detail—a detail that fits all the puzzle pieces."

He grinned. "You're welcome."

I rolled my eyes. "Don't you even want to hear—"

"Spill it!"

"A mummy moved to a different location, and decapitated. It was Seti I. She was working at the digsite of Seti I."

I could practically see the gears whirring in Jack's head.

He sat forward, hands clasped on the table. "So, she was working at the Seti tomb—Belzoni's tomb, the one he discovered. Your parents went back to stop him from discovering it—"

"If they were trying to stop Belzoni from discovering Seti, it must have been to stop Giada from working at that digsite later, when she went back to the Harem Conspiracy. They figured if they could keep Belzoni from finding the tomb, she'd never go there, and never get started looting."

He pounded the table with one fist. "That must be it! But," his shoulders dropped. "Why so complicated a plan? Why come here to Venice, to stop Belzoni? Why not simply go back to the Ramesses III time and intersect Giada there, to stop her?"

"Maybe they'd already been there. Or at least too close to that date. If so, the only way to stop her was to keep her away from Ramesses III completely. And the only way to do that was to keep her from her digsite project on Seti I."

I was ready to dance a jig in the middle of the cafe, but Jack gave me only a slow and thoughtful nod.

I did some quick mental math, then gasped at the answer. The numbers lent an air of destiny to all of this.

"Jack, I've been to 1458 BC to see Hatshepsut's Mortuary Temple, been to 1325 to see Tut-ankh-amun's tomb, and been to 1075 inside Seti's tomb on the day they moved his mummy. Ramesses III's Harem Conspiracy was in 1155 BC." I paused to let him feel the ramifications.

He shrugged, obviously missing my point.

"Don't you see, Jack? The Harem Conspiracy happened exactly eighty years before my trip back inside Seti's tomb. This means we can *do* something! We can go directly back to Ramesses III and stop Giada ourselves! Well, at least I can. Have you been near 1155 BC?"

He rubbed at his eyes. "No. Never."

I grabbed his hand and squeezed.

He returned the grip, almost desperately, gratefully.

We sat in silence for a moment, but then Jack's expression crumpled.

"Sahara, there's something you're missing."

I steeled myself. More lies coming to light?

"If we do this... if we go back to stop Giada during the Harem Conspiracy in 1155 while she is still young? It could destroy us both."

# CHAPTER THREE

*December 23, 1974*
*Philadelphia, Pennsylvania*

The stately *gong* of the doorbell of her Society Hill mansion surprised Giada.

She glanced away from the half-packed suitcase splayed across her sumptuous bed to check her watch.

Who would make an unannounced visit at nine in the evening, and so close to Christmas?

Not that Christmas traditions meant much in this house. In fact, by the time the holiday arrived, she and Colin would be in Spain.

"You expecting someone?" Colin's voice, pitched low and suspicious, drifted from the top of the winding stairs that led to the entrance hall.

"No."

Colin moved into her Georgian mansion in the ritzy section of the city six weeks ago, giving her a feeling of added security. Even with a bevy of occasional staff on call—housecleaners, gardeners, handymen—the hundred-year-old house felt eerie on lonely nights.

Despite his darkly striking good looks and almost sensual way of moving through the world, Colin had a violent streak she admired, though she would never admit it. He knew how to handle danger.

She could barely hear him heading down, his footfalls nearly silent on the thick plush of poppy-red carpet treads.

Giada slipped from the master suite, to the head of the gleaming wood staircase, and peered over.

She couldn't see the grand ivory-paneled front door from her perch, but she heard the soft sweep of it, as Colin pulled it open to their visitor.

"I'm here to see Miss Moretti." A feeble and thin male voice.

"She's not expecting anyone."

"I have a business proposal for her."

Giada's jaw tensed. Business? This late at night, and at her home? Why hadn't he called to make an appointment with her secretary? Requested a meeting at the Moretti Foundation's downtown office where she spent the days she wasn't traveling?

"Then you should call her office."

She half-smiled. Colin sounded more like bodyguard then boyfriend. Good man.

"She'll want to hear this privately, I'm quite sure."

The tension returned, this time to her neck and shoulders.

Her foundation remained beyond reproach, providing a charitable cover for her more clandestine activities. The money for her lavish lifestyle was purported to have come from an inheritance. Only she, and now Colin, knew it flowed from a stream of black-market antiquities sales, rather than an early windfall.

A stream that was running dry, hence the needed trip to Spain.

"As I said," Colin's voice took on a gravelly tone, "call her office."

"You're the paramour, I take it? Her young man? With that Irish *brogue*." The stranger leaned on the last word, rolling the R, in a parody of an accent.

"You have me at a disadvantage, Mr...?" Colin's scornful sarcasm bled through his polite question.

Giada circled the banister, her hand skimming the polished walnut, and headed down to the entrance hall.

"El-Rassul. My name is Ahmed Abd el-Rassul."

The name drew her up short, her hand suddenly slick on the rail.

But it couldn't be him, could it? Not here, in what would be his future.

"Well, Mr. el-Rassul, as I said—"

"I've got it, Colin." Giada recovered, sailed down to the front hall, and pasted on a smile for the visitor.

Framed in the doorway, the man seemed very tall, but advanced age had stooped his shoulders. His steel-gray beard glowed against the deep bronze of his skin and hung to the middle of his chest. He wore the rounded *taqiyah* skullcap of a devout Muslim, paired with a shabby black suit.

"What can I do for you, sir?"

"Ah, Miss Moretti. I believe the two of us should speak. Alone."

Colin opened the door wide enough for the man to enter, but huffed a laugh from deep in his chest. "Not a chance."

El-Rassul stepped over the threshold. "Such nervousness over an old man?" He waved a hand at his aging body. "What harm could I be?"

Giada faced him down, folded her arms. "As I said, sir, what can I do for you?"

"I believe we can help each other, miss." He glanced at Colin, then shrugged. "I assume your beau is well-aware of your business dealings. Since you picked him up in Ireland, after your amazing find of the ninth-century Viking silver hoard in that boggy crannog."

She straightened. "You've done your homework, I see. But why would I possibly—"

"Because I, for one, don't believe what the magazines and papers report about your 'sixth sense' for what digs to fund.

Only twenty-five years old, and yet such a knack for finding just the right spot to dig, where something miraculous will be discovered." He smiled, but it was all teeth, like a predator. "Miraculous. And might I say, *lucrative.*"

"The Moretti Foundation is a non-profit—"

"Oh, of course, of course." He waved a hand again, dismissing her defensive comment. "Yes, so much good work done by your foundation. So much money given to the work of archaeology. And yet, it is circular, is it not?" He peered at her from under bushy salt-and-pepper eyebrows. "The work that is funded in turn yields the money behind the scenes to fund more work?" He spun a finger in the air. "Round and round it goes, and Miss Moretti only gets richer and richer as she gains fame as a great philanthropist."

"Listen, mister," Colin rounded on him, one hand on his chest, "I don't know what you're implying—"

"Oh, I think Miss Moretti knows." He smirked at Giada. "I think she knows exactly what I'm implying. About her ability to somehow *know* just where to dig. As if she had... prior knowledge."

Giada's heart tripped over a beat and her fingers went cold.

"Shall we sit in the parlor, Mr. el-Rassul?" She waved a shaky hand toward the spacious room to her left.

She followed the old man into the parlor, ignoring the daggers in Colin's eyes.

"If you've an interest in archaeology, sir, then I'm certain you're aware of the coincidence of your name?"

Mr. el-Rassul lowered his stooped frame to the ivory sofa, somewhat painfully it would appear.

"Not a coincidence, my girl. Not at all. We have something in common, you and I. The Ahmed Abd el-Rassul you know of—he was my grandfather."

Giada sat in a floral tapestried wing chair opposite the man and tightened her fingers into the soft upholstery. "Fascinating."

Colin leaned against the doorframe, arms crossed and face steely.

"But I'm not sure why that gives us something in common."

"Because just as my family profited from years of antiquities never catalogued or documented, well, all this—" he swirled a hand again to indicate the parlor, the entire mansion—"all of this has been similarly purchased."

"What's he talking about, Giada?" Colin's eyes didn't stray from the old man.

Colin was well-aware of where the money came from. So she answered the question he was truly asking.

"Mr. el-Rassul's grandfather, and namesake apparently," she nodded toward the old man, "was one of two brothers who stumbled upon a magnificent royal cache of mummies and grave goods in Egypt, when their goat fell down a shaft into what is now known as TT320."

At this, the old man chuckled, as though he had knowledge she didn't.

"Rather than report their find to the Department of Egyptian Antiquities where the goods could be removed properly and teach us much of ancient Egypt, the brothers systematically looted the cache for a decade, selling off pieces to collectors and getting rich in the process."

She bowed her head toward el-Rassul. "I congratulate you on the wealth of your family, gained at the expense of your people."

"Ha!" He leaned back on the sofa, then struggled through a fit of coughing, as though the effort to laugh taxed him. He pulled a thin, cylindrical pipe from his pocket, along with a lighter. "You don't mind if I smoke?"

She flicked her wrist vaguely.

He lit the *medwakh* pipe, and the acrid scent of the traditional *dokha* tobacco drifted to her.

It was a smell that carried her back to Egypt, to her university days. Back when she and Alexander and Renae were the closest of friends, before everything went wrong.

He took a drag on the pipe, then coughed again.

"That stuff will kill you, you know."

He shrugged. "Perhaps. But I will die a happy old man. And that is where you come in, Miss Moretti."

So now they were getting down to it. Was he here to blackmail her? But what proof could he possibly have?

"I'm not sure what you think you know—"

"I know you have the power to change history. That's what I know."

It was her turn to rock backward in her chair.

"What?"

"Ah, I see my words have found their mark. That paleness of face, that slight tremble in your voice. You betray yourself my dear."

"Alright, that's enough." Colin pushed away from the doorframe and advanced on the old man.

But el-Rassul held up an imperious hand, not taking his eyes from Giada. "Does he know? Does he know how you do it? All those marvelous *discoveries?*"

Giada chewed her lip. Colin knew everything, of course. She couldn't do it without him, in fact. But how could this man know of her strategy...

Understanding struck like lightning.

"Your grandfather was—was—"

"Was like you. Yes. A traveler through time."

Giada exhaled and sagged against her seat. "And the goat story?"

"All a fabrication, of course. My grandfather, and his brother Mohammed, they had gone for a bit of an ancient holiday, to see some of the great temples and tombs in their glory. Imagine their surprise at being conscripted to be part of a secret relocation project, moving mummies and grave goods to a royal cache to protect them from tomb raiders."

"Ironic, since they returned to raid the cache themselves."

He chuckled, then blew a puff of gray smoke. "Yes, ironic." His smile faded. "But perhaps not so fortunate as you seem to believe. The story of the goat arose when the Antiquities Department traced the artifacts back to them, and then tortured them for days to give up the location."

"I'm afraid I feel little sympathy."

"No? I am surprised, given your line of work."

"Why are you here, Mr. el-Rassul?"

"I am here, my dear girl, because the wealth of my family dried up years ago, and I want to see it returned. But I do not simply want my *future* changed. I want more than to ensure a fortune for my son and grandson."

"You want to change your own past."

He smiled. "Ah, now you are catching on." The smiling words ended in a phlegmy cough.

"And you think I can help? Why would I?"

Colin crossed the parlor and sat opposite el-Rassul, leaning forward with forearms braced across his knees and hands loosely clasped, as though ready to attack the old man if necessary.

"We shall get to that. But first, you must hear my plan."

"Go ahead, then."

"I will do it better this time. Be more discreet and careful with the way items are sold. We will do it much more slowly, over a period of many decades, and we will not get caught. You will tell them where and how to invest the money." He grinned, looking almost childlike with excitement for a moment. "And, oh, the wealth that is there. Far grander than even TT320. The greatest find in all of Egyptian archaeology."

She raised her eyebrows. "You're talking about King Tut's tomb? You want to raid... I don't understand."

"I want you to go back eighty years, and get a message to my father, and to me at the age of seven. Explain the location of the tomb, and the way it must be done."

"But even if I could do that, within a few years people will be searching for it. And certainly if artifacts keep showing up, Carter will have even more reason to believe the tomb of Tutankhamun is there. He'll find it even sooner."

"And that is why you must also kill Howard Carter."

"What?" Giada leaned forward, mouth agape.

"Now hold on here," Colin stood, fists clenching.

El-Rassul reached into his jacket, as if for more tobacco, but instead his hand emerged with a pistol.

"Sit down, boy."

Colin drew himself upright at the sight of the weapon, but did not sit.

El-Rassul kept the pistol resting on his knee but trained on Colin. He glared at Giada. "Keep your Irishman on a leash, Miss Moretti."

She could practically feel the heat from Colin's hatred. But she needed to hear this out.

"So you want me to kill Howard Carter to prevent him from eventually finding the tomb, and to instruct your father and your younger self how to exploit it. I get it. But that will seriously change your past. You'll have dual memories, possibly even split your sanity into pieces. Trust me, I've seen it happen."

He shrugged, then took another drag of the pipe. "I probably only have a few years left. Why not live them in luxury, leave a fortune to my family, and remember a past filled with all the good things wealth can bring? The memories of poverty will fade. I will let them go."

"And you? Did you inherit the family ability?"

"To travel? Yes. But not to change the past. And an eighty-year trip backward to meet my younger self would be ill-advised, to say the least."

"Assuming I could do as you wish, you said we could help each other. What's in it for me?"

"My silence." He exhaled another cloud, the pistol still propped on one knee.

"That's it? You're blackmailing me?" She forced a laugh. "As if any reputable newspaper or government agency is going to believe I've made my fortune by time traveling into the past to set up future discoveries for myself."

"Perhaps not the newspapers. Not the government. But Tempus Vigilia will believe it."

Giada sucked in a breath.

Five years ago, the Tempus Vigilia inducted her into their membership, after she witnessed Julius Caeasar's assassination and answered a simple question about the dictator's last words. A bit less than five years since she, Alexander, and Renae returned to their university digsite with the fantastic surprise that Alexander was a Revisionist, and Giada claimed her first discovery of the necklace he'd buried for her near the steps of Seti's tomb.

That first "find" had changed her life. Given her a taste of recognition, and what it meant to be valued for what she offered.

And now, only a few years out of college, Giada had rocketed into the public eye of archaeology by becoming the "woman with the nose for ancient gold," as one paper had coined her. A clipping she kept in her desk drawer, to re-read whenever the old childhood fear of insignificance flared.

The old man was correct. She'd stayed under the radar of Tempus Vigilia these past few years, but if el-Rassul went to the Society with what he knew, she would be blackballed.

And a person did not ever, ever want to be blackballed by Tempus Vigilia.

The Society had high-ranking members in all sectors of global power—banking, government, education. Within a month, she would likely find her fortune mysteriously wiped out, her reputation tarnished, and possibly even herself incarcerated for illegal activities they would find a way to pin on her. All without ever revealing the existence of the Society, nor of time travel itself.

"You're crazy."

A lame response, but she was at a loss, scrambling for a way to get out of this disaster.

"Perhaps. But I have thought much about my plan. The first find, the royal cache, was a lucky accident when my grandfather witnessed it being buried. There is no way to pinpoint another time in which so vast a fortune was buried in a tomb we still have not found. But to go back only eighty years, to be certain of the location and the riches of a then-undiscovered tomb, in my lifetime… it is too good an opportunity to pass."

Giada glanced up at Colin, still standing a few paces from el-Rassul's gun and not looking at her.

"And Miss Moretti, you will not go completely unrewarded. Of course, you have my silence about your activities, but I'll be happy to have you arrange payment of some of the goods, perhaps to your own grandmother as a young woman? I have read you come from humble beginnings—"

"Leave my past out of this, el-Rassul."

He held up a hand, the pipe pinched between thumb and forefinger and his palm outward. "Apologies. But I do understand what impoverishment can do to a person." His eyes narrowed. "It makes them hungry. And sometimes even angry."

Was it a deal she was willing to make? To perhaps change her own past? But if nothing else, to ensure her future.

"I may be able to arrange getting this message to your father." She braced her elbows against the arms of the wing chair and steepled her fingers. "But I am not having Howard Carter, or anyone, for that matter, killed."

The pistol slowly swiveled away from Colin, to point at her own midsection. "Then my plan will fail. And it will be your fault."

He coughed, this time with some violence, the gun wavering in his hand.

Giada winced with each hacking sound, her eyes on his trigger finger.

She lifted her chin, forced her attention to his face. "So now you are saying you will kill *me* if I don't do what you ask? Shall we get the threats clear between us, Mr. el-Rassul?"

He set the pipe on an ebony side table, pulled a handkerchief from his breast pocket, wiped his mouth, and shrugged one shoulder. "I believe we understand each other."

Colin growled from the back of his throat. "Enough of this." He advanced on the old man, hand extended to grab the frail wrist.

But el-Rassul anticipated him, raised the gun, and was ready when Colin reached him.

The sharp percussion of the gunshot echoed off the Rococo plastered ceilings and the mahogany wainscoting. A sound so foreign to the elegance, it seemed to have traveled here from some other place or time itself.

The bullet pitched Colin backward. He fell face-up on the Persian carpet, a red stain blooming across his chest.

Giada rocketed to her feet, then fell beside Colin.

"What have you done?" She threw the words like pebbles against el-Rassul. "Colin!" She pressed her flat palms against the wound in his chest, her own heart racing, the smell of blood assaulting her.

"Call an ambulance!" she screamed to el-Rassul, half her brain knowing the request would be ignored. "Do something!"

But Colin's eyes were already glassy and staring and unresponsive.

Giada sat back on her heels and studied her bloodied palms.

"You stupid, stupid man." She hissed the words at el-Rassul.

"Defending myself, my dear. I'm an old man—"

"And in the process you've destroyed your own plan." She used the back of her hand to smooth the hair from Colin's forehead. "You understand nothing, you old fool. Colin was the Revisionist. *Him.* Not me. There is nothing I can do in your past that will have any meaning. You have killed the only person who could."

At this last, the words hitched in her throat, and a strangled cry followed them. She bent her forehead to touch Colin's, hot tears falling across his face.

Theirs had been a complicated relationship, since that day in Ireland when they met, when after a strange, evasive-yet-hinting conversation over coffee, they recognized each other as fellow time-travelers. Since then, they'd taken eight trips to the past, each time with Colin revising history and enabling her to make an amazing find when they returned. They were business partners in that sense. But they had become so much more. Giada hadn't thought her heart capable of anything—not since Alexander—but Colin was at least a start in the right direction. He was the only person who truly understood her.

And now he was dead.

"Not the only person."

"What?" She looked up at el-Rassul through tear-blurred eyes, and the word tasted bitter in her mouth.

"He was not the only person who could change my past. There are others."

Others, yes.

"So what do you expect me to—"

"I expect you to find another Revisionist. And to do whatever you must, to accomplish my plan."

She needn't ask what he would do if she refused. Besides the blackballing and the destruction of her life and career, proof of what el-Rassul was willing to do lay bloody and unmoving on her carpet.

But she knew of only one Revisionist who might be willing to save her life.

Or would Alexander turn her away once more?

# CHAPTER FOUR

*December 19, 1922*
*Thebes, Egypt*

*G*    *oing back to stop Giada could destroy us both.*

I did not want to think about Jack's warning.

After a quick overnight stay in a run-down hotel in Venice, Jack and I began the trek back toward Luxor.

I kept my head in a book during train journeys and stayed in my cabin for most of the ship's journey.

So much to avoid.

Not only my hunger for Jack's continued presence, like a gravitational pull I could barely resist, but also his repeated protestations and comments about the foolishness of my proposed plan.

I wanted to ignore his fears altogether, but for the four days of stomach-churning passage across the Mediterranean, I succumbed to his warnings and then resisted a dozen times.

Traveling to the Harem Conspiracy of 1155 BC, to change the course of Giada's looting history could keep my parents safe from her attempts to exploit them. And if safe, my parents would never have to take their fateful trip to Venice in 1905, and I wouldn't lose them. I understood returning from stopping her, to find the past seventeen years transformed, might have an impact on my mind.

"Possibly devastating," Jack had said.

And what did I know, really?

Still, it seemed worth the risk to me.

My struggle was not in whether to gamble my mental health.

But how could I risk Jack's? How was that fair?

Because as surely as changing the young Giada's future in 1155 BC would save my parents, it would also drastically alter the course of Jack's life. Giada's looting of the past through unscrupulous Revisionists made her wealthy. Would all of Jack's memories of his wealthy privilege while growing up be erased? The whole course of his life changed? Would he even go to Egypt to meet me? And what would it mean if he didn't? Would he disappear from my presence somehow?

The possibilities overwhelmed me. So I focused on keeping food down and thinking about the work waiting in Luxor, where the threatened rain had spared the tomb from destruction.

On the morning I showed up at KV62, fresh from the train from Cairo, Howard took my arrival in stride, as if I'd never been gone. And indeed, though it felt like a lifetime, first to Rome and then to Venice, it had only been about two weeks. Lord Carnarvon and Eve would be back at Highclere for the holiday by now, but there would be little time for festivities here in Egypt.

I passed through the newly installed steel gate and paused in the doorway of the antechamber to let my eyes adjust.

"Good. You're here." Howard looked up from a gorgeous alabaster cup, shaped like a lotus in full bloom, and nodded once. "We've got our work cut out for us." He waved a vague hand toward the tomb entrance. "The Met's loaned us Burton for the photographs, but he's still catching up."

I smiled at the floor. Worldwide fame had not altered the man, and likely never would.

He scowled. "And of course, in exchange, they'll try to get their hands on whatever they can for their collection."

"I would guess everyone will have their hands out."

Howard set the cup aside, climbed to his feet, hands on his hips. He surveyed the tomb's contents, still a wild cacophony of discovery. "You've no idea. The British Museum, of course, should have their choice. But the Egyptians aren't having that. I'm predicting a war over all of this."

"I hope it'll be archaeology and scholarship that wins the war."

Howard frowned in my general direction. His own interests were rarely so impartial.

"Yes, well. I could use some sketches made of this piece. It'll take Burton some time for proper photographs."

"His wife Minnie is here." I jutted a thumb toward the desert behind me, where Minnie paced. "She says you sent a donkey to bring her out."

"Busybody," he muttered under his breath. "The woman wasn't going to give me a moment's peace until I did." He stood, wiped his hands on his trousers and half-grinned. "Sent the donkey, though. Not the Ford."

"Yes, I heard about your big purchase in Cairo. Our very own digsite automobile to haul loads, rather than those poor camels."

He brushed past me on his way to Minnie. "It's all going to be different now, Sahara, you'll see. The eyes of the world are on what we do here."

A tiny thrill ran through me at the words.

Despite my ongoing, and somewhat emotionally desperate, search for my parents, this digsite and this discovery still meant the world to me.

I followed Howard outside.

Minnie patted the back of her skirt as if to remove the donkey-dust, then removed her pith helmet and wiped a yellow polka-dotted handkerchief across her forehead. Despite her obvious discomfort, her coifed hair remained perfectly in place, along with the ever-present pearl necklace.

"Your husband's over there," Howard jutted a thumb. "He's got his very own darkroom in KV55, Queen Tiye's tomb." He crossed to the shade of a tent, poured something from a flask, and lit up a cigarette. "And we've got our own quiet little laboratory down there in KV15, where we can work on the conservation of everything we bring out."

Minnie seemed disinterested in all but the contents of the tomb, so Howard soon escorted her into the antechamber.

I grabbed a sketchbook and pencil and trailed them, feeling disconnected from the project after my time away.

So why was I thinking of disappearing again?

If I were to travel back to 1155 BC to stop Giada from whatever she learned at the Harem Conspiracy, I would have to preserve my changes upon my return, use my "Revisionist" superpower, and come back to time passed, however long it took me to accomplish my goal in the past. And with only one shot to make it happen in 1155, I would want to get there early enough to ensure I had enough time to stop Giada.

Another risk to my career seemed unavoidable.

I spent a hot morning on Howard's requested sketches of the lotus-shaped cup, carved from a single piece of near-translucent alabaster, as wide as my hand-span, and twice as high. Engraved hieroglyphs, filled with blue pigment, circled the rim and were inscribed in a square in the center of the cup.

"Here," Howard pointed to the symbols inside a cartouche, signifying Tut-ankh-amun's name, "more proof we've found his tomb."

As if I didn't recognize the king's nomen inscribed in the oval, with its symbols for the god Amun, the bird and bread loaves for Tut and the ankh symbol of life. Below these, the crook signifying his kingship and the symbols for Thebes completed the naming inscription.

I had to bite my lip to keep from mentioning I'd seen this same cartouche chiseled into the door of the tomb, only two months after the king's death.

"We'll get Gardiner to translate these." Howard ran a finger along the rim. "Right now, we need to catalogue."

By late morning, Howard had approved my sketches, and I flagged down one of the drivers loitering near the site to head back toward my room at the Met's American House for a meal.

With the building looming, I spotted two figures on the road leading to the house, in what seemed a heated argument. A moment later, their identities became obvious.

"Pull over here, please. I'll get out here."

"*Sayida?* You are certain of this? I can drive you—"

"Here, please."

Already the raised voices of Jack and his Aunt Giada's goon, Reuben, filtered into the vehicle.

They both turned as I slammed out of the automobile.

The driver roared away, kicking up dust.

We all set our backs to the flurry of sand and shielded our eyes.

I waved a clear spot in front of my face and glared at Reuben. "What is he doing here?"

Reuben half-bowed, as though he were a polite gentleman, meeting me for the first time. "As I told you in Rome, I followed you back here. It's my job."

"That doesn't mean you need to be slinking around here." I jabbed a thumb at the American House. "This is my *home.*"

Reuben smirked. "I go where Jack goes. And apparently Jack goes here."

I flicked a glance at Jack. "So, what are you doing here? I thought we weren't meeting until this evening."

Jack pulled off his hat and swiped at his forehead. "Yeah, I was going to tell you—I got a room here."

"What?" Was there no possible way to avoid this man?

"One of the Met guys went back to the States, and Lythgoe said I could rent his room for a few weeks."

Reuben shook his head. "A few weeks? Come on, man. You know the longer this goes on, the more likely—"

Jack whirled on Reuben, nostrils flaring and jaw tight. "Then go back now, and tell her I *am not coming back.*" He spit the last words one at a time, eyes boring into the other man.

I started forward. "Jack—"

"Don't say it, Sahara. I don't want to hear it."

"Listen, man," Reuben's tone softened. "If I go back now and tell her you're not coming, she's only going to send two others back to get you."

"Aarrgh!" Jack stalked away from us both, hands on his hips. "Why can't she leave it alone?"

Reuben lit up a cigarette, took a deep drag, and shrugged at me, as though the answer were unknowable.

Jack spun back to us. "Fine. Stay here longer. Follow us around. Do what you came to do." He reached for my hand. "Let's go get some lunch."

I took his hand, pushed past Reuben, and joined him on the road. I could feel the red-haired man watching us from behind. Where would he go? The odd sense swept me that somehow he would simply disappear.

"Catch me up, Jack. I feel like I'm missing something. What was that about Giada sending back people to get you? And what is Reuben really supposed to be doing?"

Jack sighed as though weary of all of it.

"So, you know I left 2002 in November for my sightseeing trip to ancient Egypt. Giada was there beside me when I left, saying goodbye and telling me to have a good time. I'm not a Revisionist, so by the time she said goodbye, I should have been saying 'I'm back!' and telling her all about it."

"But you didn't come back."

"I didn't come back."

"Which means…"

"Which means I either die here in 1922, or farther back in the past, or I decide to never go back. To stay in the past."

"Why didn't you tell me this?"

He closed his eyes briefly. "Because it seemed a little intense. I didn't want to scare you into thinking I'm going to get myself killed somehow. I knew you'd stop letting me help you. And we haven't known each other long. To tell you I'm planning to... to stay with you... for good..."

The words trailed away. His eyes strayed to the horizon, as if he wished to escape.

But my heart was here, total and complete. Beside Jack.

It seemed unfair to push further. He hadn't wanted to say those words to me. Not yet. Reuben forced his hand.

"So what was he saying about Giada sending others to bring you back? Is that possible?"

"Yes. Two travelers, even Observers, if they each take a hand of someone else, can bring that person with them when they jump. It's a bit more complicated than that, but you get the idea."

"I think I'd like to hear it all."

"You can't do it with anyone—the person being pulled back must also be able to time travel. Or a child who will eventually develop the ability. That's how your parents have been able to bring Persia with them, even though it's unlikely her abilities have started yet."

"I hadn't even thought of that. But you're saying it can be done against the person's will?"

"Yes."

"Wow."

"And if Reuben returns to Giada and tells her I'm refusing to come home, she may send two others to snatch me back to 2002, whether I like it or not."

"Then we'll convince him to tell Giada you're dead." I shuddered at the word, even though a lie.

"That might be worse, actually. She'd be even more motivated to find a Revisionist—you, your sister, your parents—to change the past and save me."

I clenched my fists. "Is there no way to stop this woman?"

"Well, if there is, I've never found it. She always gets what she wants."

We'd reached the steps to the American House, but slowed to finish our conversation in private.

"There is a way. I'm going to 1155 BC to change everything."

"Sahara, it's too risky. When we return—"

"Not we. Me."

I started up the steps to the verandah.

He caught my hand and pulled me back.

"Jack, listen, I've thought about this. Thought about everything you've told me about time travel, and how making changes to the past affects people."

His eyes narrowed, and he nodded once. "I'm listening."

"You said if Revisionists change the past when they return, they'll have two sets of memories, but for everyone else, the changed past will be normal. It'll be the only past they've known. Right?"

"Right. So?"

"So, if I go alone, you're safe. I mean, you might have a different life, and that's no small sacrifice. But it won't mess with your mind."

A flutter of yellow at the door above us drew our attention.

Minnie Burton waggled a few fingers in Jack's direction. "Lunch is ready, Mr. Moretti. Will you be joining us, then?"

I suppressed a smile and looked up at Jack, eyebrows raised. "Seems you've made yourself at home already."

Jack tipped his hat toward Minnie. "Be right in, Mrs. Burton. And thanks very much for the kindness."

Minnie's glance darted between the two of us a moment longer, but when it became clear we weren't following her, she whirled and disappeared into the house.

As soon as she was gone, Jack grasped both my hands in his, brought them to his chest, and trapped them there.

"Listen to me, Sahara. Your plan, while logical and even admirable, is unacceptable to me."

"But—"

His fingers tightened on mine. "If you are successful in changing the entire course of my aunt's life, and therefore both our lives, when you return, I will have never met you. You'll remember me, but to me, you'll be a stranger. And I am never going to let you be a stranger."

"And if we go together, and still change both our lives—"

"Then when we return to a new reality, we will remember and find each other."

His arguments whittled away at my logic, but I still searched for an alternative.

"And I'm beginning to see you're right, Sahara." Jack's gaze traveled the length of the road we'd walked, as though he could still see Reuben out there somewhere. "What choice do we have? She won't stop until she's brought me back to 2002. She won't stop until she's found you or your family and tried to exploit your abilities." He released my fingers and ran the back of his hand across my cheek. "We must undo all the harm she's caused. It's the only way to keep us all safe."

I looked toward the Theban hills, toward the Valley of the Kings, where we would once again travel to the time of the ancient pharaohs.

"Well then, I think we have some studying to do."

Jack pecked a quick kiss on my cheek. "But first, lunch."

# CHAPTER FIVE

*December 27, 1974*
*Philadelphia, Pennsylvania*

Giada's breath, a puff of ash in the dark winter air, clouded her view of the narrow stone home across the street. She set the briefcase down, leaned against a lamppost, and exhaled again, watching her breath in the fading red lights of the taxi.

She'd driven past this historic little home in Chestnut Hill more than once in the past four years. Thought about what it would be like, to live here. For her to be the one pushing the navy-and-white baby carriage with a little girl tucked inside. To watch, smiling, from the window as Alexander trimmed the low-hanging branches from the Japanese Maple which this evening traced graceful, leafless shadows against gabled windows lit from within like gold-wrapped gifts and the whitewashed front porch.

But she did not live here. Renae lived here. Renae, and Alex, and their sweet little girl who was big enough now to skip down the sidewalk, each hand held by one of her adoring parents.

Giada raked a hand through her hair and pushed her shoulders back. Enough of this wishing for what could not be.

The image of Colin, bleeding out on her Persian rug, threatened to derail her. She could not allow it. The old man, el-Rassul, gave her no choice. She must get Alexander to help her make the old man's dream of riches a reality. If she didn't, her life as she knew it would be over. And perhaps even her life itself.

She swallowed hard, lifted the briefcase, and crossed the street.

A moment later, she stood on the porch and pressed a fingertip, white-hot, against the bell.

The door swept open, spilling that golden light into the night air, outlining Alexander.

"Giada?"

The shock in his voice wounded her, for some reason.

"Hello, Alexander."

"I didn't realize—come in, come in. It's cold out there."

She stood in the entryway as he pushed the door closed behind them.

"It's good to see you, Giada." Uncertainty tinged the friendly words, and perhaps insincerity.

"I know it's been a long time. And the last time we spoke—"

"Who's at the door, Alex?"

Renae's voice was followed by Renae herself, cranberry-red dish towel in hand and smiling.

She looked the same, still. Even this close and not from a parked car across the street. Motherhood hadn't aged her, no stubborn pregnancy weight still hugging her body. Beautiful as ever.

"Hi, Renae."

Renae's lips parted, and she glanced at Alexander, perfect eyebrows raised.

He shook his head slightly, as if to say *don't look at me, I didn't invite her.*

Renae recovered and extended a hand toward a room off the

foyer. "Come, Giada. Let's sit. Tell us what's happening with your life."

Giada followed Renae into their front room, its furnishings worn, perhaps second-hand, but tidy. Little touches of the two of them called from everywhere. Terracotta statues and faience jugs from their travels, jade green embossed leather-bound books tumbling together on shelves. A parchment map spanning the wall above the sofa. Everything you would expect from the modest home of a time-traveling university professor.

"Your house is lovely."

And she meant it. Despite the contrast in luxury with her Society Hill Georgian, this little stone home *was* lovely, in all the ways that meant anything.

"Mommy! I ate all my peas!" The little-girl voice drifted from another room.

Renae smiled apologetically. "That's Sahara, wanting her cookies."

Giada nodded and tried to smile.

Renae disappeared, but Alex sat in a nearby leather chair and held a hand to invite her to the green brocade sofa.

"What brings you here tonight, Giada?"

Getting right to it, then. But she couldn't blame him. They hadn't parted on good terms, and now here she was, showing up unannounced.

She set the briefcase by the curved wooden leg of the sofa and lowered herself to sitting.

"I—I need your help, Alex."

Renae returned, leading Sahara by the hand. "This is Miss Moretti, Sahara. She is Mommy and Daddy's... *old friend*." She nudged the little girl forward. "Say hello."

Sahara crossed the room to stand in front of Giada and study her with serious eyes. She wore a periwinkle-blue romper over a blue gingham-checked shirt. The girl had Renae's beautiful dark hair. But those were Alexander's eyes.

"Hello. My name is Sahara. Like the Sahara Desert."

"Hello, Sahara."

"She's not old, Mommy."

Giada exhaled a little laugh and touched the girl's hair. "No, I suppose not. Though I sometimes feel that way."

Alexander crossed one leg over the other and tilted his head at her. "Renae, Giada has just been saying she needs our help."

"Really? That is surprising."

The unmistakable undercurrent needled her. They all knew Giada had money enough to hire any help she might need.

"The truth is," she sagged back against the sofa, "I've gotten myself in some trouble."

Alex frowned. "I'm afraid that's *not* surprising."

A little spark of anger flamed to life in her chest. "I get it. You don't approve of my business—"

"Business?" Alex leaned on the word with sarcasm. "I can think of better words for it."

"What, then? Scam? Swindle? I'm not hurting anyone, Alex."

Renae took Sahara by the shoulder. "Let's go get those sugar cookies, sweetheart. Leave Daddy to talk to our friend."

Giada watched them go. "We don't all fall into the perfect life, like the two of you have."

"There's a wide gap between perfection and deception, Giada."

She took a breath. This wasn't going well. And she needed it to go well.

"Listen, Alexander. I have a problem, a problem you can help fix, and I can make it very worthwhile for you. You know I can."

"I don't need your money, Giada."

"No," she glanced around the room, "no, I know you don't. But think of Sahara. What you could do for her in the future. Education, travel—"

"What is this problem?"

Renae came to the doorframe of the kitchen, leaned against it to listen.

She spilled it out, then. Everything about el-Rassul's visit, how the well-known story of the goat falling down a shaft was the fabrication of two time travelers who'd stumbled on a way to get rich. And now their old-man grandson, wanting to improve upon the scheme. Needing a Revisionist to make it happen. His threat to blackball her with Tempus Vigilia if she didn't comply.

"Giada, I'm afraid you're only reaping what you have sown. We both told you, years ago, you couldn't continue this way without getting caught. What we thought was a simple initiation into a fun fraternity turned out to be the Society's tracking method. And they keep too close an eye on their members for your wealth, and its origin, to go unnoticed forever. Still driving that BMW, I assume?" He glared down at her as if she were a troublesome student. "If you're going to mess with history, you're going to suffer for it."

She would ignore the condescension. For now.

"There's more than that, though." Giada glanced at Renae, then past her to the kitchen, where Sahara must still be busy with her cookies. "I think he might kill me."

She'd left Colin out of her story. She sensed that if Alex and Renae knew el-Rassul had already killed someone over this, they would be more likely to go to the Society themselves than to help her.

"Oh, Giada." Renae crossed the room, sank to the sofa beside her, and clasped her hand. "What have you gotten yourself into?"

"It's not my fault! He came to me. Threatened me." She turned away from Renae's pitying expression. "Please, Alex." She lifted the shiny black briefcase. "I have everything you could possibly need, to go back eighty years, right here. Three plane tickets to London—I knew you wouldn't want to go alone, and I thought you could make it a holiday—all the money you need when you get to England." The words came in a rush. "Plenty of nineteenth-century British Pounds, which will get you far in 1894. A complete bio on Howard Carter, and even an artifact I bought years ago, so you'll have an introduction to him and can find a way to divert him from digging in the Valley. Details about where to find el-Rassul as a boy and his father, and what to tell them. And I checked the university schedule—I know you're on Christmas break right now—"

"Giada, stop."

"No, Alexander—"

"I said, *stop.*"

She breathed against some of the tightness in her chest, but it would not loosen.

"Giada, I do not have many regrets in my life. But one of my biggest is the day I buried that necklace near the steps of Seti's tomb, for you to find when we returned."

"What? Why would you regret—"

"I blame myself for getting you started down this path, Giada. The changes we made to history that day still haunt me. And just because we *can* revise history does not mean we ever *want to* again."

"We?" Giada turned to Renae, in time to see the exasperated look she threw at her husband. "You are *both* Revisionists?"

"It doesn't matter, Giada. We're not going to do this thing you're asking."

"Doesn't matter? You sit there and judge me?" Giada straightened, feeling the heat pour into her face. "When the two of you—not only travelers, but both Revisionists—have defied the Society to get married, and…" She trailed off, her eyes darting to the kitchen doorway. What amplified abilities must that little girl have, the child of two Revisionists?

Renae stepped into Giada's line of sight, as if to block her view, and even her thoughts, of Sahara. "We've taken the censure of Tempus Vigilia for it, Giada. Believe me. Alexander could be one of the foremost scholars—"

"None of that is important." Alex stood. "Our family is our business. And we don't want any part of yours."

Yes. Their family. Alex made it all so very clear, after their semester digging in Egypt. He and Renae were in love. Getting married right away. Alexander was *so sorry*, if Giada had mistaken his feelings of friendship for something more.

And then Sahara, born less than a year after they married. The perfect little family.

Alex was still standing over her, an obvious signal of the end of her visit.

"She's about the same age as my nephew, you know." Giada jutted her chin toward the kitchen. "My sister's boy, Jack. You remember my sister, Angela?"

"Last I heard, she was unwell."

Giada laughed, dry and humorless. "That's a nice way of saying it. You'd think she was sixty, to look at her, instead of thirty."

"Sounds like she's shown the same poor judgment with her gifts as her sister."

"Alex." Renae's soft voice was a gentle reprimand.

Too late, though. The anger boiled into Giada's words. "They're so fragile at that age, aren't they?" She looked again toward the kitchen, where Sahara emerged, cookie crumbs around her lips.

Giada hated herself for the words, but they kept coming. "So easy for them to have an accident, get lost, even… taken."

Renae was standing now. "Get out." A mask of fury fell over her face. Mama bear, defending her cub. "Get *out*. Now."

Giada stood eye-to-eye with her two former friends, letting ice pour into her veins and cool the anger.

"You've made your own choice, then. Nothing that happens after this can be blamed on me."

She was through the foyer, out the door, and halfway down the walk before she remembered the briefcase full of money, still propped against the living room sofa.

*Let them have it.*

A parting gift from an old friend they'd never see again.

# CHAPTER SIX

*December 29, 1974*
*Philadelphia, Pennsylvania*

*R*enae paced her tiny living room. Past the frayed sofa, the second-hand coffee table, the pistachio-green upholstered chair—a wedding gift from her mother. Then a turn and back again. She checked the wall clock for the hundredth time, but its hands read 9 PM, only a few minutes since the last time.

When would Alexander return from his Haverford College library?

And more importantly, what would he have learned?

In the two days since Giada's outrageous visit, they came to the most difficult decision of their lives.

"How dare she?" Renae had hissed when Giada finally closed the door of their little stone home, their refuge from the demands of academia.

Alexander stood at Renae's back, gripped her arms. "She's gone now, so it doesn't matter."

Renae whirled on him. "Doesn't matter? She's spent four

years getting rich as Croesus, while we survive on your teacher's salary, and then has the audacity to come to us for *help*?"

"I don't think she would have, if she weren't desperate—"

"And why does she find herself desperate, Alex?" Renae glanced at little Sahara, framed in the kitchen doorway, and forced her voice into something more pleasant. "Through her own actions, that's how."

"I know, Renae. It's nothing I didn't just say to her."

Renae pulled in a breath through her nose, exhaled through her mouth. The effort did little to calm her.

"And to threaten us, Alex?" She whispered the horrible word, though Sahara hopefully had no reference to understand a threat. "When you have kept her secret from Tempus Vigilia all these years?"

"Not only me—"

Renae huffed and threw herself onto the sofa, beckoning for Sahara to come to her. "Fine, I kept her secret as well. But we both know it was for your sake, not for hers. Because you still feel some kind of ridiculous guilt. As though you could have prevented her from falling in love with you."

Alexander closed his eyes and rubbed at his temples. "Well, I thank you for the compliment about my irresistibility, but still, it's more than that. We were once all such great friends. I feel... loyal, I suppose."

Renae bore holes into him with her eyes until he finally looked at her. Looked at Sahara, snuggled against her chest.

"And now? Do you still feel such loyalty to her now? Or does your loyalty lie with your family?"

Alex sighed. "Of course you and Sahara are my highest priority, Renae. I would never let anything happen to you, but I can't believe Giada—"

"She's betrayed you, Alex. When are you going to see that?"

At the mention of betrayal, a memory tickled in Renae's mind, then bloomed.

From Alexander's expression, he'd retrieved the memory at the same moment.

"That woman we met—during our semester digging at Seti."

Renae nodded, biting her lip. How did it fit?

"She warned me—made me promise we would run—"

"But how could she know?"

"It doesn't matter." Alexander squared his shoulders. "We have to trust her reasons. And we need to leave here. We need to run, together, just as she told us."

"Run? Where? How?"

They were questions with no answers, not that night. But in the two intervening days, they discussed several possibilities.

There was no question of simply relocating somewhere else in the country, or even the world. Giada's wealth opened too many doors, gave her the power to ask questions even in remote corners. No, they needed to move backward through time, and stay there, at least until they believed the threat passed.

Hence Alexander's late-night visit to the dusty library on the campus where he taught Egyptian Studies. Research. And hopefully a decision.

One more glance at the clock. 9:05.

"Mommy..." Sahara's sleepy voice drifted down the steps like a wisp of sweet-smelling smoke. "I'm thirsty."

Despite herself, Renae smiled. These days, Sahara seemed to be always hungry or thirsty. Perhaps it was a growth spurt.

Renae climbed the steps to Sahara's room and nudged the door open.

The tiny nightlight her daughter insisted upon barely lit the edges of the room, where the wallpaper mural of an African savannah surrounded the little girl's bed. A cartoonish lion, half-hidden in emerald grasses, and a smiling zebra bending to a sapphire pool protected Sahara from scary things in the night.

Giada's words intruded, the subtle mention of how little children could get lost, or have accidents, or even be taken from their parents. Cartoon animals could not protect her daughter from a woman like that. From a world more like a real jungle than this idealized child-version.

Sahara stirred in her bed, a tiny splotch of midnight blue

pajamas, with yellow stars splashed in constellations across her belly.

"You have water right here, sweetheart." She reached for the purple cup always at the girl's bedside.

From below them, the familiar creak and sweep of the front door filtered up the steps.

"That's Daddy, finally home," she whispered, and pushed hair from Sahara's damp forehead as the girl sipped her water. "You'd better get to sleep, or Daddy will think you've been out hunting lions again."

Sahara smiled, heavy eyelids drooping, and curled into her fleecy pink blankets once more.

Alexander appeared in the doorway a moment later, framed by the light of the hall.

Renae tried to smile against the fear gripping her for the past two days. "Well?"

He entered, eyes on Sahara.

"I'm still not sure. But I've got some good ideas."

"Shouldn't we be making a decision quickly? If we're truly—" she glanced at Sahara, whose breathing was deep and even —"truly in danger?"

He nodded, but said no more, and she felt the heaviness in him, at leaving the profession he loved so much, the city where he'd grown up, the home they'd built together.

Renae felt it, too. The dark cloud of regret and resentment and even fear surrounding them the past two days. She went to him, took his hands in hers, and pulled him to their own bedroom.

Much later, arms still entwined around each other, a dull thud sounded from somewhere downstairs.

Alexander tensed, pulled her tighter.

"What was it?" She whispered against his ear, barely audible.

"Stay here." Alexander slid from her grasp, bent to the floor, then stood with his usually hidden baseball bat firmly in his grip.

He wore striped pajamas, reminiscent of the baseball uniforms of bygone days, and the image of him standing there with the bat would have made her laugh. If not for the stomach-churning fear.

Had Giada sent someone to hurt them? To do something to Sahara?

Alexander was gone a moment later, disappeared into the dark hall.

She winced at the tread of his feet on their creaky stairs. If she could hear him, wouldn't any intruder also know he was coming?

She slipped from the bed and yanked on a pair of pants and a sweater. Somehow she felt less vulnerable fully dressed. She went to the doorframe, ear tuned to every sound.

But the sounds were unintelligible. A grunt, some rumbled words, a sharp cry. A crack like wood on stone. A soft thud.

And then pounding footsteps. Up the stairs.

Renae froze, unable to decide whether to dash to Sahara's room, or lead the intruder away from the little girl.

She gasped in relief when Alexander's face appeared in the dark stairwell.

"Get Sahara. We have to leave. Now."

"But we haven't packed—"

"Now, Renae!" Terror, rather than anger, charged the words and seemed to knock the breath from her lungs.

She was in Sahara's room in half a moment, scooping the sleeping girl into her arms, dashing back to the hall.

Alex reached for Sahara, a pair of shoes for herself and him in his hands, a blanket draped over his arm.

Renae shook her head. "I've got her."

He led the way down the stairs.

Renae tried in vain to keep Sahara's feet from bumping the wall.

The child stirred in her arms. "Where are we going?"

"Sshh, Mommy and Daddy are taking you on a surprise adventure, sweetheart. But you must be quiet."

At the foot of the stairs, Renae gave only a glance toward the living room as they hurried to the front door. Enough to see a prone figure on the carpet.

"What have you done, Alexander?"

He didn't answer. Only opened the door and pushed them gently through it.

Winter darkness slapped her cheeks, and she clutched Sahara closer.

"Mommy?"

"Sshh."

Alexander was still pushing them. Across the unlit porch, down the steps, into the grass already sharpened with frost.

She winced as the grass bit into her bare feet and turned toward the car.

Alex pulled her back.

"What—?"

"Across the street," he hissed. "Run. And stay there. I have to go back for him." He dropped the blanket and shoes to the grass.

"Go back for—what are you talking about?"

He clutched her arms, turned her to face him, and spoke over Sahara's head, the words barely audible.

"There's a bomb."

"What?" Her knees weakened, and Sahara suddenly seemed too heavy to carry.

But Alexander still gripped her arms, and thankfully did not let go.

"Now, Renae. Across the street, into the park. I will meet you at our bench."

"No! You can't go back!"

"I knocked him unconscious, Renae. I can't let him die in there."

"No!"

Should she put Sahara on the grass? Restrain him?

But Alexander was already running back to the porch. He yelled over his shoulder. "You need to get her safe!"

He disappeared into the dark house.

He was right. Sahara came first.

She grabbed the blanket and her shoes, barely managing to hold all of it and her daughter, and ran across the frozen street, across the tree-lined sidewalk, into the manicured park where they'd enjoyed so many afternoons.

But even a park can be menacing at night. Especially when you are running for your life.

She held back a hiccup of fear, clutched Sahara tighter, tried to stay upright on her numb feet.

She was still running when the blast tore apart the winter silence of their once-peaceful neighborhood.

"Mommy, you're hurting me! Put me down!"

"You're fine, honey. Mommy forgot your shoes and the grass is very cold, so I will carry you."

The last few words fell out broken and grief-stricken.

Was she alone in the world with Sahara? Did Alex make it out?

She reached their bench, the one where they'd spent hours watching Sahara play. This late, even the lamppost was unlit.

She fell to the bench, Sahara still on her lap, tucked her freezing feet under her legs and wrapped the blanket around them both.

Dared to look up.

In the pale moonlight, leafless trees clawed shadow-hands across the dirty remnants of last week's light snowfall, piled like tiny mountain ranges along the sidewalks.

But across the park, through the trees, the unmistakable orange glow of what was once their home.

Unreasonably, the thought of her favorite pink azalea, burning, caused a physical pain in her chest.

"What was that *boom*, Mommy?"

Tears burned hot in her eyes, down her chilled face.

"Mommy?"

"Just some… fireworks. Nothing to worry about."

Could Sahara see the flames? Would she know where they came from? At only four years old, it was already clear their daughter was brilliant.

Renae turned Sahara slightly, shifting her line of sight.

But Renae couldn't turn away. Not from the street where—

"Alex!"

*He was there.* Running. She knew the outlines of his tall figure even in the dark. Carrying something.

She hauled herself to her feet, still holding Sahara, and half-ran toward him.

A moment later, his arms were around both of them and his tears flowed as hot as hers.

"When I saw that ticking clock, I was so afraid. So afraid you two wouldn't get out..."

"We're safe, Alex. We're all safe." She pressed her head against his shoulder. "Did you—did you get the man out?"

Was it wrong to hope his answer was negative?

"He wasn't there."

She gulped, stared up at his face.

"I guess I didn't hit him that hard. He woke up. Got out somehow."

Renae's strength hit its limit. She pushed Sahara into Alex's arms and searched the darkness beyond him. "Do you think he's still looking for us?"

"I don't know."

She bent to retrieve what Alex had dropped when he reached them. His shoes. And... the black briefcase Giada left behind.

She held it aloft, a question in her eyes.

"I know. Of all the things to grab. I'm not sure why I did, but it was like instinct or something."

"Come." She led them both to the bench, where they slipped on their shoes, then wrapped the blanket snugly around Sahara.

Alex lifted the little girl once more, and in silent agreement, they moved deeper into the shadows of the park.

Minutes later, they reached the opposite border, dropped to the last bench they'd encounter, and sat in silence, attention turned toward their neighborhood.

She couldn't see the fire from here. But sirens split the silence of the park.

No dangerous figure appeared out of the shadows.

Were they safe? At least for now?

"What are we going to do, Alex?"

"What we planned. We're going to leave. Clearly, it's not safe for us here."

Heat poured into her chest, a white-hot fierce protection of those she loved.

"I will never forgive her for this."

Alex wrapped his free arm around her shoulder. "Focus on the future right now, Renae."

Sahara squirmed against his chest. "Daddy, I'm cold. And I don't have any shoes."

Alexander was silent.

Renae glanced at his face.

Twisted with grief, his eyes clenched against tears.

Sahara had no shoes, it was true. But they had lost everything else as well.

Everything but the clothes they wore, Alexander still in his ridiculous striped pajamas. A single blanket.

And a briefcase.

She lifted the leather case from the ground, rested it on her thighs, and popped the latches open.

As promised, it contained a large amount of cash. A stack of new bills, as well as a wrapped bundle of what must be bills from around 1894.

A clay-colored folder of typed pages lay in the bottom, information about Howard Carter, it appeared. And a tiny stone cup, with faded markings of a king's name inscribed inside an oval cartouche. Tutankhamun's, no doubt.

"That's where we're going to escape." Alexander's voice was low, but solid again.

"What? Even after what she's done—"

"Think about it, Renae. It's the last place she'd think to look for us."

"I'm not helping her!"

"No, that's not what I'm saying. We won't do anything to

prevent Carter from his path. Won't go to Egypt to find this el-Rassul character. But we've got plane tickets, a way to get introduced to Carter, and a briefcase full of currency for London in 1894. In what other period in the past would we have any kind of start to a life?"

"And you don't think she would think of that? Follow us there, or send someone after us?"

He chewed his lip. "We'll lie low for a while. Be careful."

"And when would we come back? How could we know it was safe?"

Alexander turned back toward their house, as if he could see its burning remains from here. "What do we have to come back to, really?"

"Your job, for one thing!"

"But if we revise… We'd have to let the time pass when we return, or we'll be right back in the same trouble. They aren't likely to invite me to step back into the position I abandoned with no warning."

"So, 1894… forever?"

He closed his eyes and leaned his head back. "I don't know. Maybe until Sahara is old enough."

"Old enough to time travel, you mean?"

He nodded, eyes still closed. "Until she can keep herself safe from the Giada Morettis of the world."

"And our parents? What will they think has happened?"

"We'll get a message to them. Your mother, my father—perhaps they can visit us in the past…"

It was too awful to contemplate, all of it.

Renae pulled a few current bills from the stack of cash, then snapped the briefcase closed. "Let's go find a taxi."

Alexander shifted Sahara in his arms, and the girl opened her eyes again to stare into his.

"Daddy?" Her breath puffed white in the moonlight.

"Yes, sweetheart?"

"I'm hungry."

# CHAPTER SEVEN

*December 21, 1922*
*Valley of the Kings, Egypt*

hree days later we had a travel plan, I'd crammed my brain with every detail of Ramesses III and his Harem Conspiracy, and we'd created a tale for my colleagues about a last-minute trip to Cairo for Christmas, to introduce me to Jack's visiting family.

That last part was Jack's idea, and I objected at first.

"They will all think we're... a couple. A serious couple."

It was after nine in the evening, and we hovered over the table in the American House's kitchen, sharing a huge wedge of Panya's apple pie. The house cook loved to bake even more than I did.

Jack playfully pushed my fork away from the perfect bite of golden crust I was aiming for.

"Yes. Yes, they will."

I glanced up.

He didn't meet my eyes.

"Fine. Christmas in Cairo." I stabbed the pie crust.

Jack nodded. "And since I'll get back here to 1922 the same

moment as we leave for our trip to Ramesses' time, I'll find a place to wait it out in Luxor, until you return."

I relaxed against the wooden chair, belly comfortably full. "Jack, what if…"

"What?"

"What if, while you're waiting for me, Reuben makes good on his threat to return to 2002, and then Giada sends two others here to drag you back? What if you're gone when I come back?"

"I'm not going to let her do that."

"Come on, Jack. You know she could make it happen. They could show up while you're sleeping." I waved my fork at the air of the kitchen. "We don't exactly have security here."

"Then we need a meeting spot." He grinned. "Like Valentine's Day, on top of the Empire State Building."

"What's the Empire—"

"Never mind. Not built yet. A spot somewhere in the past, obviously. A place and time we agree on now, if we should ever get separated."

"That's good, yes. It should be in Egypt, since this is where we're more likely to have a problem."

"So what's a famous happening we can pinpoint?"

"Deaths are always useful, since they're so well-documented in the records. Lesser-known events and the years they occurred can be so uncertain. I suppose the future's not like that—now that everything is documented in books and photographs?"

Jack laughed. "You'd be surprised at how even printed media can be manipulated to tell us things that aren't true."

"Well, I'm sure my parents chose Nero's death for our meeting time because it's a known date."

"How about Cleopatra?" Jack winked as he said the name.

I laughed. "Oh, so you want to meet the most famous seductress in history, do you?"

He shrugged. "Hey, we have to pick somebody."

"Okay. She'll work. But we're aiming for the day of her death, so I'm afraid you won't get much time with her."

"Hmmm. Too bad." He finished the pie, smiling.

"So, 30 BC, the day of Cleopatra's death, in Alexandria."

"Got it. But if we do get separated, no running back to 30 BC immediately. You might be in the past somewhere, revising history, and might be on the way back, or just figuring something out."

I drummed my fingers on the table top. "Then, three weeks. Three weeks alone, before we'll meet at Cleopatra's palace in Alexandria on the day of her suicide."

"Another suicide, like Nero? Geez, why are these people always killing themselves?"

"Because it was better than the alternative."

We sat in silence, as though the idea cast a pall over our entire plan.

Not that we had much of a plan, beyond getting back to 1155, inserting ourselves somehow into the Harem Conspiracy, finding a young Giada in the midst of all the craziness and stopping her from learning whatever it was she used later.

Oh, and not getting executed.

I was armed with all the knowledge we had, but it wasn't much.

"It's getting late, Jack. Helen or Minnie will be in here soon, raising their eyebrows over us."

He pulled me closer. "Then let's give them something to talk about."

I slipped from his grasp, stood, and cleared the pie plate and forks.

He studied me, mouth downturned. "Sahara, I'm not giving up, you know."

"I know."

And I did. He continued to help me search for my parents, at risk to himself. I no longer suspected him of being so loyal to Giada that he would deceive me.

So what held me back from giving in to the one thing I was beginning to want, as much as I wanted to find my family or leave a legacy in Egypt?

Mostly one undeniable fact. Jack would have to remain in the past. Never return to his life, his family. Just like my parents had done.

I said goodnight to Jack in the hall outside my bedroom, slept fitfully, and met him back in the kitchen before daybreak.

We both carried satchels, packed as if for a Christmas jaunt north to Cairo, and wore traveling clothes. He would need his belongings while he waited for me to return, and would hold on to mine.

Despite the early hour, Helen Winlock was already drinking her coffee in the kitchen.

"Headed to Cairo, then?" she asked. "Unchaperoned?" Eyebrows raised, of course.

I forced a smile. "Only until we join Jack's family, later today."

Jack winked at Helen. "Don't worry, Mrs. Winlock. I'll be on my best behavior."

She sipped coffee and watched me over the rim of her cup. "I should hope so."

I'd arranged the day before to have my favorite Egyptian driver, Chefren, outside at dawn, and he did not disappoint.

"No digging today, *sayida*?" Chefren pointed to my traveling clothes with the stub end of his ever-present cigar.

"To Medinet Habu this morning, Chefren." I nodded toward Jack. "A bit of sightseeing."

We traveled the two-and-a-half kilometers south, to the edge of the Nile floodplain, in tense silence. Thus far, Jack had refused all information about our destination, the Harem Conspiracy, and Ramesses III. He claimed I would give him too much history and it would interfere with his ability to be "in the moment." I was dying to prepare him with at least the basics, but it seemed best to wait until we were free from an audience.

Chefren rolled the Fiat to a stop at the entrance to the Medinet Habu site and the massive Mortuary Temple of Ramesses III.

"How long you wish me to wait, *sayida*?"

I glanced at Jack, a feeling of *deja vu* sweeping me. Nearly two months ago, I asked Chefren to wait outside the tomb of Tut-ankh-amun while I traveled in time. Except I hadn't returned, and Chefren eventually left. Perhaps he wondered if today would be a repeat.

But no—today, today Jack would be returning to the moment we left.

I held on to that fact, pushing away the question of whether Jack's mind would be intact. He was strong.

"Uh, yes, I suppose we'll be here about thirty minutes, if you want to wait. Or we could walk into town—"

Chefren waved away my suggestion. "I will wait."

We climbed from the automobile and slammed the doors, raising a cloud of desert dust.

Jack lifted my satchel strap over his own shoulder. "I have a feeling when I return here without you, that guy is not going to be happy."

"Hmm. Yes, you'll have to tell him I'm doing some drawings or something. Tell him you'll come back for me in a couple of hours."

We crossed into the wide courtyard of the ruins of Ramesses III's palace and temple.

"And how *will* you get back to the American House once you've returned?"

"Well, you'll know how long we were in the past, so you'll know when I'm getting back, right? You can arrange a ride for me."

Jack smiled. "You're getting the hang of this. Sure, I'll figure out someone to send, to give you a ride. So you can meet me wherever I'm lounging."

"That would be great. Thanks."

Jack elbowed me. "I'm joking. I will be here myself. Trying not to pass out from holding my breath."

We stood for a moment, gazing up at the top of the first pylon wall, some twenty meters above our heads. I scanned the carved reliefs of men and plants, but suppressed the urge to explain each to Jack.

"Let's get inside. Away from Chefren's watchful eye."

We passed through the huge doorway, into the first court-yard, lined on our right with six pillars fronted by carved statues of Osiris, and on the left by the columns in front of the first temple.

Jack took in the well-preserved site. "So, Ramesses's palace? Or a temple? Or where he was buried?"

"Yes." I laughed. "Mostly. This is his mortuary temple, where Egyptians worshipped him after his death. The palace connected to it, over there." I pointed. "But he was buried in the Valley, in KV11."

"Okay, I'm ready for my history lesson. Just make it brief. I don't have a memory like yours."

I wandered to the back wall of the courtyard and ran my hand along the bas-reliefs, Jack following. "See how deep these carvings are? Made it harder for successors to chip them out and erase their predecessor's victories."

"What are those round holes?" Jack pointed to the upper part of the wall.

"This place went through a few variations of use over the years. The Romans used it as a military post. And those holes were likely for beams used in a Coptic church built inside the temple here."

"Okay, but what about the Harem Conspiracy, and all that?"

"Right. So, Ramesses III was the last significant king of the Twentieth Dynasty, following after his father, Ramesses the Great."

"Sounds like Dad was a lot to live up to."

"He was. Ramesses III also had political chaos to deal with, attacks from the group known as The Sea Peoples, and a famine probably caused by fallout from a massive volcanic explosion in Iceland and the cooling period it caused."

"So things weren't good."

"No, not good. Egypt was slipping economically and politi-cally. And when the famine meant he couldn't supply food rations for the workers constructing this site and his tomb, he ended up with the first recorded labor strike in history."

Jack traced the ridges of the carved hieroglyphs, as I had done. "So, I'm guessing the harem wives had their own complaints?"

"Not all of them. One secondary wife in particular, Tiye. Ramesses had declared the son of his chief wife would follow him, Ramesses IV.

"Creative with the names."

"Well, they had other names, but the dynasty relied on naming conventions to preserve the line. But his secondary wife, Tiye, wasn't happy with his chosen successor, and wanted her own son, Pentawer, put on the throne when her husband died."

"Understandable."

We drifted into another chamber, admiring the painted walls.

"So Tiye enlisted a handful of court officials and overseers to assassinate the pharaoh."

Jack chuckled. "Hmm. That's more problematic, I guess."

"Yes, she had all the overseers—of the harem, the cattle, the treasury, the palace butler—all in her pocket, carrying messages out of her restricted access in the royal harem's Western Tower, in a big conspiracy to kill Ramesses."

"And?"

"And it doesn't appear she was successful. We know the names of all the conspirators because they were all executed after their trial. Her son, Pentawer, was allowed to commit suicide."

"Generous. What about Tiye herself?"

"Unknown."

Jack sucked in a breath, chest expanding. "Okay, so what's our plan? We're heading into a conspiracy, with everyone trying to murder the pharaoh. But where and how do we intersect my Aunt Giada? And derail her nefarious future?"

I laughed. "Wow. Dramatic."

He shrugged and grinned.

"But that's one question I can't answer. All we know is that she somehow returned to her university digsite with knowledge of where to find a valuable piece. We can assume she didn't bring it back with her, or even change its location so she could find it later, since she's not a Revisionist. And since Ramesses' tomb has been empty for hundreds of years, it probably wasn't hidden there."

"So, we'll need to hang out with her a bit, to figure it out?"

"If by 'hang out' you mean spend time with her, then, yes. Is that going to be difficult for you?"

Jack surveyed the inside of the temple ruins, brow furrowed. "Not difficult, no. Just odd. But I don't think we should tell her who I am, who we are. We're already treading dangerous ground, messing with history—mine and yours. I'd prefer to keep the damage to a minimum."

"Agreed. So if we're not Sahara and Jack, who are we?"

"Hmm. Was it just the pharaoh who had concubines?"

"Very funny."

"Fine, you can be my wife."

"And we're visiting... from Syria. Claiming to be foreign smoothed over lots of issues for me when I was with Senamun."

"Syria. Got it."

I wandered through the lofty arch of the second pylon into the second courtyard. "Let's move into a side chapel, over here. Hopefully quiet when we show up in 1155."

"And when exactly are we showing up?"

"Exactly at daybreak on the fifteenth day of the third month of the Shemu summer season."

Jack laughed. "Could you be more specific?"

I grinned. "The conspiracy is well-documented in the judicial papyrus. It was during the Beautiful Festival of the Valley."

Jack scanned the sky above us. "They were celebrating this valley as beautiful? I thought it was all about death."

"They were celebrating death."

"Ah, of course."

"The commotion around the festival helped distract from the conspiracy."

"Ok, so we're hitting daybreak on the morning of the

conspiracy. What if that's not soon enough? What if Giada gets up to no good before that?"

"We need something specific to aim for when we travel. And I've been thinking about that possibility, but Giada would have needed a specific moment as well. And I think that's what she would have chosen—the day it all happened."

"Smart."

"I see only one possible problem. It's our dating chronology. Scholars don't always agree on exact dates for events, for reigns and deaths of kings. We're cutting this one close, since we believe I've already been to 1075, exactly eighty years prior, to see Seti's mummy relocated."

"Well, we won't know until we try."

"So, let's try."

We chose what was believed to be a chapel inside the mortuary temple. But did we know for certain? What if we "appeared" in the center of a busy kitchen?

It was beginning to feel familiar, this touching of ancient places, head down, mind fixed on a point in history. Jack and I placed hands on the wall inside the chapel, fingers interlaced, heads bent together.

I didn't mind the spinning, the vertigo, the slight twinge of nausea. As long as it worked.

And Jack was there when I lifted my head, so all was well.

We emerged into 1155 BC against the same wall of the chapel, but instead of stone chips at our feet, the glazed floor met a flawless wall, with a few reed baskets of ochre fabric stacked beside. I ran a hand through the fabric to ground myself. Robes for priests, it would seem. So our assumptions about the use of this chamber were correct.

The chapel lay in deep shadow, with the light of the rising sun blocked by walls and pylons. But enough light for us each to scan ourselves, and the other.

Jack looked identical to how I first saw him in Tut-ankh-amun's palace, The House of Rejoicing, when he pretended not to know me. Bare chest, white triangular skirt knotted at his hip. Shaved head, kohl-painted eyes.

He ran a hand over his head and cursed. "I forgot about the bald thing. Makes me feel like an old man."

I skimmed his muscular chest with my gaze. "You don't look like an old man."

His lips twitched into a smile. "Well, thank you, ma'am. You are looking quite fine yourself."

I put a hand to my beaded hair and smoothed the white sheath dress, hugging embarrassingly close to my curves.

Jack held out a hand. "Let's go find my aunt."

I grasped his hand with my own. "And derail her nefarious future."

# CHAPTER EIGHT

*Fifteenth day of the third month of Shemu, 1155 BC*
*Thebes, Egypt*

$\mathcal{I}$ expected the temple to lay in shadow and silence at this hour, hoped even priests would not yet be about.

Perhaps because of the festival day, or perhaps every day was crowded here, but the chapel churned with people, and more than one of them did a double-take at our sudden appearance—eyes widening, heads shaking as if to refuse what their minds told them.

But when faced with a choice between people appearing out of thin air or some trick of the light, wouldn't anyone opt for the latter explanation?

"So what's the plan?" Jack touched my lower back possessively.

I pulled him aside. "I couldn't really make a plan. We have no idea what we'll encounter."

"And we have no idea what my Aunt Giada was doing here."

"If she's anything like the person I met more than fifteen years later, my guess is she's trying to insert herself into the center of the Harem Conspiracy."

"Sounds like you know her about as well as I do."

Resentment tinged Jack's words. The woman had betrayed his trust.

"So, logic dictates we make our way to the harem wing ourselves."

Easier said than done. We slipped from the temple chamber and began to work our way toward the adjoining palace. The usual frescoed walls and lotus-petaled columns painted in vivid shades of red, blue, and gold were near-twins to the House of Rejoicing we'd wandered in the time of Tut-ankh-amun.

"The air is different, though," Jack said, as if reading my mind about the similarities.

I eyed the sky above the open courtyard we crossed, the cobalt blue of our last trip to ancient Egypt muted by a slate gray.

"The volcanic ash, perhaps?" I pulled in a deep breath, half expecting to taste or smell the ashes, but all was desert dust, as usual.

We slipped into a palace hallway, and my sandals scuffed gritty flagstones. Yes, something about this place seemed dirtier. We were meeting ancient Egypt at the start of its slow decline.

Servants, priests and priestesses, and various officials criss-crossed courtyards and the hallways, ignoring us. Perhaps only trusted visitors reached this far into the palace. Still, we moved quickly, avoiding eye contact with anyone who might ask questions, looking purposeful, even as we had no idea of our destination.

"How will we know we've found the harem wing?" Jack jutted his chin toward a pair of bulky, iron-chested guards at the end of a corridor ahead.

"That would be one indication, probably."

"But we're not getting past them by looking as though we belong here."

We detoured quickly, and in perfect synchronization, before either of the two guards took note of us.

Jack tangled his fingers in my own and pulled me into a small storage chamber off the courtyard.

We took a breath in the dim light. Our first moment alone since arriving.

"Listen, Jack. If Giada is in the harem, we'll only find her if I go in alone."

"No way. Not going to happen."

"Splitting up is unavoidable. This whole thing today—the festival, the attempted coup—it all centers around the harem. There's no way we can get close enough to the action if we stay together."

Jack exhaled a ragged breath and glanced through the narrow doorway to the lush courtyard beyond, still busy with people.

"Can't I go in as a servant, or something?"

"Perhaps some male servants are allowed into the women's quarters, but I would guess only those who've been approved and are well known. I, however, might be able to pull off convincing them I'm a new member of Pharaoh's harem."

Jack's glance swung back to me, eyes stormy. "Okay, now I am definitely not on board with this. Why can't you be a servant? Why do you have to go in as Pharaoh's next conquest?"

I smiled. "Trust me, kings of Egypt were far too busy dealing with foreign invaders and local issues, not to mention big festival days and potential conspiracies, to be thinking much about spending time with their harem ladies."

"Yeah, not so sure I believe that. I've read about these guys having dozens and dozens of children. Somebody was spending time with somebody!"

"Fine. I guess they found time between politics." I grinned. "But I think we can feel confident it won't be today, with everything else going on."

Jack was still scowling, but at least he'd stopped arguing.

I nodded. "Good. Let's figure out a place to meet, and give me about an hour. I promise I won't stay away longer than that." I grabbed his arm. "And no going back to 1922 without me!"

*Or 2002,* I wanted to add, but I bit back that little touch of fearful sarcasm.

"Not funny." He shifted to peer through the open doorway, separating me from the corridor. "Back here. In this room. In less than one hour." He held my upper arms and even in the shadows, the intensity of his gaze pinned me. "Don't do anything risky. Come and get me." He tilted his head. "Are you even going to recognize her if she's in there?"

"Good question. She was, what, about forty when I met her? And now she's closer to twenty?"

"And dressed like an Egyptian."

I glanced down at my own dress, the white sheath that was beginning to feel like the uniform of ancient Egyptian women. This one did have a bit of colorful tasseling and some beads, at least.

"I guess I'll look for someone who seems as out of place as I do. Or maybe someone sneaking around, trying to steal priceless artifacts."

Jack shook his head. "There's nothing she can take from here, remember? She's not a Revisionist. The only thing that can help her in the future is knowledge. She must have learned something here, about where to dig in the future. And the only way we're going to stop her is to intercept her before she gets that information."

"Or…" I bit my lip, thinking. "Or, if we know what she learns, I can change it before I leave. Move it or destroy it. Something."

Jack sighed. "I guess it's all we have."

I took a step toward the door, but he wasn't letting me go yet.

He pulled me against his bare chest, hand around my head, pressing my cheek against his skin.

A little flare of something, deep within me, felt dangerous. I pushed away.

He caught my face in my hands and kissed me, his lips bruising mine as though he feared he'd never see me again.

I broke away, breathless. "I'll be fine, Jack. I promise. Let me locate her, and then we'll figure out what to do next, together."

I pulled from his embrace and melted into the corridor again.

In truth, I was far less confident than I sounded. Finding a woman I'd met briefly as a teen, when she was decades older than the version I'd meet today, sounded impossible. A twentieth century needle in an ancient haystack.

Shoulders back and eyes trained straight down the corridor, I marched toward the guards without meeting their glance.

As expected, they stepped together into the center of the hall. Wordless.

I could play that game. I lifted my eyes, looked at both of them, and raised my eyebrows in indignation. Said nothing.

"No unauthorized visitors." The brute on the right practically yawned as he delivered his command, and I had to focus to push past the initial mismatch of lips and words that happened each time I traveled to another time. His eyes roamed past me, sleepy and inattentive. Was guarding the harem so boring? It was about to get more interesting before the day was over.

"I am authorized. I am the newest wife of Ramesses, who is Powerful of Strength and Rich in Years. I'm newly brought from Syria."

The guard on the left chortled. "Another one?" He glanced at his compatriot. "How many new wives can one king acquire in a week?"

His friend lifted one of my braids over a callused and thick forefinger. "This one isn't nearly as fresh as the other two, though."

More laughter. "Probably got a litter of brats back in Syria already."

I huffed, pulled my hair from his creepy touch. "If you will excuse me…"

They stepped aside.

Shocking, but I'd pulled it off.

Although perhaps I owed credit to the two younger women, recently added to the harem ahead of me.

Younger women? Could one of them be Giada?

Regardless, we had found the right corridor, and I was one

step closer to stopping that evil woman from a lifelong pursuit of ill-gotten gain through exploiting people like those in my family.

I glided down the corridor, glancing from the corner of my eye through open doors, into lavishly decorated chambers of lounging and milling women. If our knowledge of Egyptian harems was correct, I would encounter more than just these two muscled guards at the entrance. Somewhere, the overseer of the harem—what was his name?—would be keeping the women in check.

*Panouk*, that was it. And Pentawer was the son whose mother had arranged what was soon to come. The other names of the guilty cited in the judicial document, frustratingly, also started with the same letter. Pebekkamen, Panhayboni, Pendua, Pairy. They all held roles in court, from overseeing the royal cattle to the royal treasury, but I only bothered with remembering the man in charge of the harem and the prince at the center of the conspiracy.

I reached the end of the corridor with no obvious direction on how to find Giada. But I was far from giving up. This trip to the time of Ramesses III would be the last time I searched history for my parents. It was all going to change today.

I felt the determination in my chest, and it scared me. What exactly was I willing to do, to stop Giada?

First, I needed to find her.

I slid into the chamber at the end of the hall, eyes on the half-dozen women scattered around the room.

Much like Ankhe-sen-amun's ladies-in-waiting when I traveled to ancient Egypt months ago, these women barely registered my entrance. A few sideways glances, then back to their clothes and jewels and makeup.

But no, there was something else in those furtive looks, and the studied way they did not acknowledge my entrance.

They knew. They all knew something was about to happen, and they were trying to stay out of it. Or thought I was part of it.

Good. Let them avoid me. More time to examine each one in

turn, searching for someone who belonged here no more than I did.

That one? Lounging across a lion-headed narrow bed that rested on four clubbed feet like paws? She was young and pretty and thin, with the looping wadjet eye paint and a lipstick that shimmered gold in the light. But was her skin tone perhaps a bit too dark for Giada's European heritage?

She flicked a glance over me, sensing my attention, but then her eyes moved on.

No, she seemed too... at ease. Too comfortable here.

I sauntered toward a wide wooden chair tucked into the front corner of the room, and lowered myself to it, then leaned back with half-closed eyes to study each of the other five women.

This one, wrapping robes around herself—too curvy. That one, fitting a jeweled collar of tubular turquoise stones tight against her throat—too short.

None of them seemed to fit the description in my memory. But nearly twenty years had passed for me, and more than the same undone for her.

The oddness of it all swept me.

My memory of Giada had always carried a whiff of fascination, of a sheltered teen girl encountering a sophisticated older woman. And now we would meet again, nearly in reverse.

Would Giada find *me* older and sophisticated?

I snorted a laugh, then covered my mouth when a few heads jerked in my direction. The laugh stayed in my chest, threatening to escape.

*Lock it down, Sahara.* The excitement of the day was already getting to me, before it had begun.

As if on cue, a shout from the corridor put every woman in the chamber on alert.

*No, not yet!* It was too early for the conspiracy to launch into full swing! If we didn't find Giada before it all began, our chances would fall to near zero.

I leapt for the doorway, darted into the hallway, and took quick stock.

Something happening at the end of the corridor. Two shorter men, arguing with the guards.

I took advantage of their distraction and trotted for the next open chamber door, then pushed into it before they saw me.

I rounded into the room, too fast and too desperate.

Only four women here, but every one of them stared at me, open-mouthed.

No doubt put on alert by the same shouting I heard.

Two of the women, young girls barely old enough to be marriageable, grabbed each other's hands and backed away from my sudden appearance.

The other two, who weren't much older, seemed more... amused?

One of them tall, with an athletic build and carefully applied kohl outlining striking blue eyes.

The other... Oh, my stars and glory...

Did the floor suddenly tilt and the sun snuff out?

The other woman was my mother.

# CHAPTER NINE

*Fifteenth day of the third month of Shemu, 1155 BC*
*Thebes, Egypt*

alf a moment after I locked eyes with my mother, someone knocked me flat to the tiled floor.

Air whooshed from my lungs. I choked in a breath and stared at the blurred pattern of blue stone under my forehead. Braced my fingertips on the tiles. Lifted a shaky glance to the two women.

Two women. Giada. And my mother.

Both in their early twenties, perhaps, neither with any idea of who I might be.

In fact, neither seemed aware of my presence.

"It is beginning!"

A lean man stood above and behind me, also ignoring the woman he'd flattened.

My breath returned in short hiccups of emotion and I teetered to my knees. The room still seemed off-kilter, and the air hazy around the edges of my vision.

How could this be?

Had Giada somehow found my mother already in the past?

Had she given up the search in Venice and come further back in time?

I pushed myself to my feet.

The older man jostled me aside.

A short fuzz of white hair ringed his shaved head, above a smooth, tanned face. He wore the traditional knotted white skirt and sandals. Impossible to guess his age, or his position. Was he one of the major players?

"Who are you?" His voice took on a strident tone.

I lifted my head. The jumble in my brain allowed for no ready lie to give him.

But he looked past me, to Giada and my mother.

So young. They were so young.

Wait… Giada could not have chased my mother here after losing her in Venice, when both were in their thirties. For these two women, Venice had not happened yet.

For that matter, *I had not happened yet.*

Another pass of vertigo. I flung a hand out to steady myself and found empty air.

Two staggering steps to my right, to the wall. I clutched at a stone bust of a woman, perched on a narrow pedestal. Her blank, kohl-lined eyes stared at me from under a conical headpiece.

Giada stepped in front of my mother. Was that a protective gesture?

She lifted her head to the man.

"We are new to the harem. What is beginning?"

The older man's forehead puckered and he took a step backward, as though regretting his earlier words.

But the two young girls in the back of the chamber scrambled toward him.

"Where is he, Panouk? Where is Pharaoh?"

"He is coming." The man's high, thin voice hinted at his status as a eunuch, probably the overseer of the harem. "He is coming to Tiye's chambers."

"It is too soon!"

This from Giada, speaking to my mother.

And they both looked... disappointed?

"I told you we should have come yesterday."

The first words I'd heard my mother speak in over seventeen years.

Words that changed everything.

Giada and my mother came here *together*. They were... friends.

Panouk shook his head, but his eyes narrowed on the two newcomers. "Everything is in place as expected. But you will want to be elsewhere when it happens. Pharaoh's guards will not tarry."

The harem overseer whirled on his sandals and disappeared deeper into the harem wing.

The two young girls clutched hands and followed after him through the door, but turned the other direction in the corridor, toward the courtyard.

Across from me, Giada and my mother faced each other, still oblivious to my presence.

"So? Stay here? Do you want to see it all the way through?"

My mother's voice matched my memories. Fun-loving, upbeat. Always ready for a challenge.

"That's what we came for. I'm not leaving yet!"

And Giada as well—a younger version of the headstrong woman I met at Highclere Castle.

"Fine, but we need a plan. And we need to find Alex. I'm not taking..."

But the rest of her words were lost to me.

My father. Here in ancient Egypt. Close enough to see him, to fall into his warm hug. To hear him whisper my name.

A shift in my balance, like tectonic plates sliding under my feet, nearly knocked me down again. I gripped the teetering stone bust with damp hands.

The rocking of the pedestal drew the attention of the two women.

"Are you... are you well?" My mother crossed the chamber,

her attention on me for the first time. "Did he hurt you, when he knocked you down?"

I shook my head and backed against the wall.

All I wanted in the world was to have her touch me. Embrace me. But somehow, the physical touch seemed to embody every bit of danger in traveling to the past and messing with your parents before your birth. What harm had I already done, simply by *seeing* her?

"Fine. I am fine." The words rasped from my dry throat, quiet as a whisper. At least the hysterical laughter remained pent in my chest.

Her eyes roamed my face, then my body. "You seem unhurt. But you need to stay hidden. This place is about to turn to madness."

A bubble of laughter escaped. As if anything could be more insane than facing your mother, more than ten years your junior.

She paused another moment, lips parted as though she wanted to say something more. Ask me something else. Her questioning eyes filled with the same empathy I remembered poured over my skinned knees and bee stings. Did she feel the strange sensations that dizzied me, as though time had warped, and with it, everything else? She smelled of lavender. Not the perfume she always wore in my youth.

And I was taller. Taller now than at fifteen when she disappeared, a few inches taller than her. As though I'd grown in an instant. Did Lewis Carroll's Alice feel this strange in Wonderland?

Giada grabbed her arm from behind. "Leave her. We're not going to see anything here."

I reached my free hand toward the past, but let it drop.

"Take care of yourself," she whispered. "Find somewhere to hide until all of this is over."

The two slipped from the room, in the direction Panouk had taken, toward the end of the hall where I began my search.

I followed.

No way was I letting either of them out of my sight.

The two young girls must have heeded Panouk's advice and disappeared from the harem wing, but it seemed the rest of the women, most of them closer to my age, chose to congregate *en masse* in the largest chamber at the end of the corridor.

Giada, my mother, and I stumbled past the two guards at the door, into a cacophony of shrill voices, fluttering hands and arms, choking perfume, and the criss-crossing paths of women who couldn't seem to decide whether to gather their clothes and jewels and flee, or retreat to the background to watch the action play out.

Somewhere, the soothing sound of stringed music played, but its chords were as effective as a trickle of warm water running through a raging fire.

A large woman bumped against me, glared as though it were my fault, and jabbed an elbow into my ribs for the offense.

Eyes never leaving my mother, I crossed to the side of the room and pressed my back and palms against a gritty wall fresco of sacrifices being offered to the ibis-headed Thoth, and my thigh against the lion-headed couch I'd noted earlier. I licked dry lips and tried to swallow against the tightness in my throat.

What would I say to her? Could I warn Renae of Giada's coming treachery? Not without explaining who I was, which seemed like a very bad idea.

I was already calling her Renae in my mind—as if my brain refused to call someone younger than myself *mother.*

I would have to process it all later—what it meant to find my parents here—but for now, our plan remained unchanged. We must remove Giada's chance to start looting the treasures of the past.

*So, this was how she did it.* I already knew one of my parents, perhaps both, were Revisionists. They must have helped her. But why?

Another man slid into the chamber, his muscled chest heaving and drawing the attention of every woman.

Panouk shot forward and swung the heavy wooden doors

closed behind the newcomer. "What took you so long?" He squinted up at the man, a foot taller than he.

"Pairy was late getting the pass—"

Panouk waved away the man's answer. "You must prepare. Quickly, now."

The large man's glance darted around the room.

Panouk pointed to an oversized couch-bed at the rear of the chamber, luxuriously draped with white linen.

Was that a knife in the man's hand?

He circled the bed and ducked behind it.

Panouk snapped his fingers at the crowd of women. "Stop your gawking! Go about your business!"

Nothing seemed further from natural than a dozen women standing around a chamber doing nothing more than playing with trinkets or fussing with their hair.

But we did not have long to practice the act.

The double doors yanked open. Two massive guards filled the open space.

Above their heads, the white and red of the double crown of the Two Lands of Upper and Lower Egypt was just visible.

From behind him somewhere, a strident voice called out his entrance. "The Pharaoh Ramesses, Great of Kingship, the Strong Bull and Powerful Lion, Strong-Armed, the Lord of Strength."

All that strength was about to be tested.

The guards swung apart as if attached to the door apparatus themselves, and there he was.

Ramesses III, last great king of the Twentieth Dynasty.

Walking into a trap.

From the Judicial Papyrus, we knew the names of many—perhaps all—of the conspirators brought to justice. How long did it take to apprehend them? Would Ramesses suspect the imminent attack from behind the bed and refuse to even approach?

I glanced at Renae and Giada.

They stood with arms linked, as if the best of friends, and eyes wide on the scene before us.

I knew that look. The thrill of watching words in a textbook morph into images and leap from the page before your eyes.

Ramesses surveyed the room. "What a crowd of preening birds!"

The women paused in their play-acting and each of them glanced his way.

"It must cost half the treasury of Egypt to keep you all in jewels and finery."

One of the women, tall and slender, with almond eyes and a paler complexion than most of the others, sidled closer to the king and caressed his arm.

"And every one of us loves you for it, my king." Her lips curved into the satisfied smirk of a cat after a kill. "Come, my love," she pulled him toward the couch. "Come and rest. We will get rid of all of these." She waved a hand at the rest of us. "We will have privacy."

But "all of these" remained fixed in place, like statuary sculpted here to watch this drama unfold.

I split my attention between the king being lured to an attack and the two women I could not afford to lose. Thoughts for my own safety tickled the back of my mind, but remaining still through the careening onslaught of emotion commanded all my attention.

Ramesses patted the cheek of the tall wife. "Ah, Tiye, you are always so persuasive."

So this was Tiye, the secondary wife behind the conspiracy, who wished to see her son, Pentawer, on the throne instead of his half-brother.

Ramesses allowed himself to be led to the couch-bed. He removed the double crown with its falcon and snake and handed it to Panouk, then flung himself across the linens, head resting on the curved wooden arm. The red sash at his waist, like a trickle of blood against the white linen, seemed an ill omen.

His eyes turned toward Panouk, and then the rest of his audience, all of us still watching in frozen silence.

Something—perhaps a note of fear—flickered across his expression.

He sensed something amiss. Perhaps thoughts of ambush were never far from the mind of a king.

Ramesses braced a hand against the couch and began to lift himself.

Tiye pressed his shoulder downward, pinning him there for a moment.

But it was long enough.

The hidden attacker rose from behind the couch like the sudden appearance of an army on the desert horizon.

The knife in his hand flashed downward. Toward the king.

Several women screamed.

Tiye yanked her hand from Ramesses's shoulder, but not before the knife caught her forearm in its thrust.

The slash to Tiye's arm was a flesh wound.

Ramesses did not fare so well.

The knife found his throat, just under the ear, and a wide, red smile opened across his neck, reaching for the other ear.

I pressed a hand to my mouth, stifling my own scream.

The king's body convulsed. Blood poured from his slashed throat, burbled up and over his bare chest, puddled on the white linen.

So much blood.

I'd seen Nero die by his own hand, stabbing himself in the same place, just under his chin.

And while the Roman emperor's death was gruesome, Ramesses' death was nothing like Nero's.

The violation. The fleeting expressions of surprise, betrayal, fear. The glassy-eyed stare that began to fix on a distant place and grow still.

Like Florin, in an alley in Rome.

To believe yourself the master of an empire one moment and realize you have been murdered the next—I felt every ounce of the violent shift in his mind.

My hands shook, tiny tremors I could not control.

Would the lion-headed bed at my knee hide me in the dust under it?

The room lay silent for a single beat of shock. And then the screaming began.

Panouk shrieked the loudest. "The king! Pharaoh has been attacked!"

Women shoved and tripped and pushed. A mad scramble to leave the room.

But the two guards who had preceded Pharaoh burst through the doors, bronze-bladed spears blocking any exit.

They took in the scene in an instant.

One of them backed into the hall. "Seal the corridor!" He delivered the shout over his shoulder, then rocked forward into the room.

The other darted past him. Perhaps to aid the king, though the blood-saturated couch showed it to be a useless effort.

It took half a second for the guard to spot the attacker, knife still in his hand, and run him through with his spear. He yanked the weapon backward, tearing open the man's chest, and left him where he fell.

My mind thudded with possibilities, my limbs frozen.

Had the presence of my parents changed history? The Harem Conspiracy had failed, hadn't it? Ramesses's name was in the Judicial Papyrus as the one who brought the charges against the conspirators. Was it simply honorary language for a murdered king? Or were my parents revising history?

I glanced toward Renae, to see if she appeared surprised.

She was gone.

Panic stabbed my own chest.

Where had they run?

*There*, just slipping from the chamber. The guards were occupied with the king and his murderer, and a new contingent had not yet arrived to guard the door. In the vacuum, harem women streamed into the corridor, away from the grisly scene. And in the middle of the crowd, Giada and Renae.

I shoved into the fleeing mob.

# CHAPTER TEN

*Fifteenth day of the third month of Shemu, 1155 BC*
*Thebes, Egypt*

The tide of teeming bodies sucked me halfway down the corridor ahead.

Giada and Renae staggered from the melee and stepped to the side of the hall.

And they were not alone. A third person joined them from the direction of the open courtyard, no doubt summoned by the chaos.

I faced a strange, dizzying concoction of Egyptian slave and a young Alexander Aldridge. He had my father's straight nose, that same generous mouth. The build of a man who was athletic despite preferring books and ruins. But also the shaved head, the bare chest, the knotted white fabric at his waist.

A tiny spark somewhere deep in my chest burst into flame.

My father. Only a few steps from me.

He had one hand on each of the women's arms, and a stormy expression for them which reminded me, strangely, of Jack. Or perhaps all men looked at women they cared about, who'd gotten themselves into danger, in that half-scolding, half-admiring way.

I slowed at the fringes of the crowd, let it surge and play out around me. Touched one hand to the wall for support, and the other to my cheek, wet with unexpected tears.

He glanced around, at the thinning mob, at the guards rushing toward the death-chamber of Ramesses. His eyes even skimmed over me, leaning against the wall, weeping and staring.

At his look, I straightened, wiped my face with the back of my hand.

But then his attention moved on.

I sagged against the stone again.

Still with a hand on each of the two women, he pulled them toward himself.

A clot of chattering harem wives obstructed my view for a moment, and when they cleared, the three in the hall had vanished.

*No!* Not yet. I couldn't lose them, back to their future. Not before I learned more. And had we intervened in Giada's beginnings?

I shoved forward. They must still be here. This corridor was an illogical place for time travel. Too random, here in this hall, with nothing nearby but a… storage room!

The tiny chamber where Jack and I agreed to meet—they must have slipped into its shadows.

Did they find Jack waiting for them?

I pushed through, nearly heedless of those in my way, reached the doorway in a moment, and stumbled into the room.

A collective gasp at my sudden entrance met me.

Even in the half-light, I could see four figures.

"Oh, it's you." Renae stepped away from the others and touched a hand to my shoulder.

I flinched under her touch. But the fabric of space and time didn't tear apart, so that connection must be acceptable to whatever power was running this time travel operation.

She pulled her hand away, sensing my discomfort.

I tasted regret.

"You weren't hurt back there, in all that, were you?" Her eyes were as soft as ever.

I shook my head, unable to speak.

Behind her, Jack stood with his back rammed against the rear wall, his eyes wide.

My father faced him, taking stock of how much of a threat Jack might be.

But Jack's attention was on the third woman in the room.

Aunt Giada.

Jack's eyes flicked to me, an almost imperceptible tilt of his head toward Giada.

*Yes, I know who she is.* But how could I tell him who else she had with her?

And what did it mean, to find these three together? Had Jack and I been wrong about Giada? Perhaps Jack's aunt wasn't chasing my parents through history for some sinister purpose. Perhaps they'd all become friends in the past somewhere—here?—and Giada was simply trying to track them down, just like I was.

Something else tickled at the edges of my contemplation, a thought still too elusive to grab hold, dancing behind a curtain of confusion, but too important to ignore.

From behind my mother, my father spoke for the first time.

"I think... I think he's dead."

Giada laughed, a sharp, quick laugh of playful mockery. "You think? Well, I guess you didn't see that wound, did you?"

"But he wasn't supposed to be killed. The books say—"

"Ach, you and your books, Alex." Giada grabbed his arms and shook him, still laughing. "We're *here*. Forget your books!"

They spoke so freely in front of us, even though they could have no idea who we were.

My eyes found Jack again, this time with his jaw dropped. He'd heard what Giada called my father. Put it together immediately.

Now what?

The screams of harem women and pounding of guards' feet in the hall ceased. The initial chaos had ebbed, but now the true danger would begin, as the Medjay—Egypt's version of a police force—would move in and begin to hunt down the conspirators.

Four strangers in a storage room seemed likely contenders.

"We should stay quiet. Stay hidden." I whispered the words into the darkness. "They'll be looking for anyone suspicious."

The three glanced my direction, but seemed unconcerned.

"What shall we do?" Renae's eager voice, directed to her friends. "Spend the day, like we did in Rome? We could ask these two locals to give us a tour of the palace, the temples, even the Nile."

It was as if Jack and I were extra players in a theater production to them, little more than props. Jack's earlier confession surfaced. *All the people I've met in the past, they were like walking, talking museum pieces to me. They weren't real.*

But it was more than that. These three had no fear of their words changing history, changing anything. They knew once they abandoned the past, the past would lie undisturbed, still hidden like an undiscovered tomb. They could say and do anything here.

Giada shook her head. "Too much going on here for us to simply wander around. This lady is right." She jutted a chin in my direction. "They'll be looking for anyone to blame. Rounding them up and executing them." Her voice held a tinge of excitement.

"Exactly. It's not safe for us." My father's look included both of them. But not me. "We should go home. Although…"

Renae laughed. "I know that tone. What burning question must you answer before you leave?"

"It's only that all the analysis of the Judicial Papyrus has assumed Ramesses survived this conspiracy. If he is truly dead, then it changes the chronology, changes what we—"

"Fine, whatever!" Giada swatted Alexander's chest. "Go see a dead pharaoh, then."

Jack's glance met mine in that moment. He felt it, too. Something in Giada's voice, the way she touched my father.

Giada was in love with Alexander Aldridge.

A surge of nausea, the shadows shifting. And that earlier dancing thought, still just out of reach—

"Your friend is right," Jack was pulling away from the wall. "It's not safe for you here. It would be best if you went back… to wherever you came from." He looked to my father. "I would be glad to help you escort your women to safety."

*Your women.* I rolled my eyes, but he missed my look.

He had the right idea, though. The sooner we could get these three out of 1155 BC, the greater our chances of undoing whatever got started here.

"Well, I've seen enough bloody dictators in my life." Giada leaned toward the doorway, peering out. "I, for one, want to see that nasty wife Tiye and her sniveling son get what's coming to them."

"Giada, revenge for her rudeness to you seems a bit petty, don't you think?"

Giada swung her attention back to my mother.

Even in the dark, tiny flashes of anger shone in her eyes. "You two go. Renae can show you where to find the body, Alex. I'll meet you where we entered. Soon."

My father exhaled, looking between the two women. Clearly torn between his loyalty to both, and the professional curiosity that would turn him into one of London's best scholars one day.

"I'll go with you," Jack pushed past him to stand eye-to-eye with Giada.

His aunt appraised him from head to sandal, then gave him a flirtatious, one-sided smile. "Sounds good to me."

Jack's head swiveled in my direction, his own wide-eyed nausea playing over his face.

I swallowed, nodded. "You should go with her. I will… help them." Did my body lean toward my parents of its own accord? "I will meet you in the chapel." *Where we arrived*, I wanted to say, but it seemed too obvious a signal to the others.

He turned serious eyes toward me. "No returning home… without each other."

I reached to grip his hand. "We leave together."

And then the two disappeared through the doorway—the aunt and her impossibly older nephew—leaving me with my young parents.

Renae touched my arm. "You don't need to stay with us. We can find a way—"

"I want to." The words tumbled out, too eager. Too desperate. "To help you."

A slight furrow between her brows, one I remembered so well, nearly undid me.

I slipped to the door, avoiding her gaze. "I'm not certain how we can get close enough."

Renae sighed heavily. "Alexander, I don't know why you will never believe a thing unless you see it yourself. Here—ask this woman—is there any chance the pharaoh is still alive, after that brutal attack?"

I glanced between them. Ramesses lay dead in that chamber, I had no doubt. But I understood my father's need to see for himself. And I wanted to prolong my time with them.

"Don't force the poor woman to argue for you, Renae." He smiled on me. "I'm sorry. What is your name?"

The question knocked the air from my lungs. I took an unsteady breath.

"Gobi." The name of the first desert that came to mind. I would not give them my real name. And it sounded a bit Egyptian, didn't it? "My name is Gobi."

"Well, we thank you for your help, Gobi. I am Alexander, and this is Renae."

No need to disguise their names, their identities, then. They must assume their time here would be erased.

I nodded at their introduction, words caught in my throat.

"Gobi is right, Alex. No one is going to be allowed near that chamber. Certainly not until the priests arrive to begin the rites."

I blew out a breath. "Then we could be priests."

The two stared, questioning.

"I know where we can find robes. If we hurry, we could get to the chamber before the true priests arrive."

Renae grinned and extended a hand toward the door. "Then lead on, Gobi."

We slipped from the storage chamber, and I led them through the palace corridors, back toward the adjoining temple. We walked quickly, heads down, making no eye contact with the few who rushed past.

The silent walk afforded me a moment to think. To process the impossible, and yet obvious. My assumptions were crumbling.

Giada had not traveled back in time to seek out my parents, to exploit the ability of a legendary Revisionist. They had been friends.

Giada's "native" time seemed unquestionable—she was born in the late twentieth century, if Jack were to be believed. And why would he tell me he traveled from 2002, if it weren't true?

And if Giada was not born in the nineteenth century, was it possible my parents were not either?

It was only a small leap from that query to the biggest puzzle of all. What was the year of my own birth? Was it 1890, as I had always believed?

Or had I actually been born much later?

# CHAPTER ELEVEN

*December 30, 1974*
*Philadelphia, Pennsylvania*

*H*eavy, snow-gray clouds scudded across the slice of gloomy sky Giada could see from the second-floor window of her master suite.

From her slouched position in a deep-cushioned leather chair at the window, she felt she might never lift her head again.

The day started with energy. In the three days since her proposal to Alexander and Renae, she'd come up with a better incentive for the couple to help her by traveling back to 1894 and ensuring the el-Rassul family discovered another treasure cache to make the twentieth-century branch of the family rich once more.

Perhaps Alexander couldn't be pressured by hearing Giada was in danger. She should have known money wouldn't entice him, either. But one thing would.

When Ahmed Abd el-Rassul phoned her yesterday to find out when her Revisionist would travel back to do his bidding, she explained Alexander's reticence.

"You told him about me, then? Explained about my family

and TT320? That the goat story was a cover for my grandfather's time travel expedition?"

"Yes, yes, I explained it all. Told him what he needs to do. Offered to pay him well. He'll come around, I'm certain."

But she was far from certain.

And during the two days of waiting for her phone to ring, she realized something she should have thought of earlier. The best way to convince Alexander was not to tempt him with money or scare him with threats.

No, Alexander would be enticed by one thing only: knowledge. Or, more specifically, the opportunity to be involved in one of the greatest advances in archaeological knowledge to date.

She could give him that. Surely they could work out a plan, one that would provide Ahmed abd el-Rassul with the family wealth he demanded, but also would place Alexander in the right place, at the right time, with the right connections, to "discover" the tomb...

But her plan shattered to pieces this morning when she switched on the tiny television on her kitchen counter while scrambling a couple of eggs, and caught the early morning news.

*Sad news this morning, as it appears that late last night, a young family has tragically perished in a house fire...*

Alexander Aldridge, a local college professor, along with his wife Renae and their young daughter, Sahara.

Blast of unknown origin.

Giada barely noticed the crack of the porcelain bowl on the ceramic tile of her kitchen.

And even now, hours later, raw eggs puddled on the kitchen floor, drying around the ragged yellow edges, as she sagged in the chair beside her bedroom window.

The news provided too few details, but she'd used connections to learn more.

Arson, the fire department was saying. Some kind of explosive device. Alexander's body had been found, totally burned, in the bedroom. Renae's and Sahara's bodies, still unaccounted for, but the device detonated directly under Sahara's bedroom, and investigators assumed Renae was in the room with the little girl when the blast ripped apart the house.

First Colin. Now the entire Aldridge family.

The old man was insane. But no mental health diagnosis would bring back either of the men she'd loved.

Yes, loved. How was it she could admit it only now?

When the doorbell rang an hour later, she sucked in a breath at an illogical pang of fear.

But no one could connect her to the Aldridge's deaths. What motive would she have?

She ignored the doorbell. Until it rang again. And again.

As if the visitor were insane.

Fury replaced fear.

She stalked from her bedroom, down the carpeted steps, across the spacious foyer, and yanked open the door.

"What were you thinking?" Old man or not, she wanted to slap him.

He wore the same skullcap, the same shabby suit.

She didn't step aside as el-Rassul pushed past her, entering her house uninvited.

"But my dear, *you* are the one who acted without thought." He turned on her in the foyer.

"They had a child. A *child*, you crazy old man!"

*Hello. My name is Sahara. Like the Sahara Desert.*

She pushed away the pang at the thought of her young nephew Jack, nearly the same age, being taken from her.

But el-Rassul only shrugged. "Then perhaps you should not have been so forthcoming with information about myself and my family until you were certain of his cooperation."

Giada gaped. "You are saying this is my fault?"

But even as the outraged words emerged, she felt the truth of them. Alexander would be safe, along with her former friend Renae and their sweet daughter, if Giada had never gone to their house, never told el-Rassul about her Revisionist friend from her college days.

"I could take no chances, I'm afraid, with that information finding its way to the wrong people."

"So you set off a bomb in their house?"

"Well, not me, personally, of course. I sent someone else."

Giada crossed the foyer, toward the front living room, unable to hold herself upright. She sank into a sofa, bracing her forehead against numb fingers.

"I thought you were broke. How are you affording to pay hit men?"

"There are many ways to compensate the right people."

She shook her head. "I don't even care what that means. You are insane."

"Perhaps. Or simply desperate."

She raised her head. "And is money really so important?" She waved a hand at her mansion, the luxury furnishings. "All of this? Worth killing over?"

He laughed. "You ask me that? After all you have done—"

"I have never *killed* anyone!"

He shrugged once more. "You are still young."

"Get out." She stood. "I want nothing more to do with you, and I don't care what you do about it."

He raised his eyebrows. "No? I believe you forget I have information the Society—"

"You can tell Tempus Vigilia whatever you want." She spit the words out, feeling some measure of relief. "I don't care what you do to me. "

"Come now, Miss Moretti."

"You've overplayed your hand, el-Rassul. First Colin, now Alexander. You've killed the only two Revisionists I've ever known. There's nothing more I can do to help you, even if I wanted to. And I don't."

She half-expected the little pistol to emerge again. But everything felt cold now, from her fingers to her heart. Her own words returned to mock her. Was money so important that she'd allowed herself to come to this?

The old man surprised her, though. Turned away, shoulders

hunched, and pulled out that *medwakh* pipe with shaky fingers. Lit it carefully, and dragged deeply.

"This life," he said, exhaling smoke over her, "it's nothing like what others think, is it? This ability we have, to go back. To observe. To return and see how wrong everyone has gotten it. They are all so sure, so arrogant, about their ability to understand the past. But one hour in the past would leave them questioning everything they believe."

Giada said nothing, wishing he would leave her, so she could grieve in peace.

"And yet, we can say nothing to disabuse them of their folly. We must simply travel back-and-forth across the timeline of history, seeing but never telling, seeking but never finding. It is not a gift, is it? It is torture."

She closed her eyes. Unwilling to give him the satisfaction of agreement.

"No matter. I am through with it now."

Giada crossed the room, back to the foyer. "Good. Please leave."

He joined her in the foyer, even stepped to the door she opened, but it was only to flick ash onto her front step.

"Yes, I plan to leave. To leave all of this."

She sighed. "What are you talking about?"

He inhaled on the pipe, then puffed it slowly into the cold air. "I am going back myself."

"You can't be serious. It'll kill you."

As if in answer, he coughed delicately. "Ah, but you see, the doctors tell me I am already dying." He waggled the pipe in the air in explanation.

*Good.* The word bounced around her head, but she didn't regret it. She hoped his lungs gave out slowly. Painfully.

But that wouldn't happen if he tried what he was proposing.

"No one has ever successfully—"

"Oh, but do we know that? Do we, truly? Of course, no one has gone back eighty years to their younger self and then *returned*. But do we know for certain they did not survive? Did not meet themselves? Who better to keep such a secret than the very person who committed the act?"

Despite her desire to see him suffer, Giada nodded. "You're right. Perhaps you have a chance, still."

If he traveled back to meet his seven-year-old self, his father, even Howard Carter, would it change everything? As long as he never returned to 1974, would his changes persist? Would the el-Rassul on her doorstep, in his threadbare suit and tobacco-stained fingers, die in the past, while the seven-year-old boy grew up to become a wealthy man? And if so, was there a chance Alexander would still be alive, along with Renae and Sahara?

He dumped more ash onto her front step, then ground it out with his heel.

Giada bit back a comment about his rudeness.

"Good luck, then." She just wanted him gone. "When will you go?"

"I will fly to London tomorrow. To find Howard Carter. There should be no danger in that. Then on, to Egypt, and we shall see."

The smug satisfaction in his voice made her want to put her fingers around the crepey skin of his neck.

"Why could you not have simply done all this a week ago? Colin would still be alive. The Aldridges. Why?"

He chuckled. "As I said, you are young still. If you live to be my age, you'll no doubt understand. One must cling to every day in which life is still possible. We both know, I will likely fail."

She shut the door on him a moment later, leaned her head back against it, and wept.

But two weeks later, the tears had dried, and her assistant continued to report back to her every day with the same information.

The tomb of Tutankhamun was discovered by Howard Carter in 1922.

The man known here in 1974 as Ahmed Abd el-Rassul, a recent emigrant to the States from Egypt, was still missing, whereabouts unknown.

And the Aldridge family was still dead, from a blast so ferocious the bodies of mother and child could not be found.

He'd been right. He had failed.

As more weeks went by, then months stretched into years, Giada tried to keep the guilt buried, like a mummified thing in the tomb of her heart. She exploited every find she and Colin set up together before his death, and searched to no avail for a Revisionist to replace him.

The money began to dry up.

But year by year, a single plan became more logical, more attractive, more... inevitable.

She could be rich again. She needed only to find a Revisionist to visit her grandmother and slip her some information about a tomb waiting to be discovered in an Egyptian valley, where everyone believed no more intact tombs remained. Find a way to divert the archaeologist who might be alerted by any finds sold off for a tidy profit.

It was all there, waiting, not for the Abd el-Rassuls, but for her family.

All she needed was another Revisionist.

# CHAPTER TWELVE

*Fifteenth day of the third month of Shemu, 1155 BC*
*Thebes, Egypt*

"Here," I pointed toward the chapel where Jack and I entered 1155 BC. "We will find robes in here."

The chapel was blessedly empty. It seemed the residents of the entire complex retreated to behind closed doors.

I crossed to the reed baskets stacked at the base of the wall and pulled robes from the top.

Renae took the first from me, a leopard-skin drape, and held it aloft, laughing at the intact paws. "Oh, this one is for you, Alex. You'll look like the mighty hunter."

Alexander grabbed it from her, grinning. "Well, then you are going to be my priestess-in-training, and trail at my feet like any good acolyte."

The banter between them was like oil on my parched soul. I stood with fingers tangled in more robes, watching them, drinking them in.

Where had they come from? *When* had they come from?

Oh, if only I could ask them! The two people who would have all the answers, here with me now. And yet, for them, none of my past had happened yet. How could I ask them what year their daughter would be born?

Did my birth records exist somewhere in London?

But we were a long way from England.

"Gobi?" Renae tilted her head. "You are doing it again. That strange expression..."

Something in her voice, the hint of suspicion, snapped me from my reverie.

"Here, we must be quick. Before they bring the true priests."

We donned the linen robes with leopard skins, dropping them over the clothes we already wore, then reversed our path through the quiet temple and then the deserted palace.

We reached the head of the harem wing corridor. Four guards loitered there, heads together and muttering as we approached.

Alexander took the lead, and Renae and I stepped behind him willingly, despite his earlier teasing.

"We must see the king." His voice was confident, haughty even.

How often had he traveled through time? Jack said most travelers didn't develop the ability until their early twenties, and Alexander couldn't have been much beyond that age. His confidence impressed me.

The guards hesitated, with three of them looking to the fourth.

Alexander directed his attention to the leader. "Will you interfere with the king's *ka*?"

That was a gamble, as it made the assumption the pharaoh was dead.

But the question found its mark, and the guards stepped aside.

Renae and I trailed Alexander, our heads lowered as though in pious humility.

Would anyone recognize me as the woman who'd claimed to be Ramesses' new wife from Syria less than an hour ago?

But as the guards all looked the same to me, perhaps all

foreign women were the same to them. We passed unhindered and continued to the chamber at the end of the wing.

More guards here, but they let us pass without comment, presumably because they'd seen their counterparts at the head of the corridor let us through.

The pall of death hung over the chamber as we entered.

The guards moved farther into the hall, as though fearful of whatever rites we would perform.

Alexander took a hesitant step toward the crimson-splashed linen of the couch, where Ramesses' sprawled body cooled, his head lolling back to expose a throat cut open to the bone. Beside the couch, the fallen body of the attacker lay face-down. Blood pooled on the floor like spilled wine, its edges spreading outward, darkening the stones.

Beside me, Renae sucked in a breath at the sight of the gore, and wavered on her feet.

I pulled her to that lion-headed bed, where she sank down and wrapped her fingers around the carved mane.

"I told you," she whispered the words like an accusation. "I told you, Alex, he is dead."

Alexander approached even closer. "Yes. Yes, I suppose the history texts have gotten this one wrong."

"What are you doing with my father? Who are you?"

The strident voice from the door materialized as a young man, with heavy jewelry at his throat and around his upper arms, and a haughty expression.

Alexander stiffened but did not turn.

I stepped backward into the shadow of a corner. Renae and I were as yet unseen.

"I am speaking to you, priest!"

Alexander turned slowly, never glancing our direction.

"I am a priest, come to—"

"You are no priest that I know!"

I dropped my priestess robe to the floor, left it in a heap in the corner, and walked toward my father. "He has come with me.

From Syria. I am newly married to Ramesses, Strong Bull and Powerful Lion."

Was this Pentawer, whose mother had arranged for his father to be murdered? Or was it the next Ramesses, legitimate heir to the throne?

Either way, the ruse needed to work.

He scowled. "We have no need of Syrian priests here." He turned toward the hall. "Guard? Take this priest—"

I bowed my head. "My apologies. I only wanted to help."

The prince's glance flicked toward Renae, still seated. "And her?"

"She is a priestess." I bowed and addressed him with a title. "Blessed by Horus." More gambling. But whether he was legitimate heir or hopeful usurper, one could never go wrong with flattery.

"Yes, well, take them both and go."

I bowed my head again, then flicked a hand toward Alexander, as if to command him from the room.

He raised his eyebrows briefly, but preceded me from the chamber, with Renae following behind.

We reached a courtyard before any of us spoke.

"That was some quick thinking!" Renae wrapped an arm around my shoulders and squeezed.

"Who are you, truly?" Alexander peered down on me, his inquisitive eyes boring into mine.

I lifted my chin to his gaze. "I could ask you the same thing."

He smiled. "True enough."

"And you!" Renae swatted Alex's arm. "One of these days, your ceaseless research is going to get us in real trouble. I thought they were going to take you away. To separate us! Then what would I have done?"

"You should have a meeting place." I glanced to the hall behind us.

Where was Jack? Still following Giada?

Renae frowned at me. "What meeting place?"

Was Jack still trying to prevent whatever Giada did here to set the course of her future?

I waved a hand toward them both. "A time, a place, to meet. Should you ever get separated."

A pair of Egyptian men, servants by their attire, crossed through the dimly lit hall. I squinted to see if one of them might be Jack.

Renae was nodding. "It's a good idea, Alex. A fixed time and place."

"Such as?"

"Like Cleopatra's death." The words slipped from my mouth before I realized my mistake.

In the beat of silence following, I turned to face them both, cursing my stupidity.

"Who are you?" A mix of astonishment and anger played across Alexander's face.

Renae's lips parted in surprise. "Cleopatra? She isn't born for another thousand years." She stared at me, from head to toe. "Who are you?"

"I—I am Gobi. Newest wife of Ramesses—"

Alexander huffed. "Yeah, then I'm Alexander Graham Bell."

I smiled in spite of myself.

Renae pulled me into the shadows at the edge of the courtyard. "When are you from? Did you follow us here?"

What lie to tell them? I could say 1922. But was '22 in their future, or in their past? More than anything, it seemed critical they not guess who I was.

"I am from 1850." It seemed a safe distance from all the years they may, or may not, have lived through.

"Wow." Alexander stared at me. "That's before the Civil War."

"Don't tell her that, Alex!" Renae looked to me apologetically. "Ignore him."

He shrugged. "She's right, though, Renae. We should have a fixed point. Someplace we can always find each other."

Renae bit her lip. "Well, it can't be Cleopatra. We've already seen Julius Caesar."

"Alexander." My father grinned. "Alexander the Great."

Renae rolled her eyes. "Of course you'd want to meet him. But the day of his death—ancient Babylon is too hard to reach."

He nodded. "And it should be Egypt, anyway."

"Then Khufu. The day of his death. Near the entrance of his pyramid."

"That's good."

They both seemed to remember my silent presence at the same moment. They faced me, side-by-side, studying every bit of me.

My mother reached out to touch my arm once more. "So, what are you doing here? Now?"

If only I could tell them.

Seeing them here, together. It was at once both healing and so incredibly painful. I was not part of their lives. I could not be.

It was like getting a glimpse of a tomb full of treasures and then being excluded from it.

Before I could formulate a satisfactory answer, a shout went up from somewhere within the palace, turning us all in that direction.

Giada came barreling from the shadows, her face lit with the grin of a child who'd just raided the cookie jar.

"Listen to me." I wrapped a hand around Alexander's forearm before she reached us. "One day, she is going to betray you."

His eyes widened. He looked to my hand on his arm, then back to my eyes. "How—"

"Promise me you will be careful. If you ever suspect—just promise that you will run. And you won't leave—anyone —behind."

Giada was nearly on us now.

Alexander nodded, once. His face full of questions there was no time to ask.

"Come on!" Giada grabbed at Alex's and Renae's arms and pulled them toward the far side of the courtyard. "We have to get out of here! Now!"

The clatter of sandaled feet followed quick behind her.

Jack.

His eyes met mine. A quick shrug and a shake of his head.

How was I to interpret that?

And then two other men, running after Giada, spears at the ready. Were these the Medjay? Egypt's police force that would investigate the king's murder?

"Stop!"

The three friends tore from the courtyard.

The spear-wielding men ran past Jack and me.

"Jack, what's happening? Did you stop Giada?"

"I don't know! She went after the wife—it doesn't matter. We have to follow them."

He grabbed my hand.

We took off in the direction of the chase.

The three weren't running toward the chapel where Jack and I had entered 1155 BC. They weren't running for any location inside the palace or the temple at all.

They were headed for the desert. With two Medjay in hot pursuit.

"They're open targets!" I hissed the words to Jack as we ran. "They'll never make it!"

Had Jack and I altered history? Did I get my parents killed? But if things went wrong, couldn't I simply undo—

"You there!" My shout bounced off temple walls. This was no time for pondering the complexities of time travel. My parents needed me.

The Medjay flicked glances backward, but kept moving.

"What are you doing, chasing priests?" Did my voice sound authoritative?

My father slowed for a moment, turned back toward us, and met my eyes in a moment of understanding. He knew I was trying to buy them time.

I raised my voice and pointed behind me. "The pharaoh's murderer has been apprehended, but the plot is still underway! You are needed in the throne room!"

A moment of confusion, and they reversed direction.

But they grabbed at the two of us as they passed.

"Show us, woman."

I broke away, feigning indignation. "I told you, the throne room!"

More shouting from somewhere within the palace saved us. The two headed inward.

I spun toward the desert, toward the silhouette of three figures, running headlong over the dunes.

"They must have come through a tomb." I started after them.

"Sahara!" Jack caught at my arm.

"Let me go! I have to catch them!"

"Sahara, you can't. They'll be gone as soon as they get there. And what would you tell them, anyway?"

I spun back to him, buried my face against his chest. "It was them, Jack. It was my parents." My voice broke into fragments.

"I know. I know, sweetheart." He stroked the back of my head. "But now we need to leave as well."

And so we ran. It seemed we were always running.

Back to the wall beside a basket of priestly robes, and then back further still—or was it forward?—to another time, where I was no longer certain I belonged.

# CHAPTER THIRTEEN

*June 8, 1905*
*Highclere Castle, Hampshire, England*

*R*enae stuffed a third afternoon frock into her trunk, uncaring that it would be a wrinkled disaster long before they arrived in Venice, and glared at the back of Alexander's head.

Her husband absently chose an ebony cloth-bound book from a stack on a side table and added it to his own luggage, a ragged affair that had seen too many trains and carriages.

A book. As if their upcoming trip were nothing more than a chance to catch up on his reading.

She scowled and jammed her clothing deeper into her own steamer trunk, square and boxy, with a scent still reminiscent of the hazelnuts and figs they'd bought at the Globe Theatre, when they'd skipped back to seventeenth century London to catch the very first performance of Shakespeare's *Julius Caesar* and meet the playwright himself.

The anniversary trip—only last October—now seemed a lifetime ago.

"I don't see how you can be so casual about it."

Alexander sighed but didn't look up from his books. "I'm not casual, Renae. I'm *practical*. There is a difference."

The oil lamp beside his books guttered in the evening gloom, then recovered. From somewhere beyond the Mercia Bedroom, where Lady Carnarvon always put them up, a spooky moaning and series of rhythmic knocks against a tabletop signaled the start of the evening's entertainment. Lord Carnarvon was once again entertaining, with the Mme. Carrière and her "Spiritualistic Séance" as the main feature.

Renae added one more dress to the mess in her trunk—a puffed-sleeve silk with pleats and frills enough to hide her burgeoning belly. At nearly six months along now, she struggled to keep their secret. But since returning from Hatshepsut's Mortuary Temple and their surprise encounter with Joanne, they'd set a course of action, and an announced pregnancy would only complicate matters.

"How can you say I'm not being practical, Alex? We have no idea what we might encounter, how long it will take, if we will even be successful!" Her voice pitched higher and louder, but she didn't care. "How can we leave Sahara here? What if—what if—"

She pressed the heels of her hands against her eyes, pushing back the tears threatening since the start of this, their final day in England before trying one last idea to stop Giada Moretti from destroying their lives.

Behind closed eyes, she felt Alex cross the room. She welcomed the cocoon of his embrace, the tweedy scratch of his jacket and dusty smell of academia he always carried, as though he'd dropped from the pages of a library book. Hair just beginning to gray at the temples. The perfect Oxford don.

Their perfect life, in jeopardy again because of a woman they once called *friend*.

"Renae, Sahara will be well-cared for here, you know that. Porchy and Almina love her. Not to mention little Lady Evelyn."

From a room down the hall, a collective gasp would have made her smile if she hadn't been fighting the rising panic at separation from her fifteen-year-old daughter. The Spiritualist Movement was in full swing here in the early twentieth century, and their friend Porchy was dabbling, inviting guests to sit around a table while a supposed medium channeled platitudes from behind a gauzy curtain, ostensibly words spoken through her from the shade of someone's dearly departed. Despite the well-documented and repeated debunking of such charlatans, the seances were still popular in the rooms of wealthy estates like Highclere.

It was no wonder the disaster yet to come in Egypt would eventually morph into a supposed "mummy curse," befalling those who would trespass on the realm of the dead.

But perhaps all people, in all times, went on searching for something *other.*

"I know the Herbert family cares for her. I couldn't ask for more, and certainly never dreamed we'd be this close to Porchy —to all of them, including Howard Carter—this long before they find the tomb. But they are not her family." She put a hand to her belly.

Alexander covered her hand with his own. "And if we are to do the best for our family—you know what that means. We need to return to our own time. This baby, and Sahara, will have opportunities there which they could never have here."

"But shouldn't she be told—understand who she is, why we are here—"

"Renae, you know the answer. If we tell Sahara the truth now, about our abilities, her likely future, the reason we brought her eighty years into the past, and then we succeed in stopping Giada and undoing all of it, it will not only be our memories that change, but hers. The best way to protect her is to keep her in the dark. At least for now."

Renae pulled away and crossed to the window of the Mercia Bedroom, wishing she could throw it open and thrust her head into the evening air. The claustrophobic panic she'd felt since they encountered Joanne at the Temple of Hatshepsut grew unmanageable. She should feel safer. They were about to take action. Instead, she felt as though watchful eyes followed everywhere. Tracked their every decision.

She opened the shutters, though she could see little from the glass this late in the evening. In the mornings, their south-facing view spread across the lush lawns of the estate, all the way to the gnarled woodlands of Sidown Hill, with the arch of the Heaven's Gate folly in the distance. Tonight, all lay in shadow.

"We could leave now. Go home." She spoke the words against the glass, not turning to see his face.

"Renae. Return to when? To 1974? Aging us all eleven years in an instant, and returning with our four-year-old child missing and a fifteen-year-old in her place? Gamble that Giada is not still trying to kill us? Renae, you know we must stick to our original plan. After we take care of things in Venice."

Venice. Where they would undo all of this. Everything that had gone wrong since that first college trip into ancient Egypt with Giada, to witness the Harem Conspiracy.

She'd blown up their house a few years later, forced them to escape to the end of the nineteenth century, where they spent eleven years creating a new life for themselves. Until a stupid chance encounter threatened to reveal that they were hiding in plain sight, right where she wanted them. So yes, they'd go to Venice, prevent the start of everything.

And then back to 1985, to new lives. Where this new baby could be born into better medical care and Sahara would have a chance to become anything she wanted.

Although they both knew what the girl wanted—to make a name for herself as an archaeologist. Whenever Howard Carter visited Highclere or London, Sahara followed in his wake like a duckling after its mother. If they stayed, Renae had little doubt the girl would be present when Carter made the greatest find of his career.

But they would not stay. They would stop Belzoni from ever finding the tomb of Seti I. She and Alex would not work alongside Giada on Seti's tomb during college. They would not jump back together, to the reign of Ramesses III and his grisly murder.

And Alexander would never hide that stupid necklace in the sand beside the step of Seti's tomb, for Giada to find and claim. For Giada to discover Alexander was a Revisionist. All of it, everything stemming from Belzoni's discovery, would be undone.

"And what if it doesn't work?" She remained at the window, and couldn't keep the anger from her voice. "You know a million things could go wrong. Someone else could find the Seti tomb before 1974. We might remain friendly with Giada and eventually tell her our secret. Or maybe the three of us will end up at some other digsite, and the same thing will happen—you trying to impress her with your charm—"

Alexander huffed. "How many times will you make me apologize, Renae?" His voice rose, then dropped at the sound of a woman's scream from the seance room.

Mme Carrière must have rigged an apparition to appear, or had her assistant discreetly use her toes to drop coins into a glass under the table.

"Renae, you know I've chastised myself, a hundred times more than you ever could, for that day—"

"I know." Her eyes were still trained on the dark lawns, but she could hear the tension in his voice. She turned back to him. "But if we can never return, Alexander! When I first learned we would have another child, somehow the thought of this little one living through all we know is to come..."

He nodded, wordless. Eleven years ago, they dropped into Victorian England near the end of a glorious age. And the gilded Edwardian England they now called home would soon disappear into a war such as the world had never seen. But the Great War would only be followed by the Spanish Flu pandemic, then a second world war. If they remained, Sahara, and their new baby, would live through all of that, live long enough to see a bomb dropped in Hiroshima, a Cold War develop with Russia, another war in Korea, and even one in Vietnam.

"Don't you want to spare our children all of that?"

"That's why this trip must fix everything, Renae. It must."

Yes, it must. And they would go back to 1985, with nothing more than Giada's money to get them started, if it were still hidden where they left it before their hasty departure from 1974.

"I still say we should take Sahara with us to Venice. To 1814, even."

Met with Alex's silence, she returned to packing. She separated belongings they wouldn't take into two trunks they would leave here in the Mercia Bedroom at Highclere.

What kind of world would they return to, in 1985? At Alexander's college, before they left Philadelphia, there was talk of engineers at various research institutions beginning to link up their computers using telecommunications technology. Where might such incredible research lead? The world of the twenty-first century, if they could get their children there, could offer them so much. Even their beloved field of archaeology must be much advanced. Here in 1905, ground penetrating radar was in its infancy. In 1975, it was becoming commercially available. Perhaps by 1985 it would have changed every digsite in the world.

Since making their decision, neither spoke of the dual memories they would carry, what such a change might do to their minds. They must do this, for their children.

She lifted a small box from the corner. Souvenirs from their travels—must go into the trunk that would stay here.

Alexander's collection of ancient coins—into his trunk for Venice. They took it everywhere, as a useful way to jump through time, once they figured out they could bring even newer coins to the past, if held between two Revisionists.

She lifted a headband from the dresser, a piece she brought back from their trip to Hatshepsut's Temple. The scarab-and-jewels headband, given to all priestesses at the temple, felt cool in her hands, but brought back the heat of an Egypt sun. The day Giada's assistant Joanne spotted them. She tucked it into the trunk they would leave, alongside letters and other personal items. The headband, if anyone knew it was fashioned more than three thousand years ago, would be invaluable. Instead, it looked as new as though a villager in Deir el-Medina churned it out last week, with a dozen like it, to sell to tourists alongside the road. There was no getting rich for Revisionists in bringing artifacts back to their own time.

Not that they didn't find other ways.

And even an Observer could exploit a Revisionist. If she were so inclined to ignore years of friendship, to line her own pockets and turn to violence to gain her own ends.

A soft knock at the door interrupted the angry reminiscing.

Alexander opened the door to Lady Carnarvon, dressed in a lightweight blue silk that matched the silk embroidery of their four-poster bed.

She glided into the room, lips tight.

"Won't you both please join the seance? We need *someone* there who will not fawn over Mme. Carrière as though she dropped from the heavens."

Another figure popped up behind Almina.

Sahara, grinning. "You really must come, both of you. She's absolutely hilarious."

"Sahara," Renae sighed. "What are you doing still in those knickers?" The girl insisted on turning up her nose at acceptable clothing. Almina must be horrified.

Sahara glanced at her pants, buttoned at the knee. "I was cycling, Mom. You know that."

"That was hours ago, dear. Please, you must change into something suitable."

"Oh, let her be, Renae." Alexander smiled on his daughter, as usual making her feel she could do no wrong.

Yet even as Renae scowled at them both, a stab of guilt silenced her. Sahara should be wearing jeans and sandals, heading out to catch a movie with her friends. Not stuck in this stuffy decade of silk and lace, puffy sleeves and choking, ruffled necklines, her only friends a four-year-old girl and a library piled with books.

How could they ever tell her what they'd done to her?

And in that moment, with the Countess and Sahara waiting

in the doorway, Renae realized she would rather leave her daughter now and keep their lies intact, than tell her the truth and risk her rejection.

If they were successful in Venice, Sahara would never know any of this. She would remember a different past and live a different future.

"Let us finish our packing first, Almina," she said. "Then we'll join you, to watch Mme Carrière commune with the spirits."

# CHAPTER FOURTEEN

*April 1985*
*Philadelphia, Pennsylvania*

"*J*ack? You're going to be late!"

Giada remained seated behind the walnut desk in her home office, but directed her voice toward the spiraling staircase, hoping Jack would hear.

Hear, and acknowledge. At fifteen, the boy seemed to believe he no longer needed a parental figure, even though he never materialized until a moment after her driver honked from the street in front of her city estate.

"Calm down, Aunt Giada. He's not even here yet."

Jack appeared from the kitchen, the last half of a sandwich in hand. He wore his navy polo and tan riding breeches, but hadn't yet donned his muddy paddock boots, thankfully.

He crossed the room and flung himself onto the ivory sofa in the middle of her office.

Giada bit back a comment about expensive sofas and mustard-dripping sandwiches.

"Didn't school report cards come out today? I haven't seen yours yet."

Jack rolled his eyes. "Geez, I just got home from school, and had to get ready for my lesson. I'll bring it down later."

"And?"

"And my grades are good."

She leaned into the high leather back of her desk chair. "Only *good?*"

He sighed and tore a huge bite from his sandwich.

"Jack, you know my money can't open every door. You'll also need to get excellent marks in school, if you want to go to the right college—"

"Maybe I don't even want to go to college." The words were mumbled around his mouthful of meat and bread.

"Not that photography thing again?"

He finished the final bite and shrugged.

Giada tapped a pen against the bulky garnet ring she always wore. "You know I appreciate the arts as much as anyone, but it's not a career you can count on. You need to get a solid degree."

Jack lifted a heavy piece from the end table beside the sofa—a statue of a seated scribe Colin brought from a trip back to ancient Egypt years ago—and tossed it between his hands.

She watched the statue, a favorite of hers and one of the few memories of Colin, but said nothing.

"I'm only fifteen, Aunt Giada. Do I have to know exactly what I'm going to do with the rest of my life? Did you know, when you were my age?"

"When I was your age, I had no opportunities, no potential ahead of me. Nothing like what you've been given." She couldn't keep the edge out of her voice.

He returned the statue to the table with a *thump.* "I know. I know you were poor, and my mother was poor, and my grand-mother was sick." He rehearsed the facts as though nothing more than trivia from a history book.

But it was more than trivia, her past. What she left behind.

And she'd made sure Jack would have everything she never did, even at a risk to her own health. Since her sister's death, and after Jack's father took off, the boy was her only family. At thirty-seven, Jack was the closest thing to a son she was likely to have. And teenage-drama notwithstanding, she adored him.

What she wouldn't say, couldn't bring herself to say, was that the money was getting tighter, and might open even fewer doors in the future. Her investments kept her afloat, in a bull market that showed no signs of a downturn. But there was always a downturn.

She needed a few truly significant finds, to carry her for years and reduce her chances of getting caught by the Tempus Vigilia.

She crossed from her desk to sit beside Jack on the sofa.

"You don't need to have all the answers yet, no. In a few years, when you can start traveling to other times and places, you'll discover yourself in a new way." She smoothed a lock of hair from his blue eyes, then dropped her hand when he pulled away.

"And how will I even know how to do that, when you never tell me anything about traveling? Never let me meet any other—"

"In good time. Right now, you focus on your education." A car horn sounded from the street. "And that includes riding lessons." She elbowed him.

Jack shrugged and stood.

He didn't enjoy riding, and she knew it. But she'd spent too many years excluded from wealthy society to allow him any gaps that would leave him vulnerable.

An hour later, with Jack still gone, she'd combed through the first quarter financials for the Moretti Foundation once more, searching for places to cut, opportunities for growth.

She was headed for a precipice. Professionally and personally.

Her foundation did some good work, but it was critical she find something of real value, something she could sell—off the books, of course—to bolster her flagging finances.

And despite years of trying, she still had not found another Revisionist to add to her payroll. Someone who could help her with the ultimate find, the idea planted by the old man Abd el-Rassul years ago.

Divert Howard Carter from the Valley of the Kings, and plunder the tomb of Tutankhamun herself, or at least give her own grandmother the information needed to do so.

The phone rang on her desktop and she snatched it up, the bone-white plastic cold in her hand.

"Giada, it's Robert. Listen, I've been going over the quarterly reports—"

"I know. I'm sitting here with them now."

Her accountant kept track of the foundation's finances as well as her personal fortune.

"It's not good. You know I'm fine with your... crossing over... of monies into your personal account, but at the rate you're going, it's not going to last long. You need a serious influx of cash, and you need it soon."

She shoved back from the desk and paced the room, a habit she'd picked up since cordless phones made their debut, and she was no longer tethered to her desk while speaking.

"So, do you know any big fish looking to expand their philanthropic endeavors, Robert?"

"That's your department, I'm afraid."

Right.

"Or at least make a big discovery, Giada. It's been how long? Six years since you came up with something really valuable?"

She gripped the phone until her fingers hurt. "Sure. I'll get right on that. One big discovery, coming up."

"I'm just saying, whatever magic you used to work back then, you need to bring it back."

Magic. A word closer to the truth than he could imagine.

The magic was Colin, and his ability to locate and even manufacture finds for her, that created her fortune. For five years after that crazy old man killed him, she drew on artifacts still hidden for her to discover, or items in storage, waiting to be carefully parceled out to the antiquities black market. It was all gone now.

"I have to go, Robert. Joanne will be here any minute. We're going over the fundraiser plans. Who knows, maybe some rich guy is just waiting to give his money away to a good cause."

He chuckled on the other end, a laugh that somehow sounded sarcastic and unfriendly. "Right. A good cause. Would that be the BMW or the Lincoln?"

"Bye, Robert."

She jammed the phone back into its cradle. The man had nerve. She kept *him* in a nice car, too.

By the time Joanne showed up, Giada had spiraled into dark memories.

Robert's comment about her BMW had recalled to mind the last time she saw Alexander. His sarcasm and disdain.

From there, it was a short journey into the guilt that always lay beneath the surface, close enough to poke through whenever she wasn't careful.

Some things could never truly be buried.

Sahara would be fifteen now, the same age as Jack. The little girl in the romper, asking for cookies, would be... what? A sulky teenage girl giving her parents a hard time over grades and lessons? Perhaps. But better than the reality of the scorched house, the horrible headlines.

Not to mention the guilt corroding parts of Giada's soul for eleven years. She felt it like a physical thing—rusting and crumbling her insides—the responsibility of taking three lives.

"Giada?"

Joanne let herself in the front door, and her voice was too upbeat, too cheerful.

Her vacation must have done her good.

"In here."

Joanne appeared, all smiles.

"You're late."

The smile fell. "I'm sorry, I—"

"Whatever. Let's get to work." Giada shoved the financials into a drawer and pulled out the folder for the upcoming fundraiser.

Joanne sighed in frustration, the sound reminiscent of Giada's own reaction to her teenage nephew.

"Sorry. How was your vacation?"

Giada didn't really care. But it seemed like a necessary transition before they could get down to what mattered.

"It was great! You were right—Hatshepsut's Temple was amazing at its height." Joanne slid into a chair in front of Giada's desk and pulled a folder from her own leather bag.

"Oh, and you won't believe this! I ran into some old college friends of yours there!"

"In Egypt?"

"Egypt, yes, but in 1458 BC, if you can believe that."

Giada scribbled a note in the margin of the topmost page. "What friends?"

"The Aldridges. You remember, Alexander Aldridge, and Renae—oh, what was her maiden name? Giada? Are you—are you ill?"

"You *saw* them? Alexander and Renae Aldridge?" Giada's hand shook. She set the pen down. Had her earlier thoughts conjured the couple into the conversation?

"Yes, they were visiting the same day. You've gone really pale, Giada. What's wrong?"

"And, they were... they were young? In college, still?" Her chest pounded, the blood pulsing so hard she could hear it.

The three of them dreamed of visiting Hatshepsut together, but after the trip to Ramesses's Harem Conspiracy, and the "find" of the necklace Alex buried, their friendship soured. Had Alex and Renae gone back to the female pharaoh's Mortuary Temple on their own, some time before their deaths?

"Young? No, I wouldn't say that. Our age, as you'd expect. I think it was, you know, *now* for them. Although they were also doing a bit of archaeological work in the past over there, at one of the temples. Mentuhotep, I think they said."

Giada's heartbeat raced ahead, then slowed unnaturally, like a drumbeat in the distance, signaling some terrible thing to come.

126

She twisted the garnet ring until it chafed. "I don't understand. Were they in *ancient* Egypt, or..."

Joanne shrugged. "I don't know. We didn't talk long."

Giada stood and glared down on Joanne's smiling face. "What did they say, *exactly*, Joanne? Tell me what they said *exactly*!"

The woman held up a palm. "Whoa, okay. No need to get hostile."

But Giada was past caring how she sounded.

Joanne pursed her lips, and her gaze drifted over Giada's shoulder. "Let's see. They said they were doing some work on Mentuhotep's temple, which, of course, is close to Hatshepsut's."

"Did they say what year? When?"

"I asked if they were working with Howard Carter, but they said no, he was still tied up in Saqqara—something about accusations. They were working with Naville, they said."

Naville, Carter. It was enough to pinpoint. It had to be enough.

"A child? Did they have a child with them?"

"No. I don't understand why you're so angry. Weren't the three of you friends?"

"Go home, Joanne."

"What? I thought we were going to plan—"

"*Go. Home.*" Could she be any more clear?

Giada felt nothing at Joanne's raised eyebrows and huffy snatching up of her purse and leather bag. The sooner she was gone, the better.

An hour later, with multiple books pulled from the wall-to-wall bookcases and spread across her desk, Giada had reached several mind-jarring conclusions.

Édouard Naville worked on the mortuary temple of the Eleventh Dynasty Pharaoh Mentuhotep from 1903 to 1907.

The Aldridges could not have traveled to any of those years from 1974, because they were closer than eighty years.

The only way they could be present in Egypt between 1903 and 1907 was if they had been hiding somewhere here in the present until a couple of years ago, and then gone back. Or if they left 1974 for an earlier period in time and then lived through the years until 1903.

And there was no way they'd been in hiding all these years since the fire. Not here in their present time.

She scrambled through a bottom desk drawer to a folder tucked in the back. One she hadn't looked at for years. Newspaper clippings. The smiling faces of Alexander and Renae under the tragic headline.

Only one body had ever been found. A man, in the bedroom.

It had to have been the man who set the bomb, not Alexander.

*Not Alexander.*

She sagged against her desk chair.

She didn't kill them.

The strangling bands of guilt loosened.

She'd kept the feelings locked down for so many years. And now it was like unwrapping a blackened mummy only to find there was no body—only a charred bit of wood.

She pressed the garnet ring against her lips and closed her eyes, letting a couple of tears slide down her cheeks.

She didn't kill them.

But where had they gone?

There was only one logical answer. One solution that explained all. They took the briefcase she'd brought and then escaped eighty years backward, to 1894, believing themselves to be in danger. Now, eleven years later, it was 1905 for them, and they'd somehow found a way to work on a dig in Egypt.

She swept the folder back into the drawer, closed the books and thrust them back into their places on her shelves. Paced the office a few times, excitement and hope and determination vying for top billing in her emotional churn.

She could put this all right—everything—her friendship with them, her own situation. All she needed to do was find them in 1905. Explain that it was Abd el-Rassul, not her, who tried to kill them. And then the three of them could find Tut's tomb themselves. Set things up for the future, make some critical investments, leave some kind of will or something. Return to 1985 and be wealthier than she'd ever been.

It would be a hard sell, though. They were a self-righteous pair, and it would take some talking to convince them to change history for their own benefit.

And first, they would need to forgive her.

But she had to make it happen. For Jack's sake. She could not let him face life as she had, without support, and without a penny to his name.

~

One month later, Giada's rented Studebaker coasted across the gravel front drive of Highclere Castle, where her questioning in London had assured her the Aldridges were spending their summer.

She'd come to present-day London first, then back to August of 1905, knowing it unlikely they'd be in Egypt during the heat of the summer, and wanting to give herself every opportunity to track them down.

She was unsurprised to learn Alexander had found himself a position at Oxford, but the news that they were personal friends of George "Porchy" Herbert, the fifth Earl of Carnarvon, as well as Howard Carter, impressed her.

Alexander and Renae had built themselves into the Who's Who of Egyptian archaeology, well in advance of the King Tut discovery. At this rate, they'd be part of the find in seventeen years.

If she didn't convince them to make it happen sooner, and without Lord Carnarvon's patronage or Carter's oversight.

She was grudgingly shown into the Drawing Room by the stodgy butler, and disappointed it was Almina Herbert—Lady Carnarvon—who greeted her, rather than the Aldridges themselves.

But more disappointment quickly followed.

"I'm afraid they are abroad," Lady Carnarvon spread her

hands, as though apologetic. "Perhaps you would care to visit with their daughter?"

Giada inhaled, sharp and quick, at the pang in her chest. "Their daughter is here, then? Sahara?"

"Miss Aldridge is staying the summer, yes."

The girl was sent for, told a Miss Moretti from America was here to visit her parents.

Giada fidgeted at the window, making small talk with Lady Carnarvon.

But then she was there, little Sahara of the periwinkle romper and cookie crumbs, dressed as an early twentieth-century young lady.

Giada watched for a reaction—a flinch of surprise or flicker of fear—but there was nothing.

It would seem Sahara was never told Giada existed.

The girl crossed the room with a gentle hand extended, as though a Countess herself. "Miss Moretti, I am so sorry my parents are not here to greet you. Were you acquaintances when we lived in America? I'm afraid I do not remember—"

"No, no, of course you wouldn't." Giada gripped the girl's hand with both her own, took in every inch of the girl she hadn't seen since childhood. She was tall, and would one day be pretty, though her adolescence kept her from true beauty just yet.

"I will leave you two to visit, then." The Countess bowed her head toward Giada, then exited the room.

"Please," Sahara waved a hand toward a settee, "make yourself comfortable."

Giada glanced toward the window. "I thought perhaps we could take a turn outdoors, go for a walk."

"Oh." The girl looked downward, coloring slightly. "I'm afraid I'm not dressed for—"

Giada laughed. The frequent changing of clothes in this period was legendary. "Don't be ridiculous. We won't be climbing mountains."

She squared her shoulders and nodded once. "Very well."

Giada intended to learn all she could from the girl, to track down her parents and make her pitch. It had to work.

But an hour later, as she once more sat beside the driver in the red Studebaker and left Highclere behind, her thoughts were far less hopeful.

Angry, even.

Little doubt where the Aldridges had gone, in their "travel abroad."

The strongman they mentioned to Sahara could be none other than Giovanni Battista Belzoni, discoverer of Egyptian tombs. And his most famous, "Belzoni's tomb," was the very tomb of Seti I where she, Alexander, and Renae dug during their college years. Where they'd jumped back in time to the Harem Conspiracy and seen Ramesses III murdered. Where Alexander hid the jeweled collar of the royal wife Tiye and gave Giada her first chance at making an impressive find. Most importantly, it was the tomb where she discovered Alexander as a Revisionist.

And if the Aldridges planned to see Belzoni, there could be only one reason.

They knew Joanne would reveal their hiding place. They were going to stop Belzoni and undo every event since the three of them visited the Harem Conspiracy.

Her initial find of the necklace, her foundation, the years working with Colin after she understood what could be done. The money, the opportunities, the Society Hill mansion. All of it, gone.

As the car sped into the Hampshire countryside, she laughed at her own naivete.

She believed it would be hard to convince them to change history for their own benefit. But that was exactly what they intended. Saving themselves. And destroying her.

*If you're going to mess with history, you're going to suffer for it.*

Alexander's hostile indictment, eleven years ago.

Indeed.

She pressed her fingernails into her palms until the pain was a distraction.

They were long past the time for apologies. For working together. For redemption.

Once again, life proved you had only yourself to rely upon.

She'd find them, still. She'd find them in Venice.

But if they were going to revise history, she'd make sure it would be *her* on the winning side of those changes.

Highclere Castle receded in the distance. But behind its walls was a girl who could still provide the leverage Giada needed.

# CHAPTER FIFTEEN

*December 21, 1922*
*Valley of the Kings, Egypt*

*I* landed in 1922 hot, heartbroken, and breathless. With the tears of 1155 BC still wet on my cheeks.

But with Jack's fingers no longer intertwined with mine on the chapel wall.

A bubble of panic in my chest, head swiveling under the late morning sun.

But he was already there, scrambling to his feet on the other side of the chapel, running toward me.

He swung me off my feet in a crushing embrace.

I curled my fingers into his damp shirt, pressed my forehead against his shoulder, and sobbed.

"I didn't know exactly how long we stayed today," he whispered into my hair. "These last two hours, waiting for you, not knowing if you would return, or if your sanity would split in two when you did... I went crazy."

Yes, I had the presence of mind as we left the Harem Conspiracy to return with any changes I'd made to history intact, on the slim chance we managed to prevent Giada's future—

I yanked my head backward, studied his eyes. "But you remember me?"

In answer, he cupped my face in both hands and kissed me soundly.

When I caught my breath, I swiped at tears with the back of my hand, and retreated to lean against the wall. "And the rest of your memories?"

He took a deep breath and studied the cloudless sky before answering. "No double-set of conflicting memories, I'm afraid. All I know is what I knew before. Giada took me in after my mother died and my father left. She grew wealthier over the years from what I believed was a salvage enterprise. Sent me here to meet you as a birthday gift." He studied my face, frowning suddenly. "Is that—is that wrong? Do you have other memories?"

"No. No, it didn't work. We didn't stop her."

"But we found your parents."

My legs could no longer hold my weight. I sank to the dust and dropped my head against the stone wall.

He lowered himself beside me and took my hand, tightening his fingers to stop my trembling.

"Jack, if we found them during the university trip where Giada started looting, then I think she and my parents were friends at university."

He inhaled sharply. "If that's true…"

"Then either my parents weren't born in the 1860s, or Giada *was*."

He was shaking his head, forehead creased. "Giada couldn't have been born that far back. Or I wouldn't know her in my life-time, since 1970."

"Could she have gone back to the 1880s before you were born, and done her university training in that decade, with my parents?"

Jack pressed the fingers of his free hand against his forehead.

"It doesn't seem like something she would have done. Why sacrifice modern life for a long period of time? Besides, you met her in 1905, where she was older. Too close to the 1880s to travel there again."

My head throbbed, a pounding ache at the base of my skull. The rising heat didn't help.

I pointed to the opposite wall, still in shade.

Jack nodded, and we hobbled toward it, as though we'd run a hundred miles. Or three thousand years.

Back on the ground, I tried to calculate numbers.

"So let's say they all went to university together, the same year—when?"

"Giada would have entered about 1966."

"I was born when my parents were both young, only twenty-two years old."

"So that would have been the same year as me, 1970."

I tried to exhale the strangeness of belonging nearly fifty years in the future, but the strangeness didn't let go. Was I truly born eighty years later than 1890, as I always believed?

Eighty years. It made too much sense to be denied.

"Sahara, what's your earliest memory? Where? When?"

I tilted my head back and closed my eyes. "I remember our London flat. I don't know how old—perhaps four or five? My father was teaching then."

"So, could your parents have brought you from America in 1974 to London, and then brought you back in time to 1894, eighty years earlier, as a four-year-old?"

My eyes were still closed, and I tried to slow my breathing. "It's possible. But why?"

Jack was silent.

I lifted my head and found him studying his hands. "I can only assume they did it to escape Giada."

"Jack, none of this is your fault."

I expected an argument, but instead he sucked in a breath and turned wide eyes to me.

"Sahara! Do you understand what this means—"

I fought to catch up. "If I was born in 1970..."

"Then we are not from two different times!"

My heart stuttered over a few missed beats. "But then..."

So many rules and principles, both in Tempus Vigilia's blasted Codex and their Knowledge Base. How did all the limitations play into this new possibility?

Jack was thinking, too, I could see.

He started ticking off possibilities on his fingers. "Let's say you left in 1974, and that's your real time. You could return to the moment you left, without Revising. You'd be about thirty-two years old, but it would only be 1974, when you should be four years old. Your parents wouldn't be there. You wouldn't know anyone or have any kind of life set up for you. And it would be much too rough on your body to age that much in an instant."

"Also, you'd be four years old, and I'd be thirty-two."

He nodded, a brief jerk of the head, and ticked off another finger. "You could revise history, return with the same time passed as you'd been gone. Return to about 2002. Hard to say when you'd arrive, since we don't know exactly when you left, but physically you'd be okay. And no double-memories, so mentally okay, too. And we'd be about the same age, at least. I'd go back to the moment I left, November 2002, and wait for you, or you'd have to wait—"

"Jack."

"It would be fine. We could pick a time and place—"

"Jack." I shook my head. "You don't go back. That's why Reuben is here. You don't go back to November 2002."

He sagged against the wall.

"And besides, there are too many unknowns. What was the location, when—if—I traveled from the 1970s back to the late 1800s? In America? In England? How can I return without knowing the location? Can I even return by myself, if it was my parents who brought me back in time with them?"

He nodded, head down.

We sat in silence.

Were there no loopholes to find in all this insanity?

"That's it, then," Jack said. "We'll stay in 1922. That's the safest plan. We'll make a good life here."

As much as his words soothed the pain in my soul, the deep ache of once again missing a true reunion with my parents weighted me to the ground.

Not to mention that strange, prickling discomfort, ever-present when I had unanswered questions. If all of this—my abilities, my life—was the product of some higher power, wouldn't this trip have brought answers, rather than more questions? Was the universe randomly tossing me through millennia? Or was some greater purpose at work?

"If I'd known." I sighed. "If I'd known my parents would be there, I would have been prepared." I mentally kicked myself. Why had I not thought to tell them something, anything, that could have resulted in our meeting in their future?

I jerked upright.

"Jack!"

He gripped my hand and searched the chapel as though we were under attack.

"I know where to go next! Where we might find them!" I clambered to my feet and dragged him up to stand beside me.

"We're going to the Great Pyramid."

I stood at the rail, watching Luxor and the Valley of the Kings fade to a black smudge on the horizon.

The train from Luxor to Cairo chugged along the east side of the Nile, at least for now, until we crossed to the west at Naga Hammadi.

To my right, the verdant fields and green ripple of the Nile faded into the dusty parchment background of the western desert. Here at the back of the train, a cool pocket of shade protected me from the searing wind, but still I held my round cloche hat in one hand and clutched the rail with the other, my French-blue silk day dress fluttering around my calves.

Cairo lay nearly twelve hours to the north by train, and Jack had left me alone with my thoughts.

Would it be worth the trip? One more hop, skip, and jump back in time? To the day of the death of the great pharaoh who built the greatest of the pyramids?

Khufu, the man whose death my parents agreed on as their rendezvous point, should they ever be separated.

But would I find them there? And if so, at what age?

Perhaps still young, before my birth.

Or maybe at some point between my birth and the year I lost them, at age fifteen.

Or older even, than they were to me right now? I shuddered at the idea of finding them elderly, taking one last trip in hopes of finding their lost daughter before they died.

Or the best possibility... that somewhere in the seventeen intervening years since this morning, they figured out the identity of the girl they met on the day of Ramesses' murder, and now waited for the right time to intersect me there, in a moment that was the *present* for all of us at once?

Unknowable. And perhaps better to not think on it.

Over my head, clouds of steam from the engine streamed backward, as though tethering us to Luxor. But the Giza plateau beyond the city of Cairo was my only hope now.

The day passed fitfully. I paced the sleeping car's corridor, the dining car, the second- and third-class coach cars.

Each time I walked past Jack's seat at the back of second-class, he touched my arm or grabbed my hand. Asked me to sit, to share the ham sandwich he purchased, to order a lemonade.

I couldn't, not for hours.

And when I finally sank into the cushions out of exhaustion, I fell into a sleep fragmented with dreams of finding them and not finding them, the end of our story playing out as comedy, as tragedy, as fairy tale.

Jack shook me awake as the train's *clackety-clack* slowed into Cairo's Ramesses Railway Station.

I was beginning to tire of that name.

Passengers disgorged into the midnight gaslit station, talkative and hustling despite the hour.

Jack carried our luggage, ironically packed for the fictitious trip to Cairo, a trip which had become reality, though not to meet *his* family. But hopefully mine. He hailed a carriage outside the station, helped me into it, and instructed the driver toward the Hotel Windsor.

Despite being only a few days from Christmas, no red-and-green holiday cheer brightened the Muslim city.

I was too tired, or perhaps numb, to ask how he'd chosen the place, but he answered my unspoken question as the somewhat run-down hotel loomed into view, wedged into a corner of downtown Cairo.

"It's a former British Officers Club. A guy on the train told me it was recently bought to be an annex of Shepheard's."

Had it only been two weeks since we stayed at the upscale Shepheard's Hotel, with Howard, Lord Carnarvon, and Eve?

I waited in the lobby as Jack approached the front desk, taking in the entrance to an adjoining bar filled with chairs made from barrels.

Behind the desk, an elderly gentleman lifted watery eyes to Jack, then broke into a welcoming, crooked-toothed smile.

"One room, please." Jack nodded to the older man behind the desk. "And I'm not sure for how long."

*One room?* That request shook the sleep out of me.

I waited for the man to turn to the wall of keys, then raised my eyebrows in Jack's direction.

He shook his head briefly, then filled out the clerk's paperwork and took the key.

"Join me outside for a moment," he said to me.

In the midnight street, he handed me my small steamer trunk.

"I thought this through while we traveled, Sahara. We have

no idea how long we'll be back there. With Khufu, and your parents."

I loved the way he assumed we would see them.

"We don't know if you'll need to revise history when you return. I could be waiting here for you, for some time. And, well…" He shrugged. "We simply don't have enough money for two rooms, for however long that might be."

I said nothing, waiting to see if he was going to suggest the scandalous thing I expected. Though, of course, we were in Cairo. Who would know?

"I'm headed back to the train station. Plenty of benches there. You sleep well here, and I'll be back in the morning for you. If I need to wait for you when I return, then I'll take the room."

Ah. Sensible. Though perhaps a little disappointing.

The fatigue stole over me again. The thought of a room with a comfortable bed somewhere upstairs seemed to weight my eyelids.

He kissed me quickly, a light brush of my cheek. "I'll see you in the morning. Relax and sleep well."

But by the time the sun rose over the streets of Cairo, I'd been awake for an hour, drunk two cups of strong Egyptian coffee, and tapped out several verses of "You Made Me Love You" on my thigh as I sat in the narrow hotel lobby waiting for Jack to arrive.

*Today is the day. The day I find my family.*

# CHAPTER SIXTEEN

*September 18, 1737*
*Rome, Italy*

In the sliver of time in which Renae landed back in the Roman grotto of 1737, everything hung suspended, without breath, without thought.

A moment ago they were in the corridor of Nero's Domus Aurea in Rome, with a crazed woman ordering the dagger-thrust that was only inches from Persia's chest. Then a moment later, they'd jumped out of the year 68 AD, back to 1737.

Persia's shocking ability to stop time had erupted without warning, and she'd done it not once, but twice. First, to get Nero free from the Roman cohort and correct the timeline they'd affected. Then to escape the spinning dining room in Nero's palace, with two guards hefting spears and that insane woman issuing orders.

The woman who claimed to have executed Sahara in the Forum.

And now, here they were, back in the year they'd made their permanent home. Without Sahara.

Renae's knees buckled, and only Persia's grip on her hand, then her arm, kept her from hitting the floor of the grotto.

She tried to exhale, but grief constricted her breath. She leaned her head against the now-dulled frescoes of the wall behind her, a sob hitching in her throat.

"I saw her!" Persia's voice pitched high, like the little girl she once was. But was no longer.

Renae closed her eyes, shook her head. She was not yet ready to speak of any of it. The loss, the hopelessness of ever finding Sahara now. Their last chance, gone. Perhaps she was no longer even alive.

"Mama," Persia tightened her grip on Renae's hand, then pulled it to her own chest. "Do you hear me? I saw her! I saw Sahara!"

Alexander rounded on their daughter, frowning. "What are you talking about? And someone better tell me how those spears moved from the hands of guards to your hands!"

Persia glanced up at her father, then back at Renae, as though uncertain how to deliver the shock to him.

Renae shrugged. "Persia can stop time." The words rolled out, dull as marbles across the floor.

"What?" Alexander's expression was blank, uncomprehending.

"It's true, Papa. I did it three times." She bit her lip. "But I don't really know *how* I did it—"

"Did what?" Alexander looked from Persia to her.

Renae inclined her head toward their daughter. "I saw it. But Persia, it was only twice."

"No, Mama, that's what I'm saying!" The girl's eyes glowed bright in the dim subterranean corridor. "Just before we jumped —a moment ago—"

"One of you tell me right now what you are talking about!" Alexander's face had taken on a ruddy hue.

Persia sighed. "Papa, I know it's strange, but it appears my abilities have already begun. When Mama and I were trying to get Nero away from the soldiers—" She waved a hand. "Too much to explain. All that matters is that somehow I'm able to just… freeze everything."

"Freeze…?"

"I don't know how else to explain it. Everything stops around me. All the people, moving objects. Both of *you*, even. But I'm able to move around and do things. I can only hold it for a moment or two, but with Nero, it was enough. And then again in that bizarre rotating room—I stopped everything, grabbed the spears of the two guards and just… knocked them down."

Renae almost smiled at the way Alex's jaw dropped open. Persia had rendered him speechless, which was no easy task.

"But then I did it again, and that's when I saw her!"

"When?" Renae frowned and pulled herself away from the wall. "Saw who?"

"Just now! I saw that dagger coming at me, and I thought I'd be dead before you took me out of there. And then it happened again—everyone, frozen. Except, not everyone. Someone ran into the room, a moment before we left." She grabbed Renae's arms. "It was Sahara, Mama! I know it was her!"

This time Renae would have gone down if Alexander hadn't caught her.

His gentle arm around her waist contrasted with his words—roughened with emotion. "But how could you know? You've never seen her, never seen a picture."

"I'm sure of it, Papa. She looked like Mama, for one thing. So much like you, Mama."

Renae's breath locked up again.

"She was older than me, but, the right age. The right age for *now*." Persia shrugged, but they understood her meaning.

"And the way she looked at me—she knew who I was, I could tell. She reached for me, and I could see she was desperate."

"Still, it could have been someone else. A servant—"

"No! She ran into the room, when time stopped for everyone else. Everyone but the two of us."

In the silence following Persia's declaration, a flicker of hope, like a tiny green shoot of something alive at last, grew in Renae's heart.

Sahara, in Rome to find them.

She had found the coin in Tut's tomb. Been there with Porchy and Howard, just as they hoped.

She could travel in time, and she'd understood their message. Come back to Rome to meet them at the statue.

And Decima did not execute her.

Sahara was looking for them, even as they escaped.

Even as they left her behind.

Renae buried her face in Alexander's chest.

"We missed her, Alex. We left too soon."

He wrapped his arms around her and bent his head to her own, murmuring useless comfort against her hair.

But it was all too much.

She pounded a fist against his chest, wishing it would help.

Their plan, seventeen years in the making, had failed.

"Come," Alexander pulled away and reached for the rope, still hanging from the hole in the grassy field above, where they'd left it before this terrible day began. "Let's get back up there. I need some air."

A few strenuous minutes later, the three sprawled on the grass around the entrance to the grotto. The Colosseum loomed over them, its upper edge still crumbled and rough in this earlier century, before restorations would begin in the next hundred years.

"All of this was my fault again," Persia muttered. "I got us into trouble with that woman, forced us to leave too soon—"

"Stop, Persia." Alexander's tone brooked no argument. "There is only one person to blame in all of this. Since the very beginning."

"Giada." The name was like poison on Renae's tongue. The taste of bitterness she'd unsuccessfully fought to purge, and instead feared might consume her.

How had their lives become so manipulated by the woman they once called friend?

They'd enjoyed such good times in college, jumping back and forth in history, exploring and having adventures. But once Giada discovered Alex was a Revisionist—that stupid, stupid necklace—everything changed.

While they disapproved of Giada's methods, they largely ignored her. Until the night she tried to have them killed because they wouldn't help her raid King Tut's tomb before Howard Carter found it.

Then the jump back to 1894 to escape her, and eleven peaceful years. Time split between London and Highclere Castle. But still, the ache to return to the time they'd left behind. The pain their parents must have experienced when they left 1974. Were their parents even still alive?

The tentative peace of living in the early twentieth century ended the day Joanne saw them at Hatshepsut's Temple. The only way to correct the past was to stop Giada from ever learning Alexander could revise history.

The trip to Venice had been full of hope. The plan to stop Belzoni from finding the tomb they'd eventually spend a semester digging. But then, Giada again, in Venice. The terrified escape to 1720 in the midst of Persia's birth.

And then seventeen years before they gambled Sahara would find their coin and papyrus when the fabulous antechamber of Tutankhamun's tomb was finally opened.

Renae reached for her younger daughter, sprawled across the grass, and stroked the girl's arm. "Your father's right, Persia. All of this started long, long before you were born. You've been part of it, yes. But you are not, and never have been, the cause."

A small group of men appeared, rounding the Colosseum in the haze of early morning light. One carried a walking stick—an affectation that surely signified a young British aristocrat on his "Grand Tour" of Europe—accompanied by his chaperone and perhaps a guide. This site, the underground corridor that began the Renaissance, was one of the standard stops for wealthy young men and their educational rite of passage. No doubt the gentleman approaching would try to hack a chunk out of Nero's fresco to display in his drawing room back home. Far too many pieces of classical antiquity ended up in the luggage of British tourists in this century.

Renae pulled herself to sitting, then climbed to her feet. "Let's get out of here. I don't feel like socializing."

Alexander and Persia followed, the three nodding politely to the tourists.

"Where are we going?" Persia's voice was subdued. Sad, even.

Renae eyed the rows of dark arches in the Colosseum wall, blank eyes set in impassive stone. "There is nowhere to go."

They walked north in silence for some minutes, the Colosseum at their backs, then into a run-down residential district with tiny alleys and close-built homes overhanging the streets. The smell of garbage lay like a haze above their heads, rotten and heavy. The ancient city had become medieval, and was now speeding toward the end of the early modern period, into an era of steam-powered ships and trains that would once again remake the world. But they had not yet reached a new era of sanitation.

And yes, they had nowhere to go. They'd gambled on Sahara finding their message in Tut's tomb, but where would she go after 1922? They couldn't return to Tut's 1325 BC to repeat their message. Where else would a clue for their daughter find its way into her hands?

"I can't stand this infernal smell a moment longer!" Persia stomped ahead of them. "At least let's walk to the river!"

Renae and Alex followed, because there was nothing better to do.

They reached the River Tiber in thirty minutes of more painful silence, then dropped to the bank to watch a few early morning fishing boats scud across the muddy water. Above, the sun grew hot in the vacant September sky.

"I've been thinking." Persia sat between the two of them, but kept her eyes on the river.

*Haven't we all?*

"You should go back."

Renae said nothing, and Alex seemed as unwilling to talk. Though it was still morning here in 1737, they'd lived an entire day elsewhere, and exhaustion plus emotion leached the last of her energy into the riverbank.

"I'm serious."

Renae sighed. "Go back, where? We can't return to—"

"To 1922."

Beside her, Alexander stiffened.

"That's not going to happen."

"Please, Mama. Think about it. If you both returned to where you left 1905, revising history and returning to the time that's passed, you'd be in 1922. With Sahara. Then the three of you could find me—"

"Not here." Alexander's voice was harsh. "We could not return here to 1737, where we've built a life."

"True. But we could choose another time, farther back."

Renae bristled. "Persia, we don't even know you can travel yet. And even if you could—"

"Then let's find out."

Renae drew her knees to her chest, braced her elbows, and rubbed at her gritty eyes with fingers that felt numb despite the heat.

Yes, they would need to find out at some point. If not now, then some time in the future. They would need to let her break out on her own, as every time traveler must do with their adult child at some point.

But now? At seventeen?

But Persia was already on her feet, facing her parents with the river flowing behind her, hands clenched at her sides.

"I am going to try. Here in Rome. Where better? So many periods and events to choose from."

Alexander rolled his shoulders, eyes closed. "I don't care if you *are* able to travel back alone. Or even to… stop time. I'm not leaving my seventeen-year-old daughter in the past alone."

"But, Papa, it could be so simple! We go home to Venice from here, then you both go forward, first to 1814, then all the way to

1922 at St. Mark's, where you first left. I will go backward to an earlier year in Venice—oh, can I meet Michaelangelo? I've always wanted—" She shook her head, fluttered her hands. "Doesn't matter. I'll go back to maybe 1500, then once you find Sahara in 1922, you go back to that same day I've chosen. So I'll be alone in medieval Venice for less than a day. And I know Venice so well—"

"And if it doesn't work?" Renae couldn't keep the anger out of her voice. "We're to be separated then from *you* for decades? Perhaps forever? No. I will not be forced to choose between my daughters!"

Persia glared at her. "Yet, isn't that what you've already done?"

The accusation stabbed hard. She fought the hard knot of emotion in her throat.

Yes. She'd chosen Persia over Sahara. But what choice did she have?

"We don't have to decide all this now." Persia held out both hands, as if to help her parents from their prone positions on the grassy bank. "Please, let's just test whether I can travel alone."

Neither she nor Alex grasped the girl's hand.

*I'm not ready.*

And yet... again. What choice did she have?

# CHAPTER SEVENTEEN

*September 18, 1737*
*Rome, Italy*

*T*wo hours and two kilometers later, Renae followed Alex and Persia past the Campo de' Fiori, where she and Alex witnessed Caesar's assassination so many years ago. They crossed the Tiber here, then continued northward.

They entered the Vatican area like every tourist would for centuries: westward across the Via della Conciliazone, with the Egyptian obelisk brought by Caligula pointing the way toward the greenish dome of St. Peter's Basilica. It would be another two hundred years before the area would be declared a sovereign city-state, outside the purview of Italy's government. The pope would sign that agreement with Benito Mussolini in 1929, a few years into Sahara's future.

*How strange, that I can see into my daughter's future and yet cannot reach her.*

A quick trip to the run-down kiosk where tickets to the Vatican Museum were sold, and then they started off across St. Peter's Square to the right, to enter behind the long, rectangular Sistine Chapel.

"I'm going to meet him, then? Truly?" Persia's eyes glowed as they walked through the Picture Gallery, a hall lined floor to ceiling, and indeed even the ceiling, with gilded frames of Renaissance art.

Alexander shrugged. "If he's there, Persia. We can't be certain—"

"We will choose the right day, then. A day we know."

Renae followed silently, her heart pounding in her throat. How could these two be so cavalier? Whether Persia stumbled into meeting Michaelangelo in the sixteenth century could not be more inconsequential. They were about to let their young daughter travel to another time, *alone.*

Minutes later, they reached the famed Sistine Chapel, still sacredly quiet at this hour of the morning. Or perhaps the hallowed paintings left visitors awed into silence at any hour, in any century.

Despite her travels through the Mediterranean world, it was Renae's first visit to the Chapel, and she found it impossible to know where first to train her eyes. A dizzying swarm of figures covered every inch of the walls and ceiling—gossamer angels and horned demons, saints being escorted to heaven and the damned dragged to hell. Enough nudity to make anyone blush, and stories that would take hours, perhaps years, to fully understand.

At her side, Persia's tiny gasp echoed the expansion of her own chest, as though the art poured something of life into them both. A swell of unnamed emotion, senseless yet inevitable, rose within her, crested, and subsided, leaving her spent.

Michaelangelo's frescoes on the altar wall and ceiling were of course the most famous. Renae's eye drifted to the story splayed across the nine panels of the ceiling, to the *Creation of Adam*, with its iconic finger of God reaching out to connect with the finger of Adam, animating him to life. Then down to the Altar Wall, to the horrific scenes of *The Last Judgment*, inspired by Dante's depiction of hell.

"It's too much," Persia whispered.

Yes, yes it was. How could one ever absorb it all in one visit?

But minutes later, after a quick read-through of a plaque mounted nearby, their whispered plan had nothing to do with the historic artwork, and everything to do with their future.

November 1, 1512.

The day the ceiling of the Sistine Chapel was exhibited to the public for the first time.

It was as specific a date as they could wish for, yet Renae's fear only increased.

"Mama, all will be well. It's a good plan." Persia led the way to a corner, stanchioned off from public access, but at the moment unguarded.

At least she would not need to wait in agony, to know if Persia could travel alone.

Her daughter would touch the wall, attempt to move backward to that day in 1512, then return to a moment before she left. For Renae and Alexander, she would not seem to have been gone at all.

And if she did not return, if instead she slipped through their grasp into the past, they would follow on her heels and find her, here in the Chapel.

"Persia, you must *promise me*, no matter what happens, you will not try to revise—"

"I promise, Mama." The girl took Renae's hands in her own, and made the oath solemnly.

It was an unknown, not only if Persia could time travel already, but if she also carried the Revisionist ability. If so, and if she returned here to 1737 to a time later than she left, her parents would have already assumed she was stuck in 1512, and gone searching for her there.

"And if we have to come for you, we will meet you here, in the Chapel. No matter how long it takes, or what happens. You will always return here, to find us."

Persia nodded. "Here in the Chapel."

A brief flash of Renae's possible future washed over her—cursed like the hellish figures on the wall to spend day after day in this same place, waiting without end for a daughter who would never appear.

She clutched at Persia. "I can't do it. I'm not ready."

It was Alexander who pried her fingers from her daughter's arms. "Renae, we must." He kept her fingers imprisoned in his own, and turned her to him, to look into his hooded eyes, dark with concerns of his own. "We must."

"Another backup plan, then. We must have another—"

"No. One plan. Or we risk missing each other in the confusion."

He was right. They'd seen what trying to connect across millennia could do to a family.

She nodded, unable to speak.

But how could she let her go? Another daughter? She had a limb torn from her years ago, and now it was happening again. How could she go on with yet another part of her missing, ripped away?

She ground her teeth against the sob vibrating in her chest, to no effect.

Then clutched the girl to herself, weeping against her neck.

"I love you, Persia. Never forget that we loved you, so much."

"Mama, I will be fine—"

But she left off her protest, and instead circled Renae with her own arms, returning the desperate embrace. "I love you, too, Mama."

Then an arm that included Alexander. "And you, Papa. Both of you." She lifted her tear-stained face to study their own, as though memorizing their features. "Thank you both, thank you for the sacrifice you made for me..." The words crumbled away and she dropped her eyes. "If you find Sahara, tell her that I loved her, even though I never met her. And tell her... tell her I am sorry."

Renae lifted the girl's chin. "No, Persia—"

Her daughter smiled through the tears. "I will be fine. I'll be back before you know it."

Renae tried to laugh at the old time traveler's joke, but the laughter lodged in her throat, unable to escape.

One last embrace, one final kiss.

They stood at the corner of the chapel, where a satiny fabric draped the wall. Renae and Alexander blocked any view of Persia with their bodies.

Persia reached for the wall.

Renae should be watching for any militant guards, but she could not take her eyes from her daughter.

Touching the wall. Closing her eyes. Bending her head...

Then lifting her head.

A giddy smile on her lips, eyes dancing.

She reached for Renae's hand, then Alexander's.

"Michaelangelo says hello."

~

"I still do not like the idea of separating."

They'd left the Vatican area and crossed back over the Tiber. The sun baked the perspiration from Renae's forehead as they trudged through streets, in unspoken understanding that they progressed toward the Forum, where they could arrange transport back to Venice.

Rome held nothing more for them.

And she was tired. So tired. Ready for a bath and a bed. Not for this argument.

Persia, on the other hand, did not seem to feel any fatigue. She practically bounced on her toes as they walked. "We will find a time that is indisputable, easy to get to. You can get Sahara from 1922 and meet me there—"

"It is not so easy." Alexander's voice was low, that rumble in his chest that meant he was unhappy. "We have a life in this time."

"But this time is no more your home than any other time in the past."

"But 1737 is *your* home."

"I don't care about that! And listen, we can always have your backup plan, too, yes? The time and place you both have set aside to meet, if anything should ever separate you."

Yes, they always had their "backup plan," as they called it. Never getting within eighty years of the day of Pharaoh Khufu's death, keeping it sacred as a last resort should they ever be separated. They'd held onto that reassurance ever since another traveler they met during their college days suggested it. The very trip, actually, that started all this mess with Giada.

Funny how little they ever wondered about meeting that other time traveler. In the naivete of youth, they must have believed it would happen frequently, as though they would meet many more travelers at milestones throughout history, just as the three of them first met at Caesar's assassination. But, in fact, they never met another until that day at Hatshepsut's Mortuary Temple when Joanne called their names.

But that girl, back at Ramesses III's death, and the Harem Conspiracy...

Renae's chest seized.

Breath gone.

She thrust a hand out to steady herself, grasped empty air.

She stumbled through the watery gutter at the street's edge, up onto bricks and against a tenement house.

"Mama?"

"Renae, what it is?"

She braced a hand against the house, held another aloft, palm outward, holding them back.

She had to think.

Eyes closed, remembering. Remembering that girl. What had she said her name was?

Gobi. She remembered because it was unusual, even for an Egyptian. A desert name. A *desert*.

Renae desperately tried to call up the memory of the girl's face, but it was too far gone, too long ago.

"Renae?" Alexander put both hands to her cheeks, studied her eyes. "What is it? Do you feel pain somewhere?" He looked her up and down, as though he could diagnose a heart attack by looking at her.

She shook her head, put her hands to his on her face. "I think... I think it was *her.*"

He waited, but she could see the worry lines etched across his forehead, wrinkling the corners of his eyes.

"The girl. Gobi. At Ramesses. Who told us to meet at Cleopatra, but we said it had to be Khufu."

The worry shifted to confusion. He dropped his hands. "I don't—what are you saying?"

She took a breath, swallowed the fire in her chest. Felt strength returning, and with it, certainty.

"Don't you remember, Alex? The girl we met back then— another traveler—during the Harem Conspiracy? It was her suggestion, that we have a time we always kept available, if we were ever separated."

Alexander looked into the distance, forehead furrowed. "Yes. Right, she suggested Cleopatra's death, and that's how we realized she couldn't be native to 1155 BC. But what—"

And then Renae saw the truth reflected in his own eyes. The hope, washing like clean water over the muddied confusion of the past day.

"Could it have been?"

"What did she say to you? Exactly what she said?"

"That one day Giada would betray us. And when it happened, we should run. And leave no one behind."

"And then it happened. The fire, and we ran. All the way to 1894."

Persia folded her arms. "Is someone going to fill me in?"

They turned as one to their younger daughter.

Renae grinned. The words rushed out now, like they'd been pent up for more than three decades. "Years ago, when we were still in college, before we were married, before Sahara was born. We traveled back to the time of Ramesses III and met another traveler. She gave us this strange, vague warning about Giada. But she also told us to agree on a time where we would meet, should we ever get separated. That's when we decided on Khufu."

Persia was shaking her head, shrugging. Still not seeing.

But Alexander was laughing. "It was her, I know it was her. It was Sahara."

"What?" Persia straightened, put her hand to her mouth. "How?"

"I don't know." Renae leaned against the tenement house once more. "I don't know how she knew to find us there. Or why she didn't tell us who she was. But it had to have been her. And she was older than us, right, Alex?"

He nodded. "I think so. Thirty, maybe? Older than that?"

"So—so it could have been a recent trip for her. Maybe even after she missed us in Rome... today."

The three went silent, trying to piece together the confusing overlap that time travel always generated.

It was Persia who spoke the words that changed everything.

"Did she know you chose Khufu's death as your meeting place?"

Renae looked to Alex, knowing her eyes must be shining, as his were.

"She knew."

# CHAPTER EIGHTEEN

*December 23, 1922*
*Cairo, Egypt*

*N*ot even the iconic silhouette of three pyramids, backed by my eponymous desert—the Sahara—was enough to distract me today.

We bounced in a decade-old Ford through the early dawn streets of Cairo, then into the smaller adjoining town of Giza.

Jack watched the streets, packed even at this hour with heavy-laden donkeys, bicycles, honking automobiles, and broken-down horse-drawn carriages, all trying to beat the heat of the day. Drivers yelled and shook their fists, families on donkeys swerved and yelled back.

And behind it all, the Great Pyramid rose from the sand, its jagged cap of limestone the only remaining testament to the casing which once glowed brilliant white under the desert sun.

Once, yes. But I would see it today.

A tiny thrill bloomed, though nothing compared to the excitement of finding my parents. My sister.

Jack squeezed my hand where it lay on my thigh.

"I've gone over it a thousand times," I murmured. "Their conversation about meeting here one day."

"I know. And I know you don't want it to be just any day in their lives. You want it to be their *now*."

"Do you think they figured it out?"

He only smiled.

I'd asked the question, and had it answered, a half-dozen times already.

My cryptic message about Giada. *If you ever suspect, promise me you'll run. Leave no one behind.*

After Persia called my name in the palace corridor of one of Rome's most infamous emperors, they must have known I found their coin in Tut-ankh-amun's tomb. That I followed them through history. Did they remember the girl from their university days, who once overheard them plan to meet here at Khufu's pyramid? Put it together and travel here, from wherever they lived?

Well, we would soon know.

We'd arrived in Giza early, to ensure we wouldn't miss them, sometime around 2500 BC. If they showed up there to meet each other, not realizing I was on my way, there would be nothing to keep them there, except for some sightseeing, until I arrived. I couldn't take that chance.

The Ford and its aging driver took us to a roofed pavilion in the shade of a cluster of palms. A small crowd of well-heeled tourists and white-robed Egyptian guides with snorting camels milled about.

Jack paid our driver, then climbed out behind me.

Since the days of Napoleon, scholars and historians had been sketching and exploring, digging and destroying around the three kings' pyramids and the clusters of queens' pyramids, as well as the enigmatic Sphinx poking up from the sands of the plateau, like a half-buried guard dog.

Even our own strongman, Giovanni Belzoni, left inscriptions of his archaeological prowess inside the second of the pyramids built by Khufu's son, Khafre.

Three local men, in ankle-length robes and white turbans, set upon us immediately.

"A ride to the pyramids for the lady?" One of them, grizzled and burly, elbowed the others aside to appeal to Jack. "Very fine camel here. Very clean. You see?" He patted the animal's saddle, seemingly unaware of the puff of dust his salesmanship produced.

"A ride for each of us, I believe." Jack smiled at me and shrugged. "I'm a sucker for the authentic experience."

There would be no riding side-saddle here. My driver smacked the neck of his beast three times, and the camel kneeled, then settled onto its haunches in the sand.

Still, I needed a hand up, to swing my leg across the saddle, hike my dress to my knees, and secure my grip on the saddle's horn while the driver clipped my shoes into the stirrups.

Then, the crazy rocking gait, backward as the camel pushed its forelegs to kneeling, thrown forward as the rear legs came up, and back again as the animal stood upright.

I hadn't ridden a camel in some time, and forgot how much higher a mount it was than a horse.

I glanced to Jack in time to catch the tightened jaw and wide eyes as the camel lurched him back and forth.

"First time?"

He said nothing, only eyed the distance between the tourist stand and the largest of the pyramids in the distance.

"Don't worry." I grinned. "Easy as riding a horse."

"Sure. Until you fall."

"Right." I gave my guide the signal to start. "So don't fall."

Unlike a horse, the reins were not put in the hands of amateurs. Our guides each kept a grip on the lead rope and pulled us toward the pyramids in a rollicking gait that kept my hands tight on the pommel.

The three pyramids jutted from the desert, postcard-perfect, against a white-blue sky. I kept my eyes on the capstone. Once we traveled back, would it be cased in gold as historians believed?

Behind me, Jack's voice carried across the silent sand. "Will we climb to the top? Go inside?"

"We could. If you want to play tourist. But I think it's the entrance we want. That's where they agreed to meet."

The morning sun, still low in the east as we crossed toward the trio of pyramids, cut a swath across the sand, bisecting our journey.

We were among the earliest arrivals, but still not the only tourists. A couple in their fifties stood at the base, peering up toward the entrance. The woman dabbed her neck with a red-and-white floral handkerchief, as though already sweating.

Jack and I exchanged glances as our guides brought our camels to their knees and helped us dismount.

Jack's sudden disappearance from 1922 would raise no eyebrows, since he would be back before he left. My return time, however, was an unknown, and best located in private.

The boyish glee on Jack's face matched my own excitement, though perhaps for different reasons. We climbed past the couple, up the step-like pyramid about ten meters to the lowest entrance, a hole commonly believed to have been battered through in the Middle Ages by tomb robbers. The real entrance, the one used by the actual builders, yawned another ten meters above us.

At the makeshift entrance, we turned to watch the other tourists struggling up the crumbling stepped side.

I glanced to Jack, then lifted my head upward. "We need to get up there."

I wasn't about to take a chance on doing this in the open, and reappearing inside an entrance that didn't exist in 2500 BC seemed like a bad idea.

The wife below us had stopped again to daintily wipe her brow with her handkerchief. Little chance they would climb any higher than necessary.

We continued our climb, then slipped into the coolness of the crevice, then further into total darkness beyond.

Jack grabbed my hand and placed it against the wall. "You ready?"

No wasting time, then. No preparing for what might happen. We were doing this. We were doing it now.

I sucked in as much twentieth-century air as my lungs could hold, nodded once, realized he couldn't see me, and squeezed his hand.

"Daybreak on the day of Khufu's death."

"Daybreak. Khufu's death."

As it had been when I traveled to Hatshepsut's Mortuary Temple, I heard and felt a shift before I saw it.

In place of ancient mustiness, the ring of metal tools on stone, shouts of workers and the supervisors driving them, the smell of dust, and sweat, and the sharp tang of newly quarried rock.

I unclenched my eyes, made sure Jack was still with me. He was.

But we were not alone.

A pair of men, one young and one old, stood with tools in hand at the entrance. The wide, startled whites of their eyes were visible even in the dim light, and their hands fluttered around their faces and chests in a motion that in any age could be interpreted as warding off evil.

Jack stepped in front of me as if by instinct.

The older man's lips said one thing, though the word was different.

"Demon! It is the demon of In-tep, come to stop us from completing the project. Come to cut off our heads and kill us all!"

Jack raised his hand, palm outward, again in an ageless gesture of peace and goodwill, but the man jumped backwards at the movement, and metal picks rose in our direction.

"You there!" A shout from outside the entrance. "Why are you standing about? You should be working faster, faster!"

The men turned as one, facing outside but fingers pointing toward us.

"A demon! Or god, we know not which. Appeared in the form of a man to slay us!"

"What foolishness are you talking?"

The bulky figure of a man followed the voice and appeared in the sun-bright slit of the entrance.

He was bald, as the others, shirtless and not hiding his generous girth. The armbands of gold and sparkle of earrings elevated his status above the other two who saw us arrive.

He pulled up short, lips parted.

"You see? The older man shouted, pointed a trembling finger toward us. "They were not here one moment. The next moment, there they stood. He is a demon, and she is his underworld slave."

"I am no demon." Jack folded his arms across his bare chest, biceps flexing.

"No?" The laborer lifted his chin. "Then name the gods you serve. Horus? Set?"

"I don't serve any of your gods!"

*Careful, Jack.* His tone was too antagonistic for the vulnerability of our situation.

The man who seemed to be the overseer gave us a sharp look, but one more of curiosity and interest than hostility.

"You are needed below," he said to the two men, and jabbed them toward the sand and sky. "Report to Bahman."

They scurried out, likely more eager to be away from us, than get to the next assignment.

"Quickly now," the overseer pushed us inward, deeper into the pyramid's entrance. "We don't have much time. You serve the one god?"

Uh...

Jack and I traded glances.

Jack took the lead. "Yes."

It seemed like the answer this man wanted to hear. But monotheism? Here, and now? We were still twelve hundred years away from Tut-ankh-amun's father Ankhenaten, and his monotheistic heresy.

So strange. And matching nothing I'd ever studied.

"Well, I don't know where you came from, but it's not safe for you here. Especially today, when all of the Two Lands are taking care not to offend their gods, as we prepare for the king's death."

He looked Jack over, then flicked a glance over me.

"You are visitors? From, perhaps… the north?"

"Yes." Jack seemed to be in the flow, sensing the right answers.

"You have seen the king's tomb, then. It's time to move on." He peered through the entrance. "But those superstitious laborers will spread news of your heresy, or worse, faster than oil spreads on water. I must get you somewhere safe. With others who serve the one god," he added, as though it would reassure us.

"Thank you," Jack said. "What is your name, friend?"

Our benefactor turned on us, eyebrows raised as though disbelieving we didn't know his identity.

"I am Hemiunu, vizier and architect of this great feat."

Hemiunu, of course.

Hermann Junker, the dig director here at Giza, found this man's tomb about ten years ago. He had served as the engineer of the pyramid project for decades.

Hemiunu was trying to guide us out into the light.

I had no intention of leaving this entrance until this day was over. I'd wait that long if I had to, for my family to arrive.

But already, a cluster of laborers below us were talking, pointing, backing away.

"Come," Hemiunu waved us out. "We must get you down to the surface."

Jack brushed his lips near my ear. "Let's get below and out of sight. We can still watch the entrance. We will see them if they come out."

But what if they didn't come out? What if they came to this time because they'd lost each other, and once reunited inside the pyramid, they disappeared before ever emerging?

I hesitated, but a collective shout interrupted my thoughts.

Below us, a dozen or more hands pointed upward at us.
No, they pointed behind us, past us.
I swiveled slowly, heart pounding.
And there they were.
Shading their eyes. Stepping into the sunlight.
Two of them, hands still clasped, with a girl between them.
Persia, at just the right age.
Stars and glory. We had found each other.

# CHAPTER NINETEEN

*2566 BC*
*Giza Plateau, Egypt*

*E*ven with all the times, and places, and moments I imagined this reunion taking place, I remained unprepared for the wave of shock and joy, rolling upward from my toes to my head, then back to my feet.

I staggered against Jack and stared.

At first, there was no rushing headlong into an embrace. No shouted names. Only a stunned silence, as we all drank each other in, under the hot Egyptian sun.

My mother moved first.

Hesitant steps toward me. Tears, silent, but her shoulders shaking. One hand covering her mouth.

She stumbled forward, until we were eye to eye, an older and younger version of the same face.

And then, her hand on my cheek.

"Sahara."

My name, whispered like a prayer.

And then we were embracing, all of us.

My face buried against my father's chest, then in my sister's hair, as though we'd known each other all our lives, and somehow we had.

Jack stood apart. Time enough to explain him soon.

"More slaves! The demon brings more of his slaves from the underworld to serve him!"

A man, as yet unknown to us, clambered up the ramp built against the now-smooth limestone surface of the pyramid.

"Overseer, we must kill him. It is unlucky, a bad omen, especially now."

Hemiunu stepped between us and our accuser. "Perhaps, perhaps you are right." He shook his head. "But not here. Unlucky, as you say. I will take them and deal with them properly. Get your men back to work."

"As you say, Overseer."

And so we found ourselves, unbelievably, almost illogically, deposited into the chariot of the second-most powerful man in the kingdom, and if Hemiunu's guarded words to his driver were to be believed, headed for his private residence.

Away from the single pyramid, past the mortuary temple, the harbor, with the palace in the distance. But I barely registered all of it. The interior of the chariot held my attention.

I heard Jack murmur something to my father. Only heard the words *secret* and *monotheist*. At least someone had the presence of mind to keep us safe.

We spoke almost not at all for the duration of the trip. With the driver only a breath away, it seemed none of us knew where to start or what to say.

But the embraces, the hand squeezes, the long, tearful studying of each other's every angle of face and body said as much as words could have.

My sister was so lovely, now that I could study her for more than the moment I had in Rome. Her hair, clothing, and makeup were Egyptian, but I could see past all of that, to the features that felt as familiar already as my own face.

And my parents, older but still as I remembered them. My dad, tall and lean, with the crinkled eyes of a man who spent so much time with his books. My mother—more petite than me, with her full smile and sparkling eyes.

"This is Jack," I whispered at one point.

My father's eyes scanned over Jack, took his measure, seemed to indicate at least an initial, grudging approval. No indication he recognized him from their brief meeting more than thirty years ago.

In that moment, I didn't care whether my father approved, or would bully Jack in some kind of fatherly, protective outrage. The idea of having him watch over me once again was so powerful it brought fresh tears.

And then we were being hustled off the chariot, through the door of a sprawling one-story home, mudbrick but decorated with highly stylized paintings of children playing in the rushes of the Delta.

A woman met us at the door, and the driver said something we couldn't hear.

She ushered us deeper into the house, to a central courtyard that overflowed with dwarf palms and flowering poppies, with a bubbling fountain in the center and walls painted with overflowing pots of pink-petaled lotus flowers, displaying the talent of an extraordinary artist.

We stood facing each other, a little cluster of disbelief.

Persia and I had linked arms as though we would never let each other go.

"Greetings." A regal woman with dark hair flowing down her back sailed into the courtyard, dressed in the riotous colors of crimson and saffron and with tiny bells tingling at her ankles.

"I am Neferet. I am told you are visitors my husband wishes to keep safe."

Two children about the ages of ten and seven followed, the younger clinging to her dress.

"Thank you." My mother stepped forward, taking the lead as one matriarch to another. "We appreciate your hospitality. Is there a place in which we—my family—could have some privacy?"

Her voice broke on *family*, and I swallowed against the hot emotion in my own chest.

"Of course, please. Follow me."

We single-filed behind Neferet, through a corridor leading deeper into the house.

She extended a hand to an open chamber. "The room belonged to my eldest son, but he has left us to begin his own family."

The five of us clustered in the chamber, still silent.

"Please," she indicated the room's wooden chairs and narrow cots. "Rest here. I will have water and food brought to refresh you."

She was gone a moment later.

My father broke the silence, taking my upper arms in his hands and studying my face. "It was you, wasn't it? All those many years ago, the day of the Harem Conspiracy? I can hardly remember the face of the girl we met, but—" He left off, a question in his eyes.

I smiled through the watery haze. "It was me. Us, actually." I smiled at Jack.

Renae circled him and touched my forearm. "How long ago? For you, I mean? How long ago was that day?"

I laughed—a little choke of a sound that neared madness. "Yesterday. For us, it was yesterday."

We gathered the chairs into a tight group beside the cots and lingered there, sharing everything—all the missteps, the failed attempts, the near-meeting in Rome when I'd seen my sister stop time. Yes, it seemed seventeen-year-old Persia could stop time. She was still clueless as to how to control it.

"And you can travel alone already?" I asked. "At your age?"

Her eyes sparkled like my mother's. "They've only let me do it once. But, yes."

"How is stopping time possible, though?" I looked to both parents. "Have you known others who could do such a thing?"

Alexander grunted. "If there are others, they're keeping it

quiet. Bad enough we two got married, but with both of us Revisionists—"

"*Both*? You are both Revisionists?"

"We assume that's what gave Persia this extra ability."

"She's... Amplified?"

Persia grinned and waggled her eyebrows, making me laugh.

My mother ran her hand down my hair. "And you, Sahara? What have you discovered about your abilities?"

I caught her fingers in my hand and held them to my cheek. "Not much. I am a Revisionist, I do know that. And when Persia stopped everything in Rome, it didn't affect me. That's all I know. But then, I've only known time travel was possible for about two months."

"Only two months?"

I heard the anguish in her voice.

"She had no one to teach her." This from Jack, spoken quietly and without accusation.

It all poured out then, the years since we parted, time spent at boarding school and university, summers at Highclere. The war and my nursing efforts. The years on digs with Howard Carter, pursuing the illusive boy-king Tut-ankh-amun.

Something clicked as I spoke the pharaoh's name.

"You *are* from... from later. That is how you knew about the tomb. That Howard would discover it this year. Why you put the coin and the message there for me."

My father nodded, a rueful smile playing on his face. "Yes, counting on my little Sahara staying close to the action, as you always did."

"And me? What year was I born?" My voice trembled over the question.

Jack reached for my hand.

The answer was important. More important than I cared to admit.

"Sahara, we never wanted to deceive you. But you were in danger, and we had to run. The closest year to our own time was

1894, which made sense—for other reasons—and we hoped you would never remember your first few years."

"So, my birth…"

"You were born in Philadelphia, in 1970."

Jack's fingers convulsed over mine.

So it was true. I could return to where I belonged, now the twenty-first century. But without Jack. We already knew he would not return.

My father eyed our clasped hands.

"Perhaps it's time we learned a bit more about Jack, here." He leveled a serious glare at Jack's face. "Obviously, you're a traveler as well, which brings its own challenges if you two are… Well, first let's hear how you ended up here with our girl. Who are you?"

I held my breath, waiting for Jack's confession. For the truth of his Aunt Giada and how he'd come to 1922 to meet me.

"Sir," Jack's somber tone matched my father's, "I am the man who is in love with your daughter."

I exhaled, my body relaxing into something so unknown I hardly knew what to call it.

"Is that so?"

"Yes." Jack's jaw tightened. "I need you to hear and understand that fact clearly. Before the rest."

"Understood. For now. So let's hear the rest."

"I am the nephew of Giada Moretti."

From the gasp around our little circle, you would have thought he'd spoken the name of one of those Egyptian demons we'd been accused of serving.

"Explain."

The single word from my father, delivered with such hostility, pushed Jack backward in his chair.

Jack sketched the briefest outline of his childhood, his belief about who Giada was, challenged only recently. He finished by updating them about Reuben's appearance, and the news that he did not return to November of 2002.

My father broke his intense focus on Jack to look at me. "And you trust this man? You believe he is being truthful now, after everything?"

I hesitated.

Jack's revelations, delivered in mere minutes to my family, had taken weeks to unfold for me. Did I trust that we now had nothing but honesty between us?

But Jack's expression undid me. Crestfallen at my hesitation. One hand raking through his hair, the other fisted on the arm of his chair.

"Yes." I smiled at my family. "Yes, I trust him."

Jack's shoulders sagged, but he only studied the floor.

"Please, sir," grief tinged Jack's voice, "please tell me the rest of it." He raised his eyes to Alexander. "Tell me the truth about my Aunt Giada."

We talked into the afternoon, the sun slanting through the square-cut window high in the wall. Servants brought trays of flatbread and herbed lentils, with jugs of watered wine and beer.

Neferet also came, encouraging us to remain hidden, as wild rumors about us were already circulating, and we were most certainly in danger.

But they told it all. Beginning with their university days in Philadelphia, through their friendship, and Giada's claim to have found the queen Tiye's necklace in the sand. My parents' marriage and my birth within the year.

And then the souring of the friendship. Giada's lust for artifacts and the accompanying wealth driving her to make an impossible request of my parents.

As the story of her sending Ahmed Abd el-Rassul after them, and the explosion which nearly killed us all spilled out, Jack paced the floor under the window, alternately shaking his head and growling.

"It was your warning that saved us, really, Sahara."

"What? My warning?"

"Back on the day of Ramesses' murder. You warned me, if I ever suspected we were in danger from Giada, we should run, and leave no one behind."

"I—But I was talking about Venice. Trying to tell you that when you went to Venice in 1905, you shouldn't leave me—"

It was all too strange. I had somehow caused them to bring me to 1894?

"Well, with Giada trying to kill us, and 1894 ready and waiting, we made the decision to live out our lives in a different century." Alexander squeezed my knee. "One where we could keep you safe."

"So what happened? Between 1894 when you arrived in England and 1905 when you disappeared in Venice?"

"A chance encounter." Renae closed her eyes. "We ran into another friend from our university, who happened to work for Giada, while visiting Hatshepsut's time. We knew she'd tell Giada we were alive."

"So you decided to go back to 1814, to stop Belzoni from discovering Seti's tomb, so there would be no university dig when Giada first discovered you were a Revisionist."

I had managed to surprise them all—all three of them, mouths agape and eyebrows raised.

I lowered my head. "Don't be too impressed. It was my fault she found you there in Venice at all."

We pieced together the rest of it, then. Giada chasing them into Belzoni's 1814 Venice, the desperate leap back to 1720 in the midst of Persia's birth.

"We suspect it might be the reason for her newfound ability." Renae's voice was a whisper, as though anyone in earshot would believe it, anyway. "Perhaps something about her birth spanning two centuries, being born in both times, or neither time, that allows her pause all of time around her."

"Remarkable."

After years of believing my parents were ripped away from me as a teen, and months of searching for the three of them, I allowed myself at last to sink into the comfort of belonging—if not *somewhere*—at least to *someone*. Three someones.

I glanced at Jack. Maybe four.

My mother beside me seemed to sense my emotions, curled her hand around mine and smiled into my teary eyes.

"You are so beautiful, Sahara. Inside and out. I knew you would be, but it is so good to truly see you, to feel connected once more."

"I was thinking the same thing. To finally belong somewhere again, I feel as though I am no longer simply a..." I waved my hand through the air. "... a floating dust mote, with no significance."

A flicker of concern passed over her features. "You have significance, Sahara, whether we were ever reunited."

I smiled. "How can you know that, when you don't even know what I've been doing all these years?"

The concern deepened the furrow in her forehead. "Because you are more than what you *do*. You are a valuable human being, and that value isn't given because of anything you've done."

"Do you really think that's true? Even for Revisionist time travelers? I feel as though I'm meant to prove myself, with some worthwhile endeavor I haven't yet discovered."

"You have a purpose, a destiny to fulfill. We all do. But your purpose is something quite apart from your value. It's given to you *because* you are highly valued, not as a means to prove that value."

A swell of gratitude, for this moment, hearing words of advice from my mother's lips, moved me to wrap her in an embrace, leaving us both in tears.

"Hey, don't leave me out." Persia joined our hug, squeezing me tightly to herself.

As night fell across the street beyond the window, a strange keening rose up from outside the house, as though a hundred cats wandered the twilight, yowling and crying.

"What is that awful noise?" Jack crossed to the window and peered out.

My father sighed. "It is the sound of a kingdom in mourning." He flexed his fingers across his thighs. "Pharaoh Khufu is dead."

Later, Hemiunu came to us in the chamber, his expression

grim. "It is best you stay here for the night. The king—his death —" At this, his voice broke.

Neferet was behind him a moment later, arm wrapped around his waist and head against his shoulder. "Khufu was Hemi's cousin," she said to us. "They have been close since childhood."

He nodded, shielding his eyes from us. "We have been through much together. Good and bad. I will miss him."

My mother stood. "We should not be here, intruding on your grief—"

"No, no, it is best." Hemi swiped at his face and smiled. "Followers of the one god must protect each other. And as I suspected, the unfortunate incident this morning has the laborers gossiping about all of you as the cause of the king's death."

Neferet held out her hands apologetically. "I am sorry we do not have enough beds for you all."

"We are more than comfortable here, Neferet, thank you." Renae took her hands. "You have been so kind. We will leave in the morning, if someone can get us back to the pyramid, to..." She looked to Alexander, eyebrows raised.

"Our transportation to home will be there," he finished for her.

Hemi and Neferet looked between us all. Hemi opened his mouth, as if to question who we were, where we came from. But then shook his head.

"I am sorry, I—I think I will retire. It has been a long day."

"Of course." Alexander bent at the waist in deference. "Thank you again for your hospitality."

We talked late into the night, with our first priority to make a plan, to never lose each other again.

My parents and sister were living in Venice, as Jack and I suspected. But when we visited there, we searched the wrong century, since they were in 1737, not 1814 or beyond.

"You must meet us there, see our home." My mother squeezed my hand. "We have so much to show you."

We could only travel to their 1737 home once, it was true. But Venice was where we would begin. Thankfully, Jack had never been within eighty years of it.

Persia crossed the room for a jug of water. "We should have a backup, Papa. After all this time searching for her, we don't want to take any chances. What if Venice doesn't work for some reason? Or we can't get back there?"

I sighed. "I know you can't meet at Cleopatra's death. So what times have you *not* visited?"

My mother took a jug from Persia and looked to my father. "What about Solomon? We've been planning that one."

"King Solomon?" Jack smiled. "Like, the one with the mines?"

My father laughed. "You've seen that movie, then? Which one? The original? Or the 1950's version with Stewart Granger?"

"Actually, I saw it around '85, with Richard Chamberlain."

"No kidding? They made it *again*? And with that fella from *Dr. Kildare*?"

The future-talk prickled at me, as usual. "Uh, can we get back to Solomon?"

"Sure, honey." My father nodded at my mother. "Let's say the day of King Solomon's coronation, in Jerusalem."

"Agreed."

Through the late watch of the night, we talked of Rome and Venice, Luxor and Highclere, and all the places we had yet to visit, where we could plan to intersect each other in a future which was also the past.

We'd gotten only a few hours of sleep, perched on narrow cots, propped on the floor, or twisted into wooden chairs, when the shouting and pounding woke us all.

Alexander leaped to the window and kept himself half-hidden as he peered into the early morning street.

But the shouts were clear enough.

"Bring us the demon and his slaves!"

The king was dead and the people wanted someone to blame.

# CHAPTER TWENTY

*2566 BC*
*Giza Plateau, Egypt*

$\mathcal{N}$eferet's voice rose above the shouts, from somewhere within the house.

"You must speak with my husband! You have no authority—"

Her words were cut short.

The five of us stood immobile in the center of the chamber.

The heavy slap of sandals approached.

"Listen," my father turned to us all. "No matter what happens, if we get separated, we know where and when to meet." He nodded to Renae and Persia. "The three of us will return home. To Venice. Sahara, you will meet us in 1737 as soon as you can."

Jack grabbed my hands. "And promise me you'll return to 1922 without me, if it comes to that."

"What? No!"

"He's right, Sahara." My father's face turned stern. "Do what you must, to stay safe."

"And if nothing else works," Jack lowered his voice to include only me, as the shouts grew close, "we still have Cleopatra."

I nodded. There was little time for anything else.

"Here! I have found them!"

A half dozen Egyptian men poured into our chamber, then drew up short, blocking the door but unwilling to approach any closer.

"This one!" The man who witnessed our arrival yesterday pointed to Jack. "This one is the demon, and the rest are his underworld slaves, brought to serve his dark purposes."

"Careful, Jabari! He will likely become the dog-baboon before our eyes and escape!"

Neferet's stormy face appeared behind them in the doorway.

"None of you should be here! My husband is making preparations at the tomb. You must ask him—"

"Exactly why we must not delay." Another of the men stepped forward. "Hemiunu concerns himself only with the building of Pharaoh's tomb. But it is left to us to ensure the burial chamber is not defiled!"

"Take us there, then." Jack stepped forward, placing the rest of us at his back. "Take us to it, and we will return through the pyramid, to the underworld. You will have prevented any harm."

"Don't believe his lies, Waaiz. He will only curse the project. We should kill them here."

"No!" Neferet pushed through the crowd and faced them down. "Hemiunu will have you all executed for this!"

"Perhaps the vizier's family has also joined forces with the demons." The scarred and muscled worker, evidently Waaiz, stared Neferet down.

"What? No—"

"You are hiding them, are you not? Defending them?"

I advanced on Neferet, forcing my expression into a mask of anger. "What have you done, woman? We told you to ensure we were not discovered!"

Her lips parted, but then she nodded, understanding sparking in her eyes.

"Come, Sethos," she gathered the child to her hip. "Let us leave them to their discussion."

Waaiz turned on me. "Jabari says you are only slaves of this demon," he jutted his chin toward Jack. "Brought from the underworld to serve him. But perhaps you have all come to spread your ill will among the people, to keep the king from traveling to the west to become one with Ra."

I took a step back from the venom in his voice.

"What is the truth, then? Shall we free you from your bondage?" He scanned our little family group of four, with Jack still shoved to one side, but put his question to only me. "Or do you also wish to curse the legacy of the king?"

I exhaled against the impossible choice. Defend Jack and side with him, endangering us all? Or let these brutes believe we needed to be saved from him? I might keep my family safe, but doom Jack.

"I—we—" I flicked a glance toward my father. Didn't he always have the right answer?

Jack stepped between Waaiz and me, waving an imperious hand in our direction. "These people are nothing. They have no power." He laughed, a scoffing sound deep in his chest. "I brought them here, forced that woman to hide us in her home. I am the only one you need concern yourselves with."

Waaiz took him at his word. He inclined his head toward his men. "Bind him well and take him. Leave the others."

"No!" I started forward.

My father caught my arm and held me back.

He was right. I could not stop them. Interference would risk my family's safety.

Two burly men yanked Jack's arms behind his back.

His lips whitened for a moment, eyes like daggers. He glanced to me, his expression softening.

And then, unbelievably, a sad smile and a little wink.

Oh, Jack.

And just like that, he was gone, leaving the four of us in sudden silence.

"Sahara." My mother's voice, gentle. Then her arm around me. "Sahara, it will be fine—oh, sweetheart!"

I fell to pieces, sobbing against my mother's shoulder as

though they'd already sent Jack to the underworld in front of me. In the space of only hours, I found my family and lost Jack.

Persia's steely voice was for my father. "What are we going to do? We have to get him back, and it needs to be quick."

"Where would they take him?" My father and Persia were conferring as though a team. "Where would they perform an—execution?" He frowned apologetically in my direction.

I swiped at my face, swallowed against the hot pressure in my chest, and shook my head. "If they truly believe him a demon, it wouldn't be a legal type of execution. It would be more like a ritual sacrifice or something."

"Right. But human sacrifice isn't something the ancient Egyptians—"

"They don't believe he's human."

"Right again."

A throat-clearing and bell-jingling at the door turned us all in that direction.

"I've sent for Hemi." Neferet's shoulders were set back, indignation in her eyes. "He will be furious to learn his wishes were ignored." Her youngest child still leaned against her leg.

Persia slipped to the woman's side and bent to the little boy, smiling.

"Where would they take him, Neferet?" She kept her voice light and stroked the boy's hair. "If they believed him to be—what they believe—and wanted to—do him harm?"

I loved my sister even more in that moment, watching her careful avoidance for the child's sake.

"I—I don't know. We have amulets to ward off demons, and the old stories, of course. But I've never heard of a demon appearing, nor any of my people trying to kill one. It makes no sense!"

"Still," my mother folded her arms across her chest and looked through the window as though searching the streets, "they'd take him to a temple, perhaps."

"Or back to the pyramid." This from Persia, who inclined her chin toward the pyramid looming above the village.

At our skeptical expressions, she shrugged. "Think about it. If they believed his appearance would somehow curse the pharaoh's tomb, maybe they would kill him there, to... to purify it, or something."

Neferet was nodding. "It's possible."

I exhaled. "We don't have time to get this wrong." My voice sounded tight, strangled. "They will kill him quickly if they believe he's that dangerous."

My family looked to me, as though the decision lay in my hands.

And perhaps it did.

A shudder ran through me, along with the memory of Jack's bold statement last night.

*I am the man in love with your daughter.*

Was I finally ready to accept that truth? Even accept that I loved him as well, now that he was about to be taken from me?

"We go to the pyramid."

At my declaration, Persia clapped her hands together once and pointed to the door. "Right. Let's go get him."

Within minutes, Neferet had us hidden in two closed litters, borne on the backs of two sets of servants. Apparently being the vizier of Egypt came with many perks.

I tried not to think of being dragged from a similar contraption in Rome, onto the pavement of the Forum.

Neferet patted my arm and gave me a sad farewell smile. "I will send my husband to help, as soon as he arrives back here."

We jolted off.

Persia and I, alone together for the first time in our lives, glanced at each other, and then clasped hands.

"You love him, don't you, Sahara?" The shining romanticism of a seventeen-year-old glowed in her eyes.

"I love him."

She grinned. "Well, he seems rather smashing."

Despite the circumstances, I laughed. How could she sound so... so British? Here in ancient Egypt, raised by American parents in medieval Venice?

"He is. He is smashing."

"Then we will save him."

"Persia, I love your determination, but we're heading directly back to the place we barely escaped. How are we going to—"

"I don't know. But we will. Trust me, we've gotten out of worse scrapes than this one."

I winced at the "we," knowing she referred to adventures she'd shared with my parents. Without me. But at least we were all together now.

Within minutes, we regained the base of the Great Pyramid, standing alone on the Giza Plateau, awaiting the next two iconic pyramids that would form the trio so synonymous with Egypt.

Hemi's servants lowered the two litters to the sand.

The four of us climbed awkwardly out and to our feet, and conferred in hushed tones.

"He'll be inside there already, if he's here." Persia pointed upward, toward the burial chamber located above our heads, up a slope of nearly a hundred meters. "How can we know?"

It would seem now that the "demon" had been apprehended, three Egyptian women and a man showing up in litters was not cause for attention, and we were ignored.

We made the decision to spread out, see if we could learn anything, and meet back at the ramp in a few minutes.

I spent my minutes listening to a small team of laborers, first gripe about the increased work pace now the pharaoh was dead, then drift into rude comments about the woman watching them. I returned to the pyramid base with no answers.

My sister returned, hugging two jugs of water. She handed one to me and the other to my father.

"He's up there. The women are all clutching their amulets and worrying about their men. No one wants to venture upward with water for the workers. So we're going to do it."

I laughed, despite my fears. "Persia, you are amazing."

"Yes, well, we need another two jugs of water. I'll be right back."

"Listen," my father whispered as we huddled around him,

waiting for Persia, "I've been thinking about what happens next —after we rescue Jack."

I half-listened, not very interested in thinking beyond our hoped-for rescue.

"We'll leave here as soon as we're able, and technically, you and Jack could meet us immediately in Cairo, 1737. Sahara?"

"What?" I pulled my attention from the slant of smooth limestone leading to the entrance. "Yes, Cairo, 1737. Good idea."

"No, I don't think it is a good idea. We'll need to travel home to Venice, and travel is slow going in the eighteenth century. It makes more sense for you and Jack to get to Venice in 1922, and jump back to our year from there."

"Fine. Whatever. We'll do that."

"You remember the location? Where to meet us?"

"Yes, I remember." My heartbeat was speeding up. How much time did Jack have?

"And we have King Solomon, if all else fails."

I nodded, feeling words choked off.

My mother wrapped her free arm around my waist. "Now let's go find this man of yours."

# CHAPTER TWENTY-ONE

*2566 BC*
*Giza Plateau, Egypt*

*W*e single-filed up the ramp, heads down and trying to look unobtrusive, like slaves sent to bring water inside.

Once in the darkness of the pyramid interior, we lined our water jugs at the wall, and my father took the lead.

"We'll head up the Ascending Passageway here, and then the Grand Gallery beyond it, toward the King's Chamber above."

It was easier explained than accomplished. The one-meter-wide trench of the Ascending Passageway, with its ceiling less than two meters above our heads, kept us on our knees as we scrambled upward, silent. We reached the upward slope known as the Grand Gallery with relief, as the corbeled ceiling now rose nearly nine meters above, even though the narrowness of the upward slant still pinched.

How many Egyptians would be up there in the burial chamber? Would all of them be intent on killing Jack? On killing us? We had no weapons and no plan, other than trying to overpower them and get Jack back down to where we'd all arrived, at the wall just inside the entrance. It was the only way to get us all out of here.

"Persia?" I whispered to the back of her head. "Can you—can you help us somehow? Up there?"

Even in the murk, her head-shake was unmistakable.

"It doesn't happen on command. I—I don't know how or why it happens."

Six million tons of granite and limestone pressed an invisible hand against my consciousness as I climbed. Somehow it did nothing to reassure me, knowing this pyramid would still stand more than five thousand years later and would not collapse on me now. Perhaps claustrophobia, like any phobia, is immune to rational thought. I inhaled against the constriction of my chest and placed one knee in front of the other.

The strutted pieces of wood which would eventually help tourists climb this shaft did not exist, and we each slipped and slid along the smooth surface, grabbing at narrow finger-niches and toeholds to continue upwards.

Flickering torchlight and muted, echoing voices filtered down from the burial chamber.

Was Jack still alive up there?

We reached the top of the angled shaft, still on our knees, outside a waist-high tunnel into the burial chamber. My father put a finger to his lips as we assembled on the narrow platform.

A sing-song chant bubbled from within the chamber, joined by a matching voice.

Priests, intoning some kind of incantation.

A ripple of horror shuddered through me. My back and neck tingled in a prickly, clammy sweat.

Alexander leaned forward to peer under the lintel of the half-size doorway.

Persia grabbed his arm, as though to keep him from entering.

My mother placed a hand against my back in reassurance.

He pulled back and faced us in the dim light. Held up two fingers and mouthed the words "only two priests."

I chanced a soft breath. Four against two. Or perhaps five of us, assuming Jack was still alive.

*God, if you are there, please let Jack still be alive.*

My father glanced at each of our faces, eyebrows raised, the unspoken question of *ready?* in his expression.

We nodded, each of us, though I wasn't sure what we agreed to.

My father scrambled through the doorway. Yelling in Latin.

*"Ego ululantium terrere sermonibus!"*

Which roughly translated into *I am screaming words to terrify you.*

If I weren't terrified myself, it would be hilarious.

The three of us pushed in after him, joining our voices to his. The clamor bounced off the burial chamber walls.

The two priests backed away, eyes whitened and mouths agape.

Each of them wore the one-shouldered robe of an Old Kingdom priest. A leopard skin draped the neck of the shorter of the two.

The other held a knife.

In a blink, my father leaped at him, tore the knife from his limp fingers, and turned it on him.

The granite sarcophagus, thousands of pounds of weight, stood near the back wall of the chamber, waiting to be filled.

Jack lay on the floor in front of it, eyes closed and unmoving.

A swell of nausea hit me. I ran to him, dropped to my knees beside his body. One hand on his chest.

It rose and fell under my touch.

"He's alive! Jack! Wake up!" I rattled his arms as though I could shake consciousness into him.

Nothing.

I whirled on the priests. "What did you do to him?"

Persia and my mother were at my side, lifting Jack's shoulders from the cold floor, pulling him toward the chamber entrance.

One of the priests gestured with fluttering hands across his body. "Slaves of the demon In-tep! You are all cursed!"

"Yes," my father stood tall, knife gleaming in the torchlight, "and you will be cursed as well, if you try to follow us!"

I clambered to Jack's feet, helped the other two women lift his unconscious body.

"I think he's been drugged," Persia whispered.

"We can pull him down to the entrance," my mother answered. "It won't be hard."

Moments later, my father led the way downward, slip-sliding the forty meters down the Grand Gallery, slowing the progress of Jack's unconscious body, which threatened to tumble him down the length of the chute.

Persia and my mother did their best to keep Jack from taking my father down with him.

And I brought up the rear, now brandishing the knife.

Our escape was more of a controlled freefall than a steady descent. But we made progress.

The priests bent to the small chamber entrance and watched in silence from above, apparently unwilling to chance the knife I kept raised and ready.

We were doing this. We were going to escape ancient Egypt, all of us.

I pushed away thoughts of the safety of eighteenth century Venice. One task at a time.

Sunlight tunneled along the passageway connecting the outside entrance to the base of the Ascending Shaft, marking a spot like a treasure map's X where we would find safety.

We reached the bottom, the knife slippery in my sweaty palm.

My family dragged Jack toward the entrance.

*This can't work.*

The realization hit me like a physical thing, more suffocating than the Ascending Shaft.

How could an unconscious Jack place his hand on the stone and his mind on the future, to return to 1922?

A sliding sound and a yell behind us.

The priests descended, shouting to guards outside.

My parents propped the still-drugged Jack against the inner wall of the pyramid entrance.

"Down farther." I pointed to the exact spot we'd touched to arrive here.

They nudged him toward the light, but my father was shaking his head at my mother. They'd realized it, too.

Persia stood with her back to us all, facing down the oncoming priests. "We need to go, now!"

I clenched fingernails into my palms and whirled on my parents. "You three go! Take Persia back to your year. To Venice. I will find you there!"

"What?" Persia spun. "We're not leaving before you!" She glanced at Jack. Lips parted in understanding.

My father grabbed Persia's hand and Renae took the other. "We need to be ready."

Persia wrestled herself away from their grasp.

The priests were nearly at the bottom of the shaft now. Their shouts filtered out into the sunlight.

Three guards appeared, silhouetted in the bright entrance like spectral shadows.

I hovered over Jack's prone form, as though I could shield him from what was to come.

The leopard-skinned priest screamed to the guards, his voice shrill.

"The demons have escaped!"

So we were all demons now.

The four of us huddled with our backs to Jack, a tight cluster of protection for him. With nothing to protect ourselves.

"There!" The white-robed priest pointed a bony finger at us. "They shield their master In-tep!"

One guard yanked me away from Jack.

Another raised his spear, aimed for Jack's chest, and plunged it downward.

"No!" The shriek tore from my lips. It bounced against silent stone. It echoed back to me in the sudden, unnatural stillness.

A stillness that blanketed everything. Everyone.

Except me. And Persia.

She stood with arms raised over us, like a priest herself. Her face burned with a raging intensity.

"Go!" she shouted to me. "I can only hold it a moment longer! Take him and go!"

And I turned to Jack, saw the tip of the spear poised a mere breath from his heart, ready to impale.

Without thought, I wrapped my arms around his waist.

Flattened my palm against the stone wall behind his back.

Bent until my forehead brushed the top of his head.

And a moment later, we were in a different time.

# CHAPTER TWENTY-TWO

*December 24, 1922*
*Giza Plateau, Egypt*

*I* collapsed beside Jack on the floor of the pyramid's entrance, my back to the wall beside him.

He stirred, showing groggy signs of waking.

I fought the rising mix of jumbled emotion—relief and left-over panic at the danger to Jack, a crippling grief at parting from my family again, numbing shock at what I had done—dragged Jack to 1922 with me—as though he were a time travel passenger!

And above all, an illogical anger at my own foolishness, which swept over me and reduced me to shuddering sobs.

What had I been thinking? If my desperate gamble hadn't worked, I would have vanished from the ancient past and left Jack to certain death!

But I hadn't been thinking. It had been all instinct, to wrap him up and carry him out of there. An ability I suspected Tempus Vigilia, with their Codex of rules and their well-researched Knowledge Base, knew nothing about.

Jack mumbled something, brought a wobbly hand to caress my head where I wept against his shoulder.

"*Sshh*, Sahara, it's okay." The words were like pebbles in his mouth.

I swiped at my face and smiled up at him. "Are *you* okay?"

He shook his head, as though to clear the cobwebs. "What happened? I feel—strange."

"The priests drugged you. We got you out. We're back in 1922 again."

He swiveled his head toward the sunlit entrance. "But —how—?"

I breathed out, tension and confusion melting into relief. "I'm not quite sure. You were a millimeter away from a spear in the chest, and Persia stopped time for everyone but her and me, and I—I brought you back."

His shoulders sagged. "I don't understand. You brought me back... like a souvenir?"

I laughed and bent my head to his shoulder again. "Maybe let's say like a 'passenger.'"

"A *passenger*." He whispered the word as though it were holy. "Did you know you could do that?"

I sobered. "No. And if it hadn't worked—" I swallowed and went silent.

"Well, it worked." His voice was gaining clarity by the second. "But your family?"

"They got out. I'm sure. I have to believe that. And I'll meet them in Venice, as planned."

"*We*, Sahara." Jack leaned forward unsteadily. "*We* will meet them in Venice."

"Right. We." The word felt right and good.

Despite the sudden departure from my family, the plans we'd made to reconnect meant I was no longer alone in the world. I'd shed the cocoon of smothering sadness I'd carried for seventeen years.

My mother's gentle words—about a destiny bestowed on me because I had inherent value and not as a way to prove myself—

still glowed in my chest. I was a time traveler. A Revisionist. And now apparently an Amplified version. But those were only gifts to be explored, gifts given to me, but they did not define me.

I stood, then offered Jack a hand. "Ready to get out of here?"

He pulled himself upright. "More than ready. But if I'm not mistaken, we've been gone about twenty-four hours, right?"

"Oh. Yes, I guess we have." I stepped to the entrance and scanned the now-crumbling stepped slope of the pyramid below us. "I suppose our camels and guides are gone by now."

Jack joined me in the sunlight. "And no doubt wondering what happened to the two crazy tourists who disappeared into the pyramid yesterday."

As it turned out, they were doing more than wondering. The police had been summoned, the couple who accompanied us detained and questioned, the camel-guides suspected, and in the end they'd nearly given up hope of finding us—assuming we'd fallen into some unknown shaft or been trapped behind a collapsing tunnel.

"At least I don't have to explain this one to Howard," I said, as we exited the Cairo police station after an hour of making up stories on the fly of our misguided "adventure," getting lost inside the Great Pyramid.

Jack grabbed my hand and pulled me toward a small pub across the crowded street. "Yes, it's a relief to be out from under the watchful eye of everyone in Luxor for a change."

But after a quick lunch and a cab ride back to the Hotel Windsor, Jack's observation seemed to have jinxed us.

Standing in the narrow lobby of the hotel, lingering beside a small trunk and clutching a pearled handbag to her side, was none other than Helen Winlock from the American House, who'd been so concerned about our unchaperoned trip to Cairo.

At the sight of us, her lips opened to an O, but then she smoothed her hair and smiled with arms held out, as though we were long-lost family.

"Sahara? And Mr. Moretti? What a surprise to see you two

here! But of course, you are here in Cairo visiting family for Christmas, aren't you?"

Seeing Helen here stunned me into silence.

Jack said nothing.

"Ah, Monsieur and Madame Moretti!" The gentleman behind the front desk waved a hand, his usual crooked-toothed smile still in place. "I am so glad to see you have both returned. I have kept your room, of course, but as you know, your room was our only vacancy, so when you did not come back—"

"Yes, thank you." Jack sped toward the front desk, perhaps thinking he could keep the man from saying anything more if he got close enough.

But the damage was done. Helen's perfectly shaped eyebrows arched over wide eyes.

"Monsieur and Madame...?" She pursed her lips at me. "My dear, I do feel somewhat responsible for your well-being, as a single woman living at the American House."

"Thank you, Helen, I appreciate—"

But her concern flared into indignation. "I'm certain Mr. Carter would find it quite unacceptable, to hear that one of his dig team was carrying on in such a manner." She glanced at Jack. "But perhaps I have misunderstood. I'm sure when I meet your parents, Mr. Moretti, all will be explained, yes? And where are your parents?"

"They—I—" Jack glanced to me, as if I had a better answer.

"Yes, I see." Helen's mouth tightened again, to match her narrow eyes. She turned on me.

"Sahara, I'm afraid I must report this scandalous behavior back to Mr. Carter. To Lord Carnarvon, even, who has been so generous with you—"

"It's our honeymoon." Jack returned from the desk, shot an arm around my waist and tugged me toward him, grinning stupidly at Helen. "You've found us out, Mrs. Winlock. We wanted to keep it quiet."

I tried to pull away, heart stuttering. "Jack?"

What was he doing?

Helen's lips opened, then closed, then parted again. "Well, I'm simply... speechless." She peered at me. "Sahara, I knew you were smitten with this young man, but a secret wedding?"

"Oh, she's more than smitten, aren't you, darling?" Jack pecked me on the cheek. "In fact, it was all her doing. Practically dragged me to the altar. Like a *passenger*. Didn't you, sweetheart?"

This was not funny. How was I going to undo Jack's improvising?

And yet, while the surface-part of my mind raced over indignant arguments, something deeper, in my chest and belly, seemed to catch fire and glow with a warmth I hadn't thought possible.

"I—we—" I felt a blush creeping upward from my throat.

Helen chuckled. "Well. A Christmas wedding. I can see there was more here than any of us suspected."

"Indeed." Jack leaned into me. "And now if you don't mind, Mrs. Winlock, I think I'd like to get my new bride up to that room of ours."

He gave Helen a wink that must have flushed me scarlet.

Helen giggled. She actually *giggled*, then put white-gloved fingers to her lips. "Mr. Moretti, you will scandalize me yet." She took up her trunk and nodded to the desk clerk. "Thank you, sir, for calling over to the Bella to book me a room. I shall find my way there."

She smiled conspiratorially at Jack and me. "You two lovebirds enjoy your honeymoon. And don't worry," she gave me a wink, "I will keep your secret until you return to Luxor."

And then she was slipping into the street, leaving me tethered to Jack, with his arm around my waist, gaping after her.

"Monsieur Moretti, but you should have told me it was your honeymoon!" The voice of the desk clerk behind us was all pleasantry and smiles.

I turned slowly, avoiding Jack's eyes.

"Yes, certainly we would have sent a bottle—"

"Not necessary, my good man." Jack nodded briskly. "As you just heard, we've been trying to keep it quiet."

The man dipped his head, still smiling.

"Well..." Jack looked to me, as though waiting to hear what was next.

Did he think we were going up to that room, as he'd told Helen?

The idea left me short of breath, feeling my own pulse in my throat.

But Jack spoke first.

"I think we will head out for a meal."

He spoke the words into the air, and I wasn't sure if they were for me, or for the desk clerk, who couldn't possibly care what we did.

I nodded.

Jack extended a hand toward the street.

I walked ahead, though slowly, to avoid encountering Helen again.

But she had already vanished into the city.

I paused on the cracked and narrow sidewalk, analyzed a brownish weed pushing up between my feet.

"Can two American citizens even get married in a foreign country?" Jack studied the building across the street, another tallish building, perhaps a factory. "Actually, are you an American citizen, since you've been here since childhood?"

I found my voice at last. "Yes, to the second question. I'm an American citizen. As for the first, I don't know. If not, hopefully Helen won't think of that. But Jack, she's going to tell—"

"Then we'll make it true." He was still focused on red brick across the street.

My breath caught again, and I watched his profile. "What? That's ridiculous!"

He winced, as though in pain, and dropped his gaze to the street.

"I mean—not *ridiculous*, but—to go to such a length to avoid scandal..."

He stepped closer, lifted his eyes to mine. "That's not why. And you know it."

Was this really happening? Here, on a Cairo street?

He half-smiled, a little sadly. "Do you want me down on one knee?"

"Jack, we've only known each other—"

"I've known you half my life."

I huffed. "You've known an *image* of me—a caricature, practically. That's not the same."

"You're right. And I was a stranger to you not so long ago."

"Not to mention you were still lying to me until very recently!"

Again, the wounded look.

I let the statement stand, but turned my face from that pain.

"Sahara, look at me." He pulled my chin toward him with a gentle finger, and met my eyes with an intensity I'd seen him reserve for only the most serious of statements. "Sweetheart, I swear to you, I have told you everything now. And I also swear to you that I love you, and I am not leaving you."

I exhaled, unaware I'd been holding my breath.

"And Sahara, I *am* going to marry you. If you're not ready now, that's fine. We'll wait and figure out something to tell Helen and Carter and the others. But I'm as ready as I could possibly be, to be your husband."

"We'll get in trouble. With Tempus Vigilia."

Jack's face, so serious a moment before, broke into a wide grin.

"What? What's funny about that? You said two time travelers weren't allowed to marry. And if I'm a Revisionist, and even an Amplified one, I'm sure they... why are you laughing?"

He pulled me to him, kissed me hard on the mouth.

"I'm laughing because you're not saying no. You're not saying you don't love me. You're just fishing for excuses that have nothing to do with how you feel!"

I bit my lip to keep from smiling, but it was a lost cause.

"Times are changing, Sahara. At least in 2002 they are. People don't go in for all the rules and traditions so much anymore. And I, for one, don't give a flying fig what Tempus Vigilia thinks."

"I guess if my parents got away with it..."

"Exactly."

At the thought of my parents, a bubble of regret pushed against me. To get married with no family present seemed a sad thing.

But was I really thinking of doing this?

Jack seemed to sense my shift in mood and caught my hands in his.

Then bent a knee to the crumbling pavement outside the Hotel Windsor.

"Let's do this right." He kissed my fingers. "Sahara Aldridge, love of my life, will you marry me?"

I looked down on him, those blue eyes waiting for an answer, and knew there had never been doubt. Perhaps not since our first dinner in the Winter Palace dining room, when he insisted I was "intriguing."

A warmth that had nothing to do with the Cairo sun spread into the deepest places of my heart.

"Yes, Jack Moretti. I will marry you."

Jack *whooped*, jumped to his feet, and caught me up again, to kiss me scandalously in public.

# CHAPTER TWENTY-THREE

*December 24, 1922*
*Cairo, Egypt*

*D*espite the spontaneity of Jack's proposal, we could not quite pull off a whirlwind wedding.

Six hours later, we wearily descended the concrete steps outside an authentication office of the Egyptian Ministry of Foreign Affairs, certification in hand and ready to find the Ministry of Justice, where the civil ceremony could take place. We'd spent half the morning at the U.S. Embassy, filling out forms and getting notarized statements for the Foreign Affairs office.

I felt guilty about the fake passport Jack presented, which his Aunt Giada somehow arranged for him when he arrived in this time, but what else were we to do? If 1922 was Jack's new home, we'd work with what we had.

But now we were ready.

And exhausted.

We hadn't slept, even since climbing the vertical shaft to Khufu's burial chamber. Crazy.

And it was now Christmas Eve, though the city carried on as usual.

Jack paused at the base of the steps, alongside the street churning with automobiles, taxis, pedestrians and even donkeys, and turned to me.

"What do you need, to do this right?"

I held up the notarized and certified forms. "I think we have what we need."

He smiled. "To make it legal, yes. But what do you need to make it... special? A new dress? Flowers? Or maybe you want to wait—"

"We're not waiting."

He nodded, blue eyes flashing. "Then, what?"

I looked down at my beige traveling suit, with its narrow-cut skirt and blunt jacket, then let my gaze drift down the Cairo street. "A dress might be nice..."

"Done."

We wandered in the general direction they'd given us for the Ministry of Justice, until a tiny dress shop, wedged between a kabob stand and a cigar shop, caught our attention. Two elderly men sat in frayed wicker chairs outside the cigar shop, puffing on hookah pipes. The smoke wafted the scent of apples and cinnamon around our heads.

"You go ahead." Jack nodded toward the shop, then fished some money from his pocket and pressed it into my hand. "I'll be out here when you finish."

It took me less than thirty minutes, with a lovely Egyptian girl fussing over me, as soon as she heard my need, and bringing me a collection of dresses in palest lavenders and buttercup yellows to try on, then shaking her head at each, unsatisfied. Finally, she appeared with a white organza with just a hint of blush, cut narrow at the waist.

In the cramped dressing room at the back of the shop, she dropped it over my head and let the silky fabric float downward, then zipped it tight to hug my curves.

I smoothed a hand over my abdomen and down my thighs. I'd never worn anything so beautiful, so feminine, in my life.

"You are the bride, now at last, you are the bride," she said with a smile.

"Thank you, Layla."

"Ah, but wait. Also, you must have this." She disappeared, then popped back into the dressing room with a spiraling wreath of white silk flowers, which she placed reverently on my head. Then turned me to the full-length mirror, nodding.

I breathed out at the reflection staring back at me, eyes a bit wide, as though still surprised at the turn of events.

My wedding day.

What had I imagined this day to be? I cast back into my memory and found... nothing. Had I never allowed myself to imagine marriage?

And was I certain?

Only a few days ago, I insisted I would never let Jack stay here in 1922, to choose to remain stranded in the past for my sake. And yet the news that I was born in 1970 seemed to open both the past and the future and make all my protestations seem pointless.

Yes. Yes, I was certain. Jack and I found each other against such incredible odds. I would not let him go.

I paid Layla, then slipped quietly from the shop with my beige suit in a paper bag, suddenly self-conscious to appear on the Cairo street in the elegant dress and flower-plaited wreath.

But my halo of flowers could not compete with the armful of blooms Jack held, his boyish grin wide between the stems of white-and-blush lilies that perfectly matched my dress.

He delivered the bouquet to my arms, then took in my transformation, his grin fading to a smile of more wistful longing than playfulness.

"Sahara, you are..." He shook his head. "I cannot believe you said yes."

I laughed and inhaled the scent of the flowers. "That's a little concerning."

"I only mean... you are so beautiful. So wonderful." He studied my face. "I don't deserve you, and never dreamed I would ever have anyone like you in my life."

My pulse quickened yet again, and I handed him the bag I'd brought out of the shop and then wrapped a hand around his arm.

"I was just thinking how this is more than I'd dreamed as well."

"Are you sure?" His brow furrowed. "I mean, sure you want to do this? And to do it now—"

I lifted my face to his, inviting him to kiss me.

"I'm positive."

The Ministry of Justice was not far. The civil ceremony was not lengthy. We said our vows and signed our papers and were back on the street, arm-in-arm as the Christmas Eve sun faded behind the buildings of Cairo.

Married.

We paused on the street, watching the passing cars, the street vendors, a young Egyptian family wandering past. Everything but each other, in what felt like a suddenly awkward silence.

"Shall we get some dinner?" Jack's quiet voice seemed uncertain, even nervous. "A nice dinner. Anywhere you like."

And we did, at L'Amphitryon, a brand-new restaurant, ordering Veal Milanese and Chicken Piccata, and splurging on a bottle of champagne.

But it was not the champagne or the chicken, delicious as it was, that held my attention.

It was Jack's eyes, never leaving my face, as though he were drinking me in, rather than the champagne.

I pushed the remains of the meat around my plate, my appetite for food waning.

Jack reached across the table and twined his fingers into my own, turning my hand upward and rubbing my palm with his thumb.

Could he feel my pulse jumping there?

Our waiter appeared. "You wish to have the dessert?" He smiled and half-bowed toward Jack. "The orange—"

"No dessert." Jack's eyes were on mine. "We are ready to go."

I nodded, mouth suddenly dry.

We walked back to the Hotel Windsor. It was nearly twelve blocks, but neither of us suggested a taxi. We crossed the city in companionable silence.

Jack held my hand and stopped at every intersection to kiss me.

And then we were getting our key from the smiling desk clerk and ascending the steps inside the hotel, where I'd spent a half-sleepless night alone—two nights ago? Three? It was hard to reconcile the jumps through time.

Jack opened the door, stepped aside to allow me through, and then closed it quietly behind him.

And began to laugh.

I turned to him. "You're thinking this was a crazy thing—"

He was beside me in an instant, hands on my face, thumbs skimming my lips to stop the words.

"I was thinking no such thing. I was laughing because I just realized my luggage is still in a locker at the train station."

I bent my head to his hand, kissed his fingers. "So then... you have nothing at all to wear on your wedding night?"

"Sahara Aldridge! You scandalize me!"

I laughed at his impression of Helen Winlock, but then fluttered my eyelashes at him. "That's Sahara Moretti to you."

His own eyes briefly closed, and he pulled me close, inhaling against my hair. "Sahara Moretti." The words were like a sacred whisper in the hollow of my neck, all laughter gone.

I met his lips with my own, let the barrier of years and family and secrets melt away between us. Then led him further into the room.

And as it turned out, his missing luggage was not a problem at all.

# CHAPTER TWENTY-FOUR

*November 2, 2002*
*Valley of the Kings, Egypt*

Giada lifted a hand to shield her eyes against the early morning stab of the rising sun, spreading like a fire across the Valley of the Kings to the bright yellow tram she rode.

The tram jostled over a stone on the rutted road into the Valley, bringing pain she tamped down.

On her right, her assistant Fiona chirped a cry of surprise and reached out to clutch the arm of the man on her opposite side.

Giada met Jack's amused glance with a smile of her own.

Fiona made no secret of her infatuation with Giada's handsome nephew, though he was nearly ten years her senior. The girl was fresh out of college, eager to please, and had gone from intern at the Moretti Foundation to Giada's trusted personal assistant in only six months. It didn't hurt that she made no secret of idolizing Giada, either. Reminded her of a younger version of herself, in fact. With the right training, the girl could be useful for years to come. Too bad she was only an Observer.

Fiona yanked her hand away from Jack's arm, back to her lap, and laughed. "Guess I'm a little nervous." She wore a black jacket, which she'd regret as the Egyptian sun rose higher, with a red scrolled design on each arm.

Giada patted the girl's arm, her garnet ring flashing in the sunlight. "You'll get used to it. The traveling, I mean."

At twenty-two, Fiona had only been time traveling for about a year. But Giada referred only to the travel to, and immersion in, present-day foreign cultures. Today, only Jack would travel in time.

Finally.

A day nearly twenty-eight years in the making. Waiting for the discovery of Tut's tomb to be eighty years in the past.

Jack grinned at her once more. "Good day for travel, eh?" His knee bounced, foot flexed against the floor of the tram, a sure sign he was both nervous and excited.

Their conveyance out to the Valley was a cheesy tourist accommodation, the sides painted in a striped blue-and-gold like a pharaoh's *nemes* headdress, with a pharaonic gold mask in the center. The three-minute ride promised to deposit them as close to the Valley tombs as they could get on a vehicle.

Even at six in the morning, the tram held more than a dozen visitors, all hoping to beat the crowds and the heat. The Visitor Center where they bought their tickets minutes ago proclaimed more than one million tourists visited the Valley every year.

"The trip of a lifetime." Giada smiled.

Yes, she'd done everything she could to make it so. Already in Luxor, another Observer she sent back last week should be waiting with everything Jack needed—a fake passport, visa, clothes, and money, and even a couple of surprises she arranged specially for him. Her Observer would stay until Jack met up with him and completed his trip, so the arrangements wouldn't vanish upon his return to 2002.

And Jack deserved this trip. His work at the Moretti Foundation had been exceptional these past few years. The money would have run out long ago, if not for his energy and abilities.

Beside her, Fiona's gaze darted from the looming tan cliffs to the winding road ahead to the entrance gate, her head twitching toward each new vista in a way that always reminded Giada of a bird. Indeed, with her bobbed dark hair, narrow nose, and in her crimson-sleeved black jacket this morning, she was like a red-winged blackbird, perched on the edge of the tram seat and ready to take flight.

The girl's eyes alighted on Jack. "I wish you could bring me back a souvenir."

Jack laughed. "You and me both. Though you know it wouldn't be worth anything."

She nodded—a quick, fluttery movement. "It would look new, and no expert would believe it was original. I remember."

Giada had been training her new assistant in the extensive Knowledge Base compiled by Tempus Vigilia of all the known time-traveling rules.

*Only Revisionists can bring back objects from the past with them to the present.*

*Only Revisionists can change history when they return to the time that's passed while gone.*

*Only two Revisionists can bring modern objects from this present time back into the past between them.*

Yes, always the Revisionists.

Which was why Jack's trip was so critical.

Despite Giada's loose-fitting white blouse and linen pants, and even in the early hour, a dampness under the chignon knot of her still-dark hair became a trickle down her neck, under the three-strand gold chain necklace she'd foolishly worn. She flexed her shoulders against the sweat, but the tightness bothered her more. The doctor had advised against this trip, given her current treatment. She'd ignored him, as he could not know her trip had more potential to restore her health than anything he could do.

"You'll bring back something better." She jutted her chin toward the Valley. "Knowledge."

The tram pulled to a stop at the small kiosk where a guard would check their tickets, and the three alighted.

"Remember, I want to hear all about Sahara Aldridge if you can find her. What she's been doing since I saw her as a teenager. Her... abilities. What happened to her parents."

Jack stepped from the tram as it stopped, then helped Fiona jump down, and offered a hand to Giada, which she waved away.

"I've got it, Aunt Giada. You'll know more about Sahara than you care to very soon, I promise."

"Stay as long as you need, to really get a sense of... the place. And her." Giada eyed Jack, as though to pass more of a message to him. But there was no need. She'd coached Jack thoroughly all the way from Philadelphia on everything she wanted him to learn.

And he was right. The answers would be hers, very soon.

Twenty-eight years of thirsting for information had left her as parched as the surrounding sand, with the desire only growing stronger in the past seventeen years since she'd met Sahara at Highclere Castle and then lost the girl's parents in the streets of 1814 Venice.

In all that time, she'd never given up searching for a Revisionist to help with her discoveries. The recent addition to her staff of Victor Ramsey had been fortuitous, as well as personally rewarding. She'd looked forward to this year, eighty years after the tomb discovery, planning to send him back to finally achieve her plan of diverting Howard Carter's discovery and looting the tomb for herself and her family.

But once again, fate had other plans. Victor returned from a trip to Spain, where he was "setting aside" some nineteenth century *peseta* coins, with a knife wound that became fatal before she had a chance to call 911. Once again, a Revisionist died because of her actions. First Colin, and now Victor.

Although, the loss of Victor had been less painful than Colin's years ago. She hadn't let him get that close.

At least she was free of the guilt of the Aldridges' deaths, which had eaten her for the eleven years between the house fire and Joanne's discovery of them at Hatshepsut's Temple.

The entrance gate clogged with their tram-mates—a teen wearing an 'N Sync backpack, a young couple trying to corral a toddler while reassembling a stroller, a woman in a purple-floral *hajib* and white-rimmed sunglasses. Giada guided her two companions through a break in the cluster, toward the guard, where they could present their tickets and get in there at last.

At last. The thirst was growing, as though the gritty valley sand had scraped its way down her throat. A thirst that would be quenched within only a few minutes, when Jack instantly returned from his stay in the Egypt of 1922.

The three pushed through the entrance and began the trek to the first of the tombs, silent as they each took in the blank, tan sameness of it all, with only the dark tomb entrances to break up the view, like stony chutes into the underworld.

Past KV2 on their right, the Ramesses IV burial, and KV5 on the left, its massive size so recently discovered and excavated by Kent Weeks and his team, where the sons of Ramesses II were buried. They continued on, past KV7, the tomb of the father, Ramesses the Great, himself. Giada led the way, feeling the excitement of Jack at her back, and a quick-stepping Fiona following them both.

The crowd arriving with them began to thin, most choosing to linger at some of these famous tombs. A few tourists continued with the three, perhaps eager to see the famous King Tut's tomb first.

And then even those few dropped away when they passed KV62, its cracked and weathered yellow-and-black sign proclaiming the famous Tutankhamun in both English and Arabic.

"Come," she inclined her head down the gravel road leading to their left. "A quieter place."

She kept to herself that she intended to send Jack back to 1922 from the entrance of KV17. Belzoni's tomb—so named for the man who discovered the burial chamber of Seti I—and the place where everything began, back in 1969 when a young Giada, Alexander, and Renae believed that time traveling was meant only for fun.

They arrived at the tomb entrance soon enough. She gazed at the steps as though they were something from someone else's story. Had she truly dug a Nineteenth Dynasty jeweled collar from the sand right there?

Jack squared off in front of her, taking a deep breath of the desert air, and grinning like he had at age twelve, when he'd hit a home run in one of his ridiculous baseball games.

"Thank you again, Aunt Giada. For arranging everything, I mean."

She smiled and tucked an errant strand of hair behind her ear. "It's my pleasure. And I have a little surprise for you."

He raised his eyebrows, waiting.

"Besides all the paperwork waiting for you, I had my man there get you a couple of other things I thought you'd like. A press badge. And a vintage camera."

Jack grabbed her arms and kissed her on the cheek. "You are too good to me."

Fiona's hand fluttered, as though asking permission to speak. "But you can't bring back any photographs..."

"True." Jack shrugged. "But simply being able to take photos, with historic equipment, and even develop them—" Jack lifted his head to survey the terrain, as though imagining the photos he would take. "A photographer's dream."

Giada warmed at the pleasure he took from her surprise. No need to mention that his press badge would get him that much closer to the action, where he could learn more of Sahara, and her lost parents. Even Sahara's sibling, if the pregnant Renae had given birth after Giada lost her in Venice.

"Ready?" She extended a hand toward the interior of the Seti tomb.

"How far in shall I go, do you think?" Jack squinted down the recently constructed block wall corridor.

"We'll know original tomb work when we see it. But

remember—you're traveling to 1922, not to 1300 BC! I don't want you showing up during Seti's funeral!"

Fiona giggled.

"Got it. November 2, 1922. Two days before the first step was found."

A quick look backward, to ensure they were still alone. Even though Jack would return immediately, they didn't need any spectators gawking over the ritual.

*This is it.*

It had taken so long, far too long, to reach this day, when the eighty year window to the discovery was finally open, and Giada could learn all she needed about Sahara's whereabouts, whether the girl was a Revisionist and the answer to everything she needed.

Once Jack returned, hopefully with that good news, Giada would send two Observers back to 1922, to drag Sahara back to the present day, where Giada could make better use of her.

It was for her own good, anyway. The girl belonged in the twenty-first century.

*Two Revisionists can take another traveler to the past, held between them.*

But also…

*Two Observers can bring another traveler back to the present, held between them, to the moment the Observers left.*

One of the lesser-known Tempus Vigilia's discoveries, kept secret because of its volatility.

Very few knew such a thing could be done. And it was difficult on the traveler, if he were only an Observer, to come back to a new time.

They'd reached the cool interior of the tomb now, and paused to let their eyes adjust.

Giada ran her gaze, and then her fingertips, over the murals in the entry hall, still familiar after all these years.

"Right here should work."

Jack placed a hand on the wall beside hers.

She studied it—the hand of a man, no longer a boy—but still

thought of that twelve-year-old. And then the fifteen-year-old, often sullen but also so interested in Giada's tales of Sahara Aldridge, the Tut discovery. A few years later, the giddy delight at his first trip through time at age twenty-one.

She had raised him as her own, since her sister's death when the boy was eight. Given him every opportunity she could, watched over his travels and his education, and then given him a good job at the Moretti Foundation, where his charm and good looks won the hearts of wealthy donors and managed lavish fundraiser events to bring needed money into the Foundation's accounts.

But Jack knew nothing of where the wealth had begun—here at the tomb of Seti, really. Knew nothing of her own lengthy trips into the past, of Colin's activities—setting aside treasures for her to find later. Or even of Victor, more recently, adding to the Foundation's coffers.

To Jack, she was innocent of any corruption, pure-white as any academic, living off some wise early investing which supposedly made her rich.

And her desire for knowledge about the Aldridge family was only a scholar's fascination, one Jack now shared, after her carefully constructed stories prepared him for this moment.

She gave him one last smile and a nod in the dim light of the tomb.

He bent his head, palm still flat against the wall.

She waited for the head to lift, the smile of an adventure just lived, perhaps even a *whoop* and a hug for his Aunt Giada after his time spent in 1922.

Instead, Jack's form rippled, like a heat wave on pavement, and then vanished.

Beside her, Fiona gasped.

"What?" Giada thrust both hands across the space, to where Jack had been a moment before. "What—how?"

The bottom seemed to drop out of her belly. Her mouth went dry and her tongue suddenly felt so thick she could not swallow.

"No, no, no!" She waved her hands through empty air, like a blind woman searching for something solid.

Instinct told her there could be only one reason Jack did not reappear, the instant before he left.

She'd lost him.

Somewhere in 1922, or perhaps in the dark void between here and there, Jack was dead.

She heard Fiona's muffled exclamations, like a far-off bird chirping nonsense, as dark spots grew in her vision.

Strangely, in the moment before everything went dark, she had only one thought.

*This is what it feels like to die of thirst.*

# CHAPTER TWENTY-FIVE

*December 25, 1922*
*Cairo, Egypt*

I awoke slowly, as from a fog, to a strange tickling sensation at the hollow of my throat.

Which turned out to be Jack's fingertips tracing a pattern there. And then the brush of his lips, once he saw I was awake.

I ran a hand through his hair and watched the curtain flutter in the morning sunshine. "Good morning, Mr. Moretti."

"*Merry Christmas*, Mrs. Moretti."

Christmas.

And what a gift I had been given.

It seemed almost a dream, to be here in this hotel, in this bed, with Jack. To have found a place to belong, with a husband and even with a family waiting for me to visit them in the past.

I stretched and rolled to my side to face him. "And now what?"

"Now we begin our life together." He brushed the hair from my face and kissed me again.

"How about a honeymoon in Venice?"

"Now? Before returning to Luxor?"

"Why not?" I braced myself on an elbow. "We're already here, north in Cairo. And Howard doesn't plan to start clearing the antechamber until a couple of weeks into January. Why not spend some time in Venice with my family? I'll return without revising anything, and we won't have lost any time except the days of travel to and from Venice."

Jack rolled to his back, nodding. "And bonus, we'll avoid Reuben a bit longer."

Reuben. Giada's lackey here in 1922 to spy on me and report back to Giada about why Jack never returned from his trip to the past. I'd forced him from my thoughts for a while, but Jack was right. The longer we could avoid him, the better. There was no telling what Giada would do, once Reuben returned to her with the news Jack was staying with me in this time.

"So, shall we leave today?" I glanced at the window, trying to assess how late we'd slept.

"Mmm-hmm." Jack reached for me, pulling me down to himself, with a smile and more kisses to my neck. "But not quite yet."

Despite Jack's successful delay tactics, we were on a train to Alexandria, then a ship sailing for the coast of Italy by the following day.

We barely made our funds stretch, and I worried about getting back to Luxor after our time with my parents and sister.

"We'll cross that bridge when we come to it," Jack said as we stood at the rail of the steamship, watching the Alexandrian harbor slip away into a haze above the waterline.

I enjoyed this sea crossing more than the last, with my stomach not rebelling against everything I ate. Jack said I was "getting my sea legs," but whatever the reason, the trip itself felt like a honeymoon, with half of each day spent on the sun-drenched deck of the ship and the other half in the dark intimacy of our interior cabin, getting to know each other even better.

On New Year's Eve, the ship's staff launched a few fireworks off the ship's stern, to the delight of the passengers, and Jack and

I rang in 1923 as husband and wife, kissing under a red-and-green shower of fiery sparks.

By the second of January we stepped onto Italian soil, and by late that day arrived once again to the Santa Lucia Train Station in the lagoon city of Venice, exactly three weeks since we'd been here last. Three weeks, but what felt like a lifetime.

"Let's get a room," Jack said as we wandered from the train station, toward the *vaporetti* stand where several boats idled. "Not go back to 1737 until tomorrow."

I sighed. "Sounds wonderful, but can we afford it? I don't want to be stuck here in Venice when we get back, begging on the streets."

"We'll figure it out. I've still got my press credentials, my camera, and some photos of the digsite. I'll bet some Italian newspaper would pay more than our fare back to Luxor for those photos."

"Howard would kill you."

Jack grinned. "Then I guess we won't tell him."

I still felt uneasy, and tried to brush off the feelings as we strolled under the lamplit glow of Venetian streetlights, taking our time to find a place for dinner and a room for the night.

But it was more than the lack of money.

It was the truth that nothing had changed. Giada had sent Reuben after Jack when he didn't return to 2002, and at some point, wouldn't Reuben's threat become reality?

*If I go back now and tell her you're not coming, she's only going to send two others back to get you.*

I shuddered and clutched Jack's arm tighter.

Jack patted my hand, as though the damp lagoon air had given me a chill. "Let's get inside somewhere."

But Reuben's words still echoed in my brain. Jack had confirmed—it was possible for two Observers to come here from Giada's century and drag Jack back to her.

Were we living on borrowed time? Would we have little more than this honeymoon before Giada pulled him back? And what then? Once Jack left this time, would his trip to 1922 be erased? Would I even have a memory of him?

After a quick meal of pasta and fish, we spent a beautiful night in a tiny *pensione* that boasted it had been built in the late seventeenth century.

The next morning, still in our upstairs room with a view of only the building across the tiny alleyway, we placed our hands against the wall, hoping it was original.

Though we would meet my family at the prearranged Rialto Bridge in early November of 1737, we chose this room to make the jump, out of the way of onlookers, in the event I needed to revise history when returning. But why would I?

*You've said that before.*

True.

And so, with little fanfare to mark the first time we'd traveled without being chased or with questions about what came next, we joined hands, bent heads, and took ourselves back to the year 1737.

# CHAPTER TWENTY-SIX

*November 1737*
*Venice, Italy*

$\mathcal{I}$ stood with hands resting lightly on a stone half-wall, basking in the sunshine of an early morning panorama. The flagstone terrace of my parents' sprawling villa on the north side of Venice had become my favorite haunt, with this morning-moment, this view of the Italian countryside, my habit every day since we'd arrived in 1737, now nearly a month ago.

Despite the desperation which drove my parents to jump back in time from 1814 to 1720 to avoid Giada, they had created an amazing life here. The huge sum of money they brought to 1814, in their failed attempt to bribe Giovanni Belzoni into giving up Egypt, was worth even more in 1720, and my father a shrewd investor.

Within only a few years, his dealings throughout *La Serenissima*—the "Most Serene Republic of Venice"—as it was fondly known, brought wealth and reputation. His trade deals reached as far as Greece and Cyprus, and for a born scholar, he made a fantastic merchant. It would be another sixty years before Napoleon's troops brought an end to the Republic, and in the meantime, trading was prosperous and life was good.

Yes, life was good. For all of us. Our Venetian "honeymoon" could not have been sweeter, spending the time getting reacquainted with my parents, beginning to love Persia, not only for our sisterly bond, but for our shared love of adventure and her sharp wit. And Jack... Jack was becoming as much a part of the family as I.

But this morning, watching a cardinal flit from one laurel tree to another across the expansive lawn of my parents' estate, I sensed our time here was coming to an end. My stomach fluttered in response to the thought, with the sense of something new.

The *swoosh* of slippers on stone turned me away from the view, toward a figure emerging from within the villa, balancing a tray.

"Good morning, Mama."

"Good morning to you." Her smile over me was like a benediction, as always. She wore a simple patterned green silk with a white bodice, which set off her dark hair, only just beginning to show streaks of gray. "I thought you might enjoy your pastry and coffee on the terrace today."

She set the tray on the wall between us and leaned her arms against the stone, looking past the grassy lawn to the forest on the far side.

I bit into the brioche she'd brought and closed my eyes over the flaky layers.

"You'll be leaving soon, won't you?"

I eyed her sideways. "How can you always read my thoughts?"

She smiled and shrugged, her eyes still trained on the horizon. "A mother knows. Besides, it's not good for Jack to stay much longer before you get back to 1922. Well, 1923 now, I suppose."

"Should we have already left? A month seems too long to be away. Though too short to be with you." I reached for her hand.

"Jack will be fine." She returned my grasp with a sad smile. "But we'll need to plan our next time together. Where and when?"

"I need to start my own 'travel journal' as Papa always called it. I'm beginning to lose track of where I can and cannot go."

"And we'll have to coordinate a time we've never been near. Easiest—at least for the three of us—to meet here in Venice again."

"So what's happened in the past here, that you'd like to see?"

"Well, your sister has already been to 1512, to chat with Michaelangelo as he finished the Sistine Chapel."

"You're joking."

She laughed. "I'm afraid I'm not. So we'll have to stay clear of either side of 1512."

"I'm surprised the three of you haven't visited every possible time of interest while you've been living here." I brushed the remaining crumbs of the brioche off the wall, to flutter to the ground below.

"We haven't traveled much with Persia at all, to be honest. All of it felt so… risky. After we were separated from you. It used to be exhilarating, but it began to only feel frightening."

She nodded toward the tray. "Drink your coffee before it gets cold."

"Not in the mood for coffee this morning, really."

"No? Nor yesterday either, as I recall."

"I suppose not."

She glanced my way. "The smell makes you a bit… nauseated, perhaps?"

The fluttery feeling in my belly returned. A touch more nausea than excitement.

"Perhaps."

She covered my hand with her own and turned me toward her. "Sahara."

But she needn't say more.

The suspicion I had for more than a week seemed only confirmed in the eyes of my mother.

I nodded. "It's too soon to say. But I think it's possible."

And then I was in her embrace, both of us crying over the possibility. A new life, to add to my already new life.

"I don't think I truly believed I'd ever find you again," she whispered. "But now this—to meet your child, my grandchild…"

"Too soon, Mama. I can't be certain—"

She straightened and swiped at her face. "Of course. And any doctor here—" she waved a vague hand toward the canal-laced city of Venice in the distance—"won't be able to confirm until you're already feeling the baby kick. No, you must go to a doctor once you're back in 1923. They'll have blood tests there. And better medical care."

At the mention of my return, she grasped my hand. "But where—where did you—"

I felt myself blushing and cut her off before she could say the word. "I don't know, but probably before we arrived here—"

She shook her head. "But you can't be sure of that either."

It felt as though dark clouds seeped into the sky, blocking the sun. "Is that… a problem?"

The words of her journal page, found in a desk drawer at Highclere, returned to me. "You were expecting Persia when you traveled back to meet Belzoni, right?"

She frowned, the tiny lines around her mouth tightening. "A Revisionist can travel while pregnant. I've done that several times, yes. But if you—began a pregnancy—here, in this time, and then you return to 1923 without retaining your actions here…"

"Then when I return to the moment I left, the baby would be —gone?" I whispered the final word, which somehow seemed quite awful, despite the mind-bending reality that the baby would never have been.

She nodded, still grim-faced.

I turned back to the verdant view, arms braced against the

stone. "Then I must revise my history when I go back. I'm not taking any chances."

I felt her relax beside me.

"But you'll have been gone a month."

"More than that, since we left Luxor. It's February in 1923 now. Nearly two months since we left Porchy and Eve at the train station in Alexandria."

"Sahara... has Jack told you much—anything—about—the future?"

I shook my head, a sharp jerk to deny her more words. "I don't want to know. I've told him I don't want to know. It makes me feel too strange. Why?" I glanced at her serious face. "No, don't answer that."

"Strange in what way?"

I rolled a tiny pebble under my finger on the wall, pressed it into my skin until it hurt. "As though I am unreal. Living in a past history that's dead and gone, like a museum piece that doesn't know it's not alive. Nothing I say or do has any consequence. It's all been said or done already."

"And if that were true? If your whole life, everyone's lives, were already known? What then?"

"Then what does any of it mean? What's the point? And do I even have free will to choose my next actions?"

"You know we have the ability to change the past."

"But do we, really? Or is that how the past was always meant to be? Changed by us?"

"Meant to be... by whom?"

"Exactly! Now you're sounding like Jack. Asking questions about a 'Higher Power' over all of this."

"Yes. A higher power, and a higher purpose. For each of us—Revisionist or Observer. Those who can travel backward through time and even those who can only travel forward. There must be. I think the very longing for such a thing proves it must be true."

I sighed, so deeply she laughed.

"It has taken me some years, Sahara, to see the greater truth.

To stop believing myself a victim of bad luck or bad people, even to stop seeing myself as responsible for every turn that life has taken. To believe some greater purpose, some greater good, is always at work."

We were both silent, until I faced her again.

"So what is my greater purpose?"

She smiled. "I cannot answer that. But I will tell you—I suspect it may lie in the years beyond 1923."

I sighed, still unwilling to mentally fly into the years beyond anything I'd known. I'd begun to accept my value, as a person, outside of any heroic time-traveling acts. Couldn't I simply rest there? Rather than stepping into a risky future to pursue some murky destiny?

"You asked if Jack has spoken of the future. He's told me only small things. Happy things. To fly aeroplanes across the ocean will be commonplace. We will *hear* the characters speaking in the films shown in the theater instead of reading the words across the screen. But nothing of politics or disease or anything… bad."

It took willpower not to add another "Why?" to the end of my answer, and I held my breath while I watched a debate play out in her eyes.

In the end, she only nodded, smiled, and turned back toward the lawn.

But perhaps her silence was worse. The dark cloud still hovered.

"You should speak with Jack. About your return." She reached to touch gentle fingertips to my abdomen. "About everything."

And I did, before the morning fog burned away completely, standing at the window of our room on the upper floor of the villa.

His jaw dropped and the color in his face seemed to drain and then return, bringing a fire into his eyes. He caught me up in his arms. "So soon? This soon?"

I laughed. "You are surprised, after the month we have spent—"

He cut off my laughter with kisses to my lips, my cheeks, my forehead. Even on a bent knee, to my belly.

Sunlight broke through the fog and spilled, warm and golden, across the floor where he kneeled.

"But, Jack, I told you, I'm not sure yet."

He stood and wrapped gentle arms around me. "It's fine. I will be ecstatically happy until we know for sure, and then if it's not to be yet, I will be happy to wait until it's true."

"There's something else, though. My mother was quick to point out. We don't know if it—happened—here."

His brow furrowed, then cleared as he understood. "You need to Revise."

I nodded.

His shoulders sagged and he took a step backward. "A month! I'll have to wait a month for you in 1923. That's going to be torture." He raked a hand through his hair. "Not to mention if something goes wrong."

"I've been thinking about that."

"And?"

"What if we tried it again? The… passenger thing."

His eyebrows lifted. "Knock me unconscious and drag me back to 1923, you mean?"

I laughed. "Nothing so violent as that. Perhaps there is some drug that could put you to sleep?"

"Ah, so *drug* me and drag me back to 1923. Completely different." He crossed to the window and gripped the frame.

"Jack, don't be angry. We wouldn't do anything unsafe."

"I'm not angry. I'm… terrified."

"But there'd be no danger. If it didn't work, if you didn't return with me, you could simply go back to 1923 yourself, and wait out the month for me."

"I'm not terrified it won't work. I am thinking of what it would be like to be separated from you by centuries, not able to reconnect, lost to each other like you've been with your parents all these years. Never seeing you again." He returned to me and wrapped his hands around my waist. "Never meeting our child." His voice broke over the final word.

I nodded, unable to speak past my own emotion.

I had no choice but to revise history when I returned to 1923. But, like my parents years ago, would I lose someone I loved in the act of saving another?

# CHAPTER TWENTY-SEVEN

*B*ut in the end, it seemed logical to at least try to bring him back to our month passed. Better than having him wait for me in Venice. We made plans and backup plans with my parents, plans and backup plans with each other. Jack and I had Cleopatra. My parents now had King Solomon's Jerusalem for their own emergency meeting spot, though they'd sworn to never travel without each other. And as a family, we settled on the Venice of 1637, almost exactly a century earlier than where my parents and Persia made their home.

We sat around a table in a small pub in the city limits of Venice, sharing a final meal before Jack and I would return to 1923. The smoky air smelled of roasting meat and heavy cigars, and we lingered over our coffee, prolonging the inevitable.

"I've always wanted to be there for the opening," my father said, grinning over his idea.

"Really, Papa? Opera again?" Persia shook her head.

"Your father's been a little obsessed with the opera since we've been here," my mother explained.

"Obsessed?" Persia rolled her eyes. "Is that what you call going to church, just so you can say confession to Antonio Vivaldi?"

"Vivaldi lives here, really?" Jack sat forward over his coffee. "And he's a priest?"

"You see?" My father smacked Jack's shoulder. "This man knows good music." He took in the rest of us, bringing out his teacher-voice.

"The Teatro San Cassiano Opera House in Venice was the very first public opera house in the world. Opened its doors on February twenty-sixth, 1637, with a performance of *Andromeda*, by Francesco Manelli. So I think we should meet on the steps of the opera house for the show."

"But not until after the baby," my mother insisted. "It's better Sahara not travel more than necessary."

Jack reached for my hand on the table and squeezed. "After the baby."

I nodded. "And I want you three to wait the same amount of time. At least a year or so."

My mother's face fell.

I laughed. "You were planning to go to 1637 tomorrow, weren't you? Meet your grandchild tomorrow?"

She shrugged, a smile tugging at the corner of her mouth. "Perhaps. Can you blame me?"

"I suppose not. But I've given this some thought. If we are to keep meeting in the past, for the rest of our lives, I think we should do it at the same pace. I don't want to keep aging while you stay young, until I'm finally older than you."

Persia laughed. "I'd like to see that, actually."

I wrinkled my nose and stuck out my tongue at her.

None of us discussed the truth that my parents could return to 1923, or even to 2003. There was still Giada, and whatever she was trying to accomplish. And it would mean separation from Persia.

My mother had spent a few minutes the night before, trying to convince us to return to 2003. Apparently the "better medical care" she'd claimed for 1923 would vastly improve by the end of the twentieth century. Not to mention, the chance to meet my grandparents, if they were still alive. All my life, I'd believed they were not. But my mother, with tears and regret, told me of the heartbreak of leaving them in 1974.

I explained that I would not return to my "native time," because we knew Jack did not return to the moment he left 2002.

"But perhaps that's because you will bring him back as a passenger, to *your* return time," she'd pointed out.

An idea which rocked us both backward in our chairs. Why did we not think of that?

The cognitive dissonance threatened to swamp me. Did Jack not return to 2002 because something happened to him? Because he stayed with me in the past? Or was our knowledge that he didn't return actually *causing* him to not return?

Unknowable. But we would not take a chance on getting separated by centuries, not until we thoroughly tested and trusted this amplified "passenger" ability of mine.

"Alright, Sahara." My father nodded across the table, then gave my mother a stern look. "No traveling to 1637 tomorrow to meet our grandchild. Or to see the Opera House opening. We'll wait the year."

"Fine." My mother frowned. "Now, what's our backup plan?"

We left the pub not longer after, strolled to the *pensione* where Jack and I stayed our first night here, and congregated in the tiny lobby to try to say goodbye. The separation after all these weeks together, and the knowledge that with time traveling, nothing was ever certain, kept my arms tight around my mother, and then my father and sister, for so long an outsider would have thought we were parting forever.

"One year." My mother squeezed my hands, then kissed her own fingertips and placed them on my belly. "Take care of yourself. Good care."

I nodded through tears and hitched a tiny breath, ready to burst into sobbing.

"Hopefully, you will meet *three* of us at the Opera House. Do they allow babies at the opera?"

My father laughed. "They'd better."

We parted at last, my parents to the carriage that would take them home to their estate outside the city, and Jack and I upstairs to the room we paid for in advance.

It was no small feat, allowing myself to take this chance of separation from Jack. I would cling to my mother's faith, even if my own lagged. If there was truly some power at work here in my life, then I would try to trust the outcome.

We'd decided to try the sleeping idea, rather than the drugging idea. Procuring and administering a sleeping drug correctly in the eighteenth century seemed a bit risky.

But as the night dragged on, with me propped in a chair to stay awake and Jack vainly attempting to fall asleep despite the uncertainty of when he'd awaken, it began to look as though drugs were our only option.

Finally, in the wee hours of the morning, I heard his breathing deepen and become like the measured beat of a soft drum.

I gathered my skirts around me, tiptoed to the bed, placed a hand against the same wall that brought us to this century.

Thoughts on February of 1923.

And then, quick enough that he would not awaken, a hand wrapped around Jack's wrist, head bent, and the full power of my mind trained on returning with everything that had happened here still intact.

Darkness, spinning.

A moment later I felt the sun-bright room, warm around me.

I opened my eyes to first see my own clothes on my body.

And to next see Jack still asleep in the bed.

We'd made it. Together.

I shook him awake, crying in joy.

His eyes shot open, took in my clothing, and he pulled me into an embrace so tight I could barely breathe.

"Sorry, I'm sorry, did I hurt you?" He pulled me across him, to lie beside him on the bed.

I cradled his face with my palm, unable to speak.

Such a long night. I'd slept not at all, and Jack's sleep had lasted less than five minutes. It was several hours before we woke again, and another hour before we reluctantly left the room to descend the narrow steps with our luggage, ready to find a Venetian doctor who could perform a blood test.

The dim, cramped lobby of the house-turned-inn contained only one person. But it was not a desk clerk or even the owner.

A lanky man unfolded himself from a creaky chair and tossed aside a well-worn newspaper.

Even in the dim light, Reuben's red hair was unmistakable.

Jack moved to step between Reuben and me, his hand curling around mine.

"First Rome, now Venice? Giada sent the right man to track us."

Reuben shrugged. "You overestimate your ability to avoid detection. The worst part has been spending the month waiting around this godforsaken excuse for a hotel." He waved a hand at the inn's peeling wallpaper and cobwebby electric bulbs.

"So you followed us, from Luxor...?" Jack scowled.

"To Cairo. Congrats on the wedding, by the way."

My skin crawled at the thought of him standing outside the Ministry of Justice, watching us.

"I did nearly lose you when you headed back here to Venice. Wasn't expecting that. And this month." He rolled his eyes. "I was beginning to worry you weren't coming back at all. I knew the *where*, that you'd jumped from that room up there." He pointed to the cracked ceiling. "But of course I couldn't know *when*. So, good job there." He pulled a cigarette from his pocket and lit it, as though congratulating himself rather than us.

"But, now you're back, so I'm back on the job, trying to figure out why you never returned to 2002, so she can figure out how to undo it."

"You already know."

His eyes slid to me, took me in from head to toe.

I stepped closer to Jack, tightening my grip on his hand, and with the other hand reflexively pressed against my abdomen.

At least Reuben was here alone. No second Observer to pull Jack back to 2002.

I glanced around the lobby, suddenly paranoid.

"Yeah," Reuben shrugged. "I guess I do know. You're staying here. With your new bride."

"Right. So you can go back and tell her that." Jack's shoulders flexed backward. "And you can tell her a few more things for me. That I know everything now. How she tried to have the Aldridges killed back in '74. The unethical ways she's used Revisionists over the years, to make herself rich. Threatening to kill a fifteen-year-old girl, to force the girl's parents to change history for her."

That part of the story—the way Giada used her meeting with me at Highclere to threaten my parents once she found them in 1814 Venice—had been told over late-night chats at their Venetian villa. My father himself wiped away my tears of guilt over giving Giada the information about Belzoni that led to our separation, and something seemed to loosen in both Persia and my mother, as we all shared the responsibility for the lost years, but then put it behind us, forgiving ourselves for events none of us intended.

Jack's fist clenched at his side and he leaned into Reuben. "And as if all that were not enough, she then tried to *use me* to get what she wanted. I was only one more 'find' for her, wasn't I?"

"So," Reuben shrugged and exhaled a cloud of toxic smoke. "You know who she really is, what she's capable of. Or at least was once capable of."

"And what she's still trying to do—to get ahold of one of the Aldridges to change her own past."

"Can you blame her?"

I found my voice at last. "Blame her! I hold her responsible for everything that's happened to me and my family since I was four years old!"

Reuben's eyes lighted on my face, then moved away. Another shrug. "We all do what we need to do, to survive."

Jack pulled me toward the front door. "Well, you can tell her I'm doing what I need to do. Staying here with my wife."

Thankfully, he did not add "and my child." The less Giada knew about our family, the better.

"Tell Giada, there is nothing for me in Philadelphia, back with her. If she tries to force me back, I'll only leave again. And she won't find me this time."

The man was silent a moment, then nodded. "Guess I'll see you on the ship back to Alexandria, then."

"Actually, we'll be staying in Venice a bit longer." Jack pushed me out the door, into the tiny alley. "I suggest you leave immediately."

We hurried down the alley.

A glance backward revealed Reuben strolling from the *pensione*, watching us for a moment, and then turning the other direction.

Were we rid of him at last?

Perhaps. We saw nothing of him in the next five days while we waited for my blood test results, paid for by the sale of Jack's photographs, as terrible as I felt about the professional betrayal. Jack convinced the Italian newspaper to print the pictures with "anonymous" as the source. No need to burn bridges when we returned to the Luxor digsite.

And then we were back in the doctor's office, where he was all smiles and handshakes for Jack, all awkward shoulder-patting for me.

I sagged against the chair, disbelief and hope vying for top emotion.

I was going to be a mother.

Part of me had feared—when I brought the unconscious Jack as a passenger back with me, did my "Amplified" status only make it possible for him to return with time passed, or did it also make him into a Revisionist? Only our next meeting with my parents could tell us if his trip to 1737 remained in their memories. We had assumed he also revised time, but if his actions in the past did *not* remain, and our baby was conceived in 1737, what would happen to that baby?

But the questions were behind us now.

We were going to be parents.

Two time travelers, defying the stipulations of Tempus Vigilia's Codex of rules, like the generation before us.

And with me an Amplified Revisionist as well, there was no telling what kind of ability this child might have. It was a bit overwhelming, to say the least.

We stumbled from the doctor's office, heads full of instructions on how I must take care of myself once I was back in Luxor. The doctor's expression, when Jack told him I was an archaeologist, was stern enough to frighten me.

"No digging! Absolutely no digging! In fact, I see no reason for you to return to Egypt at all—such a backward place—until this baby is born. Stay here, in Italy. We will take such good care of you."

We thanked him and left, and were only a few steps down the street before I looked up at Jack with my own serious expression. "I'm not staying here. They are not clearing that tomb and cataloguing the finds without me."

"I know." He set his face toward the train station, as if he were already headed back to Luxor.

And his expression worried me. Where was the joy of the expectant father?

Did he believe Reuben would find us again in Luxor, to make more threats? Or that Giada would be unable to leave us alone, to live our lives in this century?

Or was there some other knowledge about our future, hinted at by my mother, that kept him tight-lipped, but concerned?

Whatever the reason, we were headed back to Egypt, to see the rest of our fate play out.

# CHAPTER TWENTY-EIGHT

*December 25, 2002*
*Philadelphia, Pennsylvania*

*G*iada glanced at her watch, then out the dark window of her home office to the streetlights in front of her city estate.

Above the wide doors of the mansion across the tree-lined street, a string of white lights twinkled, wrapped around swags of fresh pine, sparkling against glittery red balls.

The car should be here any moment.

She spoke into the darkness.

"You understand? Don't return until you have answers."

Behind her, Reuben audibly sighed. "Giada, how could I not understand, when you've spelled it out a hundred times?"

"Hey!" She spun on him, scowling. "Remember who writes your paycheck. And the size of that paycheck."

The quick spin and raised voice left her dizzy. She thrust a hand to a nearby upholstered chair.

Reuben's eyes followed the movement.

What was that in his eyes? Pity?

She straightened and clasped her hands in front of her.

"And you aren't to say anything to him, about what is happening here. About my... situation."

"Right." A respectful head-nod this time, rather than sarcasm.

Yes, it must have been pity she saw. The same look she'd seen in the doctor's eyes last week.

There was still time, though. There was always time. She needed to get Jack home, to undo whatever disaster had befallen him in the past and kept him from returning.

In the weeks since he disappeared before her eyes at the tomb of Seti, she'd had a surprising epiphany.

She believed for years that her money made her significant, that the money was the sum total of everything she'd done with her life. Instead, it turned out it was Jack, and her love for him, that gave her life meaning. Without him, she had nothing. And so she must get him back, no matter the cost.

And she would find a way to convince the Aldridges to help her, too. If not Renae or Alexander, certainly one of their children must also be a Revisionist.

Giada would work out that plan once she had answers. But they *would* rewrite history. She wouldn't need to spend so much time in the past, finding ways to build her wealth.

According to her birth certificate, Giada was fifty-four years old.

According to the universe, she'd lived fifteen years longer than that.

Only a steady stream of salon treatments kept people from asking questions, or silently thinking she wasn't aging well. But no salon treatment could reverse the ravages within her body.

A Revisionist could change all that. Undo everything. Like a genie in a bottle, grant Giada a fortune she was born with, one that wouldn't destroy her body in the making.

"And you have your tickets?"

Reuben patted the pocket of his wool coat. "Nonstop red-eye from Philly to Cairo, then a short hop to Luxor. I'll be on the digsite by noon tomorrow. Well, *your* noon of course. I'm aiming for earlier."

"For November—"

"Giada."

It wasn't in Reuben's nature to be conciliatory. She'd hired him for just that reason. It made the softness in his voice that much more aggravating.

She huffed.

"November 2, 1922." He nodded, a patronizing gesture.

She bit her lip and returned to watching for the driver who would take him to the airport.

How soon would that car return Reuben to her? And what answers would he have?

It had taken her nearly two months to arrange this trip, most of it spent finding and hiring Reuben, who would be more... resourceful than either Fiona or Joanne, the only other Observers she had on her staff.

Two months of failed treatments, of missing Jack like she was missing a limb, of alternating between the certainty he was dead and hope for a way to retrieve him.

And now Reuben would be gone, only for as long as it took him to fly to Luxor and back to Philadelphia, with his trip to 1922 to find Jack taking no time at all.

Within two days, she would have answers.

∾

Forty-eight hours later, Giada again stood beside her office window, watching the twinkling lights across the street.

When would they take those lights down? Christmas had come and gone.

Her first Christmas without Jack in over twenty years.

She'd attempted some normalcy. A bit of shopping in the city. The iconic Christmas Light Show at the historic Wanamaker Building. Even wandered through the kitschy "Dickens Village"—a reenactment of the story of the miserly Scrooge and his awakening as a new man.

Why had she never actually visited Dickens' London? That

would have been fun. Too late now, as she had already been to 1814. But then, it was too late for many things.

Lost in thought, she almost missed the Chrysler as it slid to the curb.

She sucked in a breath, watched for a moment as Reuben alighted from the back of the car and repositioned his hat over his mop of orange-red hair and then jogged up her front steps.

She had the door open before he rang the bell.

His face was unreadable. But it didn't seem positive.

"Don't just stand there! Get in here!"

He nodded once, removed his hat, and stepped across the threshold.

Giada led him into the front room, crossed the office to the white sofa, and sank into it, suddenly too weak to stand for whatever news he brought.

Reuben loitered in front of her, fidgeting with the brim of his hat.

"Is he alive? Did you see him alive?"

"He's fine. Alive and well."

She sagged against the back of the sofa. Whatever other news was to come, at least she had that.

"Sit. Tell it all."

It took Reuben only five minutes to devastate her life.

He'd been in 1922 for more than three months. Jack and Sahara were apparently trying to track her parents. He'd followed them to Rome, rejoined them in Luxor, then followed them to Cairo and on to Venice.

"Married? They are... *married?*"

Certainly Jack had developed an adolescent crush on Sahara, as Giada filled his mind with stories of the orphan who didn't know she was a time traveler. But in the space of three months, he had fallen in love with her and convinced her to marry him?

"Does she know—know who he is, when he's from?"

"I believe she knows everything. Because *he* knows everything."

A coldness stole into her chest, running out into her fingers, numbing her legs.

"What do you mean?"

"When I left them in Venice, he gave me a message for you."

She half-smiled, clasped her hands to keep from reaching out, as though the message were on a note, tucked into Reuben's pocket.

"He said to tell you, he knows everything now." Reuben's glance drifted, as though he were reciting from a memorized list. "That you tried to have the Aldridges killed in 1974, and then threatened to kill Sahara when she was a girl, if they didn't do what you wanted. How you've used Revisionists to get rich. And how you used him."

Was she still breathing? The room seemed a bit fuzzy.

How could Jack know all of this?

He must have met the Aldridges.

In 1922 or elsewhere, Sahara had reunited with her parents.

"Anything else?"

"He said to tell you there is nothing for him here, with you. He's staying with his wife, and if you try to get him back, he'll only leave again. Go somewhere you'll never find him."

She tried to stand. Wanted to get away from this awful man and his terrible words. She pushed up from the sofa, then fell back, her legs still numb.

"Nothing more?"

No final words of affection? Gratitude for raising him as her own son? A goodbye?

"No."

But this could not be the end. She would not allow it. She would send someone else, to explain. She must explain.

No, she would send two people. Two Observers, who could drag Jack back here with them, and then she could explain everything herself.

*Explain what? What does he believe, that is not true?*

That she'd done it for him.

*False.*

Still, if she could just bring him back. He would forgive her.

*For taking him from his wife? Undoing Sahara's very memory of him?*

"Get out, Reuben."

The man gaped, open-mouthed.

She waved a hand to soften the hostility. "I'm sorry. I need to be alone. Thank you for your trip. You'll be well-compensated, of course."

He stood, replaced the hat.

"Wait." She forced herself to stand. "Where, and when, are they now? I mean, when you left them?"

He shrugged. "I left them on the seventh of February, in 1923. Said they were staying in Venice for a bit. But I would assume the girl will want to go back to that digsite soon."

"And you never saw the parents? Renae and Alexander? Their other child?"

"Never."

She nodded and walked him to the door.

Closed it behind him and leaned against it, head back. Head pounding.

*Think, Giada.*

It would never work to bring him home against his will, erasing his time in 1922. He would never forgive her for that.

She must fix it all. Fix everything, all the past mistakes. The harm she'd done the Aldridges, the harm she'd done herself.

Everything must be undone.

How far back would the changes need to reach?

To 1985, when Joanne found them in Egypt?

Perhaps to 1974, when she'd first told the old man, Abd el-Rassul, about them? To 1814, when she herself chased them through Venice?

Or all the way back to 1155 BC, to that stupid Harem Conspiracy and the buried necklace?

Regardless, changing everything would mean Jack and Sahara would never meet. Neither one would have memories of the other.

Giada would be the only one with two sets of memories, and the knowledge of what had been. What could have been.

*I will make certain they meet. Fall in love all over again.*

Yes, this had to work.

But there was only one way to make it so. She had to have a Revisionist. Had to send two Observers back in time and escort a Revisionist to her doorstep.

And if her educated guess was right, Giada finally knew exactly where to find one.

February 7, 1923, in the tiny city of Venice, Italy.

# CHAPTER TWENTY-NINE

*February 8, 1923*
*Venice, Italy*

After the visit to the doctor and confirmation of our good news, Jack and I prepared to leave Venice immediately, to return to Luxor and the work there.

The busy hum of hundreds of passengers jostling through the Santa Lucia railway station was the sound of a happy holiday to me, as we threaded our way through a jumble of colorful tourists and uniformed station staff, weaving around piled luggage and wayward children.

*We are going home.*

The thought crossed my mind and surprised me.

But it was true. The Valley of the Kings had become a home to me, despite my American birth, my English upbringing, and my more recent adventures in the past.

Would Jack be happy, also calling it home? But of course, we would spend the hot summers elsewhere. Perhaps visiting my family, in interesting times and places in the past.

Three of us, visiting my family.

Jack tugged on my hand, guiding me toward our train and

pointing to the sign that signaled our destination. He said something, but it was lost to the sharp whistle of another train, departing the station with a huff of smoke and steam.

"What?" I craned my neck toward him.

"I said, we'll be back on another ship before you know it!"

My stomach lurched.

Thus far, I'd kept the nausea to a minimum, but ships and my stomach had never been fast friends, and with the first trimester of pregnancy upon me, how could I hope to—

Jack pulled up short.

I slammed into his back.

He held his position, ignoring me.

"Jack!" I circled him. "What—"

His face. Stunned. Horrified, perhaps.

Oh, glory. What now?

I followed his line of sight, in time to see two women, one in her fifties perhaps, and the other much younger, dart behind a wooden sign, their faces obscured but legs still visible.

And then Jack was stalking toward the sign, his face intent on the two, whose attempt to hide seemed almost comical.

I hurried after him, holding my breath.

He rounded the sign, grabbed the arm of the older of the two, and hauled her into the stream of passenger traffic.

She looked like any other middle-aged tourist, blonde hair twisted into a small bun, a traveling jacket and skirt.

"This is it, then? She's really going to try this?" He bore down on the woman like an oncoming train himself.

I had never heard such anger in his voice.

The woman withered under it.

"Jack—I—we—" She turned to me. "You must be Sahara."

"What is going on?" I looked to the younger woman, dark-haired and sharp-nosed.

She managed to shrug, shake her head, and lift her hands all in one fluttery motion.

The train whistled again, its wheels grinding and then

picking up speed as it clacked out of the station, the sound deafening.

"We're getting out of here." Jack hadn't let go of the woman's arm, and now he was dragging her toward the exit.

The younger woman and I followed, glancing at each other, like unwilling participants in some crazy street performance.

Outside the station, on the Grande Canal side, the train noise lessened. The steamy smell of the lagoon hovered over us, and Jack spun his captive to face him.

"Alright, Joanne. Spill it. What is her plan?"

Joanne?

I stepped toward the woman, who was by now nearly in tears. "You're Giada's assistant? The one who told Giada about seeing my parents at Hatshepsut's Temple all those years ago?"

She inclined her head, as if in apology. Or perhaps it was pity. "I've been with her a long time, yes."

"And you are?" I frowned at the younger girl.

She was pulling out a notebook and small pen, as though to take notes on our conversation. "I'm Fiona. I—I also work for Ms. Moretti."

"Fiona is my replacement," Joanne said. "I'm retiring soon." She smiled, as though this were a normal social visit. "Ready to spend more time with my grandchildren."

Jack folded his arms. "But first you're going to help her destroy a marriage by irrevocably separating a husband from his wife? Nice way to end your career."

We were getting some odd looks, no doubt attributed to Jack's hostile tone.

"How did you find us?" My head spun. More people from Jack's time. What did they know?

"Reuben returned, told us you'd be traveling from Venice, back to Egypt. We've been watching for you here at the train station for a few days."

I glanced at Jack. "Maybe we should go somewhere else to talk?"

Fiona nodded, a quick little motion.

"Where did you come through?" Jack's question took in both women. "From 2002." He lowered his voice. "Where did you come through, to this time?"

Joanne hesitated.

"The truth, Joanne. You owe me that."

I wasn't sure why Joanne owed Jack anything, but she seemed to agree with a weary sigh. "St. Mark's. Just inside the basilica."

"Fine. We're not going anywhere near there."

He marched toward a *vaporetti* stand.

The rest of us followed.

I understood at last. Giada had sent these two, Observers only. But between them, if they went back to the San Marcos basilica with Jack, they could return to their own time and take Jack with them.

His visit here would be erased. All of it.

I touched a hand to my belly and hurried to catch up with him.

Minutes later, the four of us were seated around a small table in the same cafe where Jack and I had planned our first day of searching the archives in Venice, two months ago.

A waitress brought espresso, which I declined, and pastry, which I devoured, trying to settle my stomach.

Fear clawed at me.

But then, wasn't Jack safe here? How did two women expect to get a grown man all the way across the city and into a church against his will?

Joanne placed a hand on Jack's arm. "I think you have the wrong idea. Giada only sent us to explain. After Reuben returned a few days ago."

He pulled his arm aside and gulped his espresso, his face souring.

"So, she received my message, then."

Joanne's voice softened. "Received it, yes. She was devastated."

Jack laughed, a sarcastic, angry sound. "*She* was devastated? I suppose she sent you to tell me it was all a misunderstanding?

The Aldridge's house fire, chasing them into the past and making threats? Even sending me, to get information?"

"She isn't making excuses." Joanne's shoulders dropped. "Not anymore, Jack. She's—I'm afraid she's sick. Very sick."

I watched as his expression fell and put my hand over his on the table.

"What?"

"She didn't get the final diagnosis until after you left. But it's progressing quickly. The chemo hasn't worked, and surgery's not an option."

"'Chemo'?" I looked to Jack, then back at Joanne, unfamiliar with the word.

"She has cancer." Jack's tone was flat, his voice subdued. "The treatment—chemotherapy—isn't working."

"Oh, Jack, I'm sorry." Despite all the harm she'd caused my family, Giada was still *his* family, and he loved her.

"So then, what? She sent you to try to talk me into returning on my own, to say goodbye? And then what? Never see my wife, who won't even remember me, again?"

Fiona shot forward in her chair, hands on the table. "No! No, that's just it! She can fix it all!"

I thought at first she meant Giada could somehow fix the mess she'd created.

But then realized Fiona was staring at me.

Oh, no, no, no.

"What are you saying?"

Joanne reached for my hand. "Sahara, you're the answer here, don't you see? You're a Revisionist, right?"

I said nothing, but pulled my hand from her grasp.

"Come back to the year where you belong. To 2003, where you and Giada can figure out how to send you back to undo everything that has happened, all the way back to when your parents first fled the States in 1974. And you can make sure she doesn't need to do all the traveling that has devastated her body, made her so sick. You'll be saving her life."

"And you'll grow up in the right century, Sahara!" This from

Fiona, all smiles. "Trust me, the twenty-first century is a much better place for women. Not perfect, but so many more opportunities—"

"And Jack?"

Joanne ran a hand through her graying hair. "Well, Jack needs to stay here for now. Because we know he didn't return to November of 2002, after he left a few months ago. But once you set everything right, he'll be back where he belongs, in Philadelphia."

"Never having left."

"Exactly."

"Never having met me."

Joanne sighed. "Yes, that's the one difficult part. But Giada will remember it both ways, and she's promised to introduce the two of you immediately. To make sure you both understand that you were once, you know, in love." A sweet smile at these last words.

"Oh, she's *promised*, has she?" I couldn't keep the sarcasm from my voice.

But Joanne turned her appeal in Jack's direction. "She's a different person now, you must believe me. This illness has... changed her."

"You are telling me Giada wants to erase my relationship with Sahara, in order to save her own life and make herself rich in some new way. This does not sound like a changed woman to me."

There was a beat of silence around the table. It seemed neither Joanne nor Fiona could think of a response.

And in the silence, Jack made one more statement.

"Sahara is pregnant."

"What—why, that's wonderful, Jack—"

The obviously ridiculous nature of Joanne's congratulations stopped her flow of words.

More silence.

Joanne sighed once more, this time with a heavy sadness

around it, and pushed her coffee away. "If Sahara returns to 2003, you'll lose more than your marriage."

"I'm not returning to 2003." It seemed to go without saying, but I said it anyway.

"No." Joanne closed her eyes. "No, of course not."

Fiona leaned forward, tapped Joanne's hand. "We can't do it, then. I won't do it."

My heart rate sped up. "Do what?"

Joanne pursed her lips, then shook her head and sighed. "Giada wanted us to... bring you back with us."

"Drag me back? Against my will?" I started to stand, fists balled.

"We won't do it, Sahara." Joanne's voice was still sad, but firm.

"Listen, both of you." Jack sat forward, arms braced on the table. "You can tell her I forgive her, if that makes it easier for you to return. That I'm sorry she's dying. You can even tell her I'm grateful, if you want—for everything she's done for me. Whatever you need to say. I don't care."

Joanne swiped at her eyes with the back of her hand.

Was she really crying over her crazy boss?

"It won't be enough. She'll die. Alone. Unhappy."

Jack's head dropped to his hands.

It was impossible. An impossible situation. I would never do what Giada asked, no matter how tempting.

Odd, I had once thought of little else besides fixing the past. Believed it was my only way forward.

But it was a lie. Going back is never the way forward. The past must be left behind. I would not fix it, would not change it. I would build on it.

I already had.

"Bring her to us." The words spilled out the same instant they occurred to me.

Joanne lifted her head. "What?"

A waitress approached, but I waved her off.

"Bring Giada to us. Not here, to 1923, obviously. She's been to 1905. But we'll figure out a place, where we can meet. Where Jack can say goodbye."

He clutched at my hand, lifted it to his lips. His own eyes were tear-filled.

"What if she won't come?"

"Then you bring her—the two of you. Would you do it? Against her will, but for her own good?"

Fiona raised her eyebrows and turned to Joanne.

But Joanne was already nodding. "It's what she needs. What she wants, even if she doesn't know it." She wiped both palms across her cheeks and sat straighter. "So where? And when? I think I know every place she's ever visited—I've been in charge of her travel schedule for years."

I let my mind drift back over places and times in the history of the world. Where was a good place to say final words to someone who had done such damage, not only to me, but to my parents and sister?

But then, of course.

Giada needed more than time with Jack, to say goodbye, even to ask forgiveness, if she was willing.

She needed time with my entire family.

"Tell her whatever you need to, to get her to Venice in your time." I nudged pastry crumbs into a napkin. "Then bring her back to February twenty-sixth, in the year 1637. Meet us on the steps of the Teatro San Cassiano, on the opening night of the first public opera house in the world."

Jack's lips parted. "But we aren't going there for a year—"

I shook my head. "My parents are waiting a year. But Giada doesn't have that long. We will go immediately. And you two," I looked to Joanne and Fiona, "will get her there as soon as you can."

# CHAPTER THIRTY

*February 26, 1637*
*Venice, Italy*

"Do you see them?" I stood on my toes, balanced on the white marble steps of the Teatro San Cassiano, searching the indigo twilight and a rainbow sea of faces, each of them hidden by a porcelain-and-sequin mask, all topped by hats bedecked with colored feathers, ribbons, and jewels.

"Are you kidding?" Jack held my elbow, as if to keep me from falling down the steps. "What was your father thinking, choosing tonight, of all nights, to meet?"

"I don't think he could have realized."

Our surprise at finding ourselves dropped into the annual chaos of *Carnivale di Venezia* was nothing compared to the surprise of seeing ourselves outfitted to match.

I wore a ridiculous burgundy satin gown in an Elizabethan style, with some kind of hoops underneath that extended my hips to more than a meter wide.

Jack's costume included a knee-length black and gold silk brocade jacket and voluminous pleated ruffles at his neck.

Added to the crazy clothing, the disorientation of searching for six individuals among thousands of costumed people milling the streets had me dizzy on the steps.

If my parents and sister arrived dressed for the *Carnivale*, and if Fiona and Joanne brought Giada to the moment here on the steps, we might never find each other.

Apparently, the operators of the Theater of San Cassiano had decided the final night of the annual Carnival of Venice, occurring like Mardi gras just before the start of Lent, would be the best night to open their opera house to a paying public, for the first time anywhere in the world. Up until now, operatic performances had been reserved for private feasts paid for by rich patrons.

A good marketing idea, but a terrible choice for a meeting time and place.

I pulled my mask into my hand, bringing my feathered hat with it, and felt my hair, pinned flat against my head in a very unflattering manner.

Jack followed suit.

Perhaps they would be able to spot us among the revelry.

Without my mask, the smell of roasting nuts and fish, and the odor of a thousand unwashed bodies, nearly undid me. I clutched at Jack's arm.

He recognized my expression at once, though the sickness typically hit me in the morning.

"This way." He shoved a path through the frenzied crowd, down the steps and into the shadowed alley alongside the theater.

I pressed my forehead against the coolness of the stone building and breathed through my mouth, willing my stomach to unknot.

It was only about six o'clock, but the sun hung low behind the homes of Venice and the carnival's legendary excess was building to a crescendo. The masks allowed all social classes to mingle in a way typically forbidden, and all laws limiting consumption were suspended. Little wonder the streets teemed with mayhem, more like a riot than a festival.

From the alley, we could hear the first sounds of a small orchestra warming up and tuning inside the theater. The discordant music calmed me somehow, grounded me with something familiar that could have been a twentieth-century orchestra at the Royal Opera House in London.

I nodded to Jack. "I'm better. Let's get back."

"Perhaps you should keep the mask on—the smell—"

"No. I'm not taking a chance on missing anyone."

We returned through the crowd, back up the steps to the entrance of the theater, and braced ourselves against the graceful curves of the stone columns. From the higher vantage point, the smell was not so bad, and the view was better.

We scanned the crowd again, and again.

A few torches, high above heads, lit the street below, along with swaying lanterns carried by revelers.

My eyes watered with concentration.

"There!" I grabbed Jack's hand. "Those two women and a man coming toward us!"

The three were masked, the women each holding the stark-white porcelain to her face with a delicate rod. The masks covered only the upper half of their faces. Crystals and gold gilded each. The man's mask concealed his entire face, his garishly painted lips frozen into a sneering smile.

"Is it them?"

But then the two women pulled their masks away from their smiling faces.

"Mama! Persia!" I started for the steps, but the theater crowd was pressing upward.

"Wait for them, Sahara." Jack pulled me back. "They're coming."

We were together moments later, with embraces and laughter over our ridiculous costumes.

Persia plucked at the mask in my hand. "Sahara, you're cheating! You must put it back on!"

But then my mother glanced around us, and her face fell.

"Where—where is the baby?" Her voice faltered on the last word, as if she were afraid of bad news.

I took a deep breath. "Things have not gone according to plan, I'm afraid."

"Oh, sweetheart—"

"No, no, everything is alright. I mean, it's not completely alright, but—"

Jack stopped me with a hand to my arm and a jut of his chin toward the steps. "They made it."

Three women watched us from street. None of them masked.

Fiona and Joanne, I recognized.

A thin, dark-haired woman stood caught between them— held upright or held captive?

She'd aged considerably since I saw her at Highclere as a teen, but I would have recognized her.

My mother's sharp intake of breath beside me signaled her own recognition.

"Alex." She stumbled against my father. "Alex, it's Giada."

My father looked to me, took in my obvious lack of surprise, then turned on Jack. "What have you done?"

"No, Papa, it's okay. It's part of the plan. We need—we need to talk to her. All of us."

His expression was as unyielding as the columns behind us, but he nodded once, tight-lipped.

"Not here." My mother's voice was steely as well. "Not here. Alex, let's go back to the apartments."

Persia put an arm around my shoulder. "Papa has rented the most elegant apartments for us. You won't believe how lovely."

We started down the steps, the five of us, before the three women at the base had moved.

Face-to-face at last, somehow it was only my mother and myself who stood inches from Giada, studying her in silence as the crowd roared in the growing darkness around us.

"Hello, Renae." A sad smile flitted around Giada's lips, then disappeared. "And Sahara. It's good to see you again."

"Oh, Giada." My mother's voice had shifted to pity. "What have you done to yourself?"

I understood my mother's feeling. This close, Giada could have passed for my grandmother. Sunken cheeks and dark circles under her eyes. Thinning hair and stooped shoulders.

And it was clear that her two assistants were doing more to keep her standing than to keep her from escaping.

"We have a place, nearby." My father stepped to Giada's side. "Let us take you there."

Giada's gaze shifted over my shoulder. To Jack.

Another smile, this one less tentative. More... imploring.

Joanne stepped away.

Jack took her place, one arm circling his aunt's waist. "We've got you, Aunt Giada."

I didn't miss the tears—sliding down Giada's weathered cheeks, and glistening in Jack's eyes as well.

~

The apartments my father had rented were more than lovely. Pink marble columns and a terrazzo floor speckled in royal blue and metallic gold, brass candlesticks with glowing tapers everywhere, and sumptuous tapestry fabrics tossed over stuffed cushions in crimson and coral, reminiscent of a still life of ripe fruit.

To be together like this—my parents and sister, with Jack and Giada—it felt surreal, as though we were still masked actors, playing a part.

With Giada lowered to a nest of cushions on a low dais, my mother pulled me aside, hands clasped around mine.

"The baby, sweetheart. Tell me." Tiny lines of worry deepened around her mouth.

"It's only been two days. For us. Two days since we left you in 1737."

Her mouth dropped. "But you made me promise to wait a year—"

I smiled and pulled her into an embrace. "I know. I'm sorry.

But I'll make it up to you. After this jump, we'll meet you some-where with the baby, but you can go right away."

She laughed. "Some things about time travel, I will simply never get accustomed to." Her expression sobered. "But now we need to hear it all."

I nodded, then glanced to the rest of our company. My father was pouring wine for the others from a crystal decanter, as though he'd arranged a dinner party for the final night of the Carnival.

I braced a hand on my churning stomach. "Do you have anything here to eat?"

Thirty minutes later, we were sitting as a group at an ornately carved walnut table, trays of cold seafood and cheese pie spread before us, and wine glasses refilled. Although when my father circled the table with the bottle, Jack covered my glass with his palm and shook his head.

"Not good for the baby," he whispered.

Another little reminder that medical science had advanced in his time.

Yet, clearly not enough to save Giada, who seemed to struggle to hold herself erect at the head of the table, where she'd been oddly seated. The regal woman I'd met at Highclere was gone.

"Thank you," she nodded as my father filled her glass. "For your hospitality." She waved a hand around the apartment. "You have done well for yourself, I see."

My mother cleared her throat. "This is not our home, Giada. Alex rented this place, as a little holiday to spend with Sahara and Jack. We were not expecting... other company."

"I see."

Jack's eyes never left his aunt's face. "Aunt Giada, I need to ask. Did you come here willingly?"

She half-smiled. "To Venice, yes." She glanced at Joanne. "I was told Sahara had been brought back, to 2003, but could not get to the States without a passport. I came to meet her." She raised an unsteady glass to me, and sipped her wine.

"But to this year—whatever year it is—and this insane carnival? No. That was entirely the doings of my two less-than-loyal assistants."

"They are more loyal than you deserve," I said. Then regretted it.

Joanne and Fiona remained silent.

We passed the breads and vegetables in olive oil, in an unspoken agreement to eat before rehashing the past.

But only a few minutes into the meal, Joanne pushed away from the table and stood. "I believe Fiona and I will explore the city."

Gracious of her, to leave our two families in private.

Giada reached out to clutch her arm. "You will not leave me —go back to 2003 without me? I'll be stranded here!"

Joanne patted her hand. "We won't leave you. I promise."

The two women escaped, and a tense silence fell again.

My mother broke it.

"Giada, I am sorry you are unwell. Clearly, traveling has not been kind to you since we saw you here in Venice seventeen years ago."

The words were kindly spoken, which was generous of my mother. But the truth of how we all got to this point was lost on no one.

"Where did you go, after that night with Belzoni?" Giada set down her bread. "I must know."

"We jumped back to 1720. To get away from you. Persia was born there."

"Persia." Giada studied my sister. "She is special, too, no doubt."

*You have no idea.*

None of us replied.

"I do wonder..." Her voice trailed off, and she circled the carved table with her sunken eyes. "I do wonder if we can change it all. So many Revisionists here, am I right? Can we not untangle the past, find a way to rewrite it?"

"And what would we lose in the process?" My father pushed

his chair from the table, arms crossed. "Persia? Conceived in 1905? And what lives would replace what we have known? Who is to say it would be better?"

Giada dropped her gaze to the platters of food. Clearly, there was one person for whom it would probably be better.

Jack reached across the table to cover her hand. "Aunt Giada. Sahara and I are expecting a baby."

Giada's head jerked upward, her eyes lighting first on Jack, and then on me.

There was no mistaking the expression in those eyes.

Joy.

And in that moment, everything I'd felt since Jack first told me his last name, and I knew Giada had separated me from my parents—all the resentment and bitterness—it all fell away.

And I forgave her.

The past spilled out then, in bits and pieces, with tears and some laughter. We each knew parts of the history, but none of us knew it all.

The seventeen years since my family had been separated. Our years before that, split between London and Highclere. The crazy skipping through time, from Tut-ankh-amun's tomb to Nero's suicide to Khufu's pyramid, trying to find each other.

Giada told of Jack's upbringing, skimming over her unethical dealings with the past, though not trying to obscure anything.

"But you must understand. Alex. Renae." Her eyes were soft and pleading. "I never, never meant to hurt you. That awful fire—I didn't arrange it. It was a crazy old man…"

I shook my head through the near-unbelievable telling of Ahmed Abd el-Rassul and his obsession with the TT320 cache of royal mummies that included the pharaoh Seti, who started it all.

"And for eleven years, until Joanne saw you at Hatshepsut's Temple, I believed you died in that fire. I—I could hardly bear it."

My mother inhaled deeply, then released the breath with a deep sigh. "And yet, when you caught up with us at Belzoni's house—"

"I know." She held up a hand. "I know. I was angry. Angry

that you were trying to erase my life. Everything I'd accomplished up until then. And I know I threatened Sahara—" at this, her eyes flitted to me—"But I never would have hurt her. You must believe me."

Silence caught up with us again, each of us studying the table, the plates, our hands.

Finally, Giada pushed herself to standing, fingertips braced against the table. "I have no right to ask this of any of you." She met the faces of each of us in turn, drawing out the moment. "But I am going to ask. I have made so many mistakes. I have been greedy and grasping and foolish. I believed I must have the money, and the fame, and the reputation, to be worth anything." She rested her eyes on Jack, half-smiling. "It turns out, I had everything without it." She faced my parents once more. "I am asking for forgiveness."

She breathed out, as though the effort cost her. As though she expected nothing.

But my parents stood as one, facing Giada.

My father lowered his head, then lifted his gaze to her face.

"You have it, Giada. You have my forgiveness."

My mother smiled, nodded. "And mine."

I stood with them, and Persia joined me.

I caught my mother's hand in my own. "If my parents can forgive you, Giada, then I can as well."

Persia grinned. "Don't leave me out. My life's already been an adventure. No hard feelings."

We four Aldridges stood facing Giada, where she stood at the head of the table, still propped on shaky hands.

But then Jack was on his feet, circling the table, taking her hands, holding her steady.

Kissing her cheek.

Wrapping her in an embrace.

And whispering against her hair. "You have been more than an aunt. You have been a mother."

She wept and shook in his arms, a leaf battered by the winds of time.

Our dinner ended with more stories told, of trips to the past, of childhood anecdotes—mine, Persia's, Jack's—told by my parents and the woman who'd been a parent to Jack for so many years.

And then the college stories. The three of them, hopping from one adventure to another.

Giada's shock when she realized she'd met Jack and me, more than thirty years earlier as the three of them escaped the Harem Conspiracy, was enough to set us all laughing.

By the time Joanne and Fiona returned, it must have seemed to them the six of us had never been estranged, had never been apart.

My mother and I helped Giada to a bedroom that night. Helped her strip down to the basic white shift under her elaborate dress, then bundled her thin body in blankets against the chill, and lit a fire in the fireplace.

Jack spent another hour with her, not leaving her side until she had fallen asleep.

She never awakened.

# CHAPTER THIRTY-ONE

*February 28, 1637*
*Venice, Italy*

*W*e buried Giada at the Church of Saint Cassian, across from the opera house.

Somehow my father arranged for the burial of our out-of-town aunt, who died unexpectedly during her visit to the Carnival. Perhaps the little vault under the church floor had been secured by a large donation to San Cassiano.

Some irony there, since my father's wealth had grown through the years from the seed money planted in a briefcase in 1974, given to him by Giada herself.

We returned to the rented apartment after a solemn time at the church.

Joanne and Fiona joined us at the church, but then said their goodbyes, to return to 2003.

"What was Joanne whispering to you about, before she left?" I asked Jack, as we sank into cushions in the luxurious apartment, exhausted though it was only mid-morning.

"Nothing. Nothing important, anyway." He studied his hands, uncharacteristically still.

I took one of those hands in mine, trying to warm it. "I'm so sorry, Jack."

He nodded, but said nothing.

"What will those two do, when they return? What will they say about where Giada has gone?"

Jack pulled his hand from mine and rubbed at his face. "Let's just not talk for a while. I'm tired."

But by late afternoon, when we had eaten and rested, it seemed conversation was inevitable.

The five of us lounged in the main room, draped across cushions and settees, discussing how long we would remain in 1637 together.

Persia paced the terrazzo floor, clearly bored.

"We haven't seen you for a year." My mother sat close to my father, leaning her head on his shoulder. "You must stay for a while."

"And we just spent a month with you." I smiled, apologetically.

Jack stood and crossed to the window, looking toward the Campo Cassiano. "We'll need to return to 1923 with our time here intact."

The grief in his voice kept us all quiet for a moment.

"Jack's right." I resisted the urge to go to him at the window. "Giada's burial. But also, I don't want to take chances with the baby." I looked to my parents. "Do we know if it's safe for an unborn child to age instantly when returning?"

"It's not." My mother's expression held concern. "Traveling while pregnant is highly unsafe for Observers, for that very reason."

"So, however long we stay here with you, we'll have missed that much time in 1923."

Across the room, Persia shrugged. "So what? You'd rather be in dusty Egypt, than here with us?"

"If we don't leave now, she'll miss the official opening of the burial chamber." Jack returned to sit beside me.

I glanced from him to my parents. "How do you know that?"

"Because I memorized the important dates before I left for Egypt."

"Jack's right." My father sat forward in his chair. "The official opening is on February sixteenth."

"And it's what... the tenth of February if we return to 1923 today?" I sat straighter. "That's barely enough time to get back to Luxor!"

"Jack." My father sat forward, arms draped over his knees. "There are—other dates—you memorized as well?"

"Yes, sir."

"Dates you haven't shared with Sahara?"

"No!" I shook my head and held up both hands. "I've told Jack, I don't want to know the future—mine or anyone else's!"

My parents looked to each other, then back to Jack, expressions too serious for my liking.

Oh, glory.

I sighed. "Do what you feel you must. If I need to know, then tell me."

My father's eyes softened. "It's Porchy. I know how fond you've grown of him over the years."

I swallowed against the tightness in my throat. "What is it?" Lord Carnarvon had been increasingly frail over the past few seasons, but surely it wasn't that bad.

The three of them seemed to toss the responsibility of telling me between them.

Persia shrugged, apparently as much in the dark as I.

My father finally continued. "It begins in a few weeks. He'll take a trip with Eve down the Nile for a few days to Aswan, and be bitten by a mosquito. The bite doesn't heal well after he returns to Luxor. He nicks it while shaving a couple of weeks later, and infection sets in. They'll take him to Cairo to try to get better medical help, but they don't have the medication in 1923 to properly treat sepsis."

I shook my head. It could not be true. Not something as simple as a mosquito bite.

"A stronger man might have fought off the infection, but you know, he's not strong."

"How long?" The words emerged, half-strangled. "When?"

Jack reached for my hand. "April fifth."

Less than two months.

Jack had lost the woman who was like a mother to him. In less than two months, I would suffer the same and lose the man who'd stepped in as a father to me.

"We can change it." I swiped at hot tears. "We can... do something."

But even as I said the words, I knew they were untrue. This was the history my family knew. Jack knew. This is what would be.

I dropped my head.

A mosquito bite.

"Sahara." My mother pulled away from my father and crossed the room to kneel in front of me, her hands covering mine. "I wish you would consider returning to 2003."

"What?"

Why had she chosen this moment to make such a suggestion?

She gripped my fingers. "Sahara, just a few years after Porchy's death, he could have been saved by the simple administration of new drugs—antibiotics—that are being developed. The twentieth century will see so many strides in medical intervention and the understanding of health. Infant mortality rates will decline by ninety percent."

"She's right, Sahara." Jack rubbed at his forehead, eyes closed. "Even more right than she knows. Your parents left in 1974. By 2003 it is even better."

My father leaned into the conversation. "With Giada gone," he paused to dip his head sympathetically in Jack's direction, "there is no reason not to go back. And now you know—you know you can take Jack with you."

My mother released my fingers, but didn't take her eyes from my face. "You know I've believed this since we discovered who Jack was. There is some larger purpose at work here, retrieving you from the past where you do not belong, sending Jack—of all people—to retrieve you, even to redeem all the pain Giada caused."

Jack's leg was bouncing now. "I don't return to November of 2002, we know that." He nodded toward me. "But I could return later. With you."

Persia tapped her foot on the tile floor. "Do it, Sahara. Travel to the future."

My sister stopped short of saying *I wish I could*, but her implication was clear.

"Have your baby in the century where he or she belongs," my mother whispered.

I blew out a breath, contemplating.

What reason did I have, to refuse?

Every argument they made was logical.

It was only fear. Fear of a future so unknown, I couldn't even imagine it.

And yet, what do any of us know of our future?

~

*February 10, 1923*
*Venice, Italy*

Hours, and nearly three hundred years later, Jack and I stood arm-in-arm inside the Church of Saint Cassian, staring at a square marker in the floor.

The box-like church was still unassuming and plain from the outside, but the interior was a lasting tribute to the Baroque style, with lofty white marble columns supporting a vaulted ceiling dressed in blue marble and pink-hued frescoes, carved into hundreds of spiraling vines and leaves. It even boasted three paintings by the famous Venetian artist Tintoretto, who was a former parishioner.

Giada would have loved it.

A slightly built priest approached us, head lowered to follow our gaze at the stone square laid into the marble tiles.

He said something in Italian, but we shook our heads.

"*Non parlo italiano*," Jack said.

I nearly laughed at the idea that in the past few months we had understood, and spoken, ancient Egyptian and the Latin of Rome.

"This stone has been here for centuries," the priest repeated in English. "Though its origin is unclear."

"It looks like a grave marker." Jack's voice was soft, reverent.

"Yes. With that name engraved—Giada Moretti—it does seem to be. But there is only those four numbers." He pointed. "Only the '2-0-0-3' and no others. No birth date or date of death. No one is certain what the numbers represent."

I squeezed Jack's hand. My father had done this, certainly. After we left the Venice of 1637 only a few hours ago. They must have stayed long enough to have it engraved and placed.

"And the words written there under her name?" I asked. "*Un caro amico*. What does that mean?"

He smiled. "It means 'a dear friend.'" He touched the toe of his shoe to the corner of the square. "If it is a grave marker, it was placed by those who loved her well."

Jack audibly exhaled, his shoulders sagging.

"Thank you," I said to the priest.

He eyed Jack with curiosity, then left us alone.

We stayed a few minutes more, and as we left, I promised Jack we would visit again.

In another eighty years.

The crossing from Italy to the northern coast of Africa, the train from Alexandria to Cairo to Luxor—it was all getting too repetitive, and I began to look forward to the faster transportation Jack promised in the twenty-first century, along with the other strange and wonderful things he had hinted I would discover.

Although when he tried to make me believe most people walked about with telephones in their pockets, I told him I could believe nothing more he said now.

We arrived in Luxor just in time for the official opening of the burial chamber.

I'd retained enough Latin to know I was *persona non grata* with Carter and the team, having been gone more than six weeks, on my "extended honeymoon."

But we had returned to absolute chaos in Luxor and the Valley, and with my official capacity at the dig, no one had the time or attention to keep me away.

It seemed Porchy had made a grievous error three weeks earlier, in agreeing to give exclusive coverage of the digsite and tomb-clearing to the London newspaper, *The Times*, for financial consideration that would benefit the excavation. But in so doing, he alienated the rest of the world's press, especially the Egyptian press, who felt insulted by the British imperialists who were now "looting" their sacred tomb.

Jack's anonymous photographs coming out of Italy didn't help matters, since no one knew the source of the leaked information.

Accusations of theft flew left and right. Howard's insistence on caution and silence were interpreted as secretive. The entire city of Luxor and even the Valley of the Kings teemed with inquisitive tourists and frustrated journalists.

We could not visit the Winter Palace Hotel without being attacked for news, and outsiders surrounded even the American House and Howard Carter's private residence, kicking up dust into a perpetual swirl of cars, donkeys, and even people on foot, tramping out to catch a glimpse.

We'd become celebrities, and the tension was nearly killing Howard and Porchy, whose friendship had become strained, to say the least.

Jack and I kept my pregnancy to ourselves, and I did my best to help wherever I was needed.

On the sixteenth of February, the official day set for the

opening of what all believed to be the Burial Chamber, we assembled for preliminary speeches, followed by an almost cere-monial removal of the first blocking stones by Howard and the Met's Arthur Mace. The two stood on a hastily erected stage, set between the two jackal-headed guardian statues, to work from the top down. The rest of us waited in chairs placed for an audi-ence and watched with breath held. One by one, the two chiseled out the blocking stones, passed them back to Pecky Callender, who passed them to Egyptian laborers, and on up and out of the tomb.

Once the hole was large enough to enter, we each took turns, two-by-two, to squeeze between the outer wall and the side of the great golden shrine Eve had described to me, back in November, when she and her father, Howard, and Pecky had snuck through the bottom.

It did not disappoint.

Through the gilded open doors, the second, sealed shrine glowed in invitation, with alabaster vessels scattered on the floor. Above it all, the linen pall draped over our heads, splashed with constellations. And then a glimpse even into a further room, with a great seated jackal presiding over more gold, gold everywhere.

It would be the work of a lifetime.

But I would not be here to see it.

~

Ten days later, the tomb was temporarily shut, and everyone went their separate ways for a bit of a break.

I said goodbye to Eve and Lord Carnarvon before they boarded a *dahabeyah* to sail upriver to Aswan on a little holiday.

Aswan, with its biting mosquitoes.

By the eighth of March, we were back cataloguing the finds from the antechamber, the painstaking process of numbering, photographing, and writing record cards stretching long into the hot afternoons.

A week later, I'd seen the angry redness of the bite on Porchy's cheek, but he was keeping it covered now. He was clearly weakening, perhaps with fever.

Eve convinced him to head north to Cairo, to see a doctor there.

Jack and I would follow, leaving the dig behind. I spent an early morning alone at the site, saying my goodbyes.

Certainly, I would visit again, in 2003, I promised myself.

What knowledge would eighty years have brought us in Egyptology? And would there be a place for me in any of it?

In Cairo, we stayed at the Continental Hotel, with Eve and her father, and I did my best to support Eve, who was inconsolable as her father worsened, rallied, and worsened again.

Lady Almina arrived by the twenty-sixth of March, and her grim determination to nurse her husband back to health took me back to our days of tending soldiers, side-by-side at Highclere Castle after the Great War.

But the blood poisoning spread with deadly fervor, and Porchy's weak constitution made pneumonia inevitable.

Armed with foreknowledge, I whispered goodbyes at his bedside on the evening of April fourth, and cried myself to sleep in Jack's arms.

By the next morning, he was gone.

So much loss, and so much gain, in the past six months of my life.

But a new chapter would now begin.

# CHAPTER THIRTY-TWO

*May 3, 1923*
*Oxford University*
*London, England*

It came as little surprise that when a young Renae and Alexander Aldridge fled 1974 for the year 1894, clutching me between them, they chose the main research library of the University of Oxford to do so.

The five buildings that represented the Bodleian Library in 1923 began with a single building erected in the fourteenth century. From here, my parents would've had more than five hundred years of history to choose from, if 1894 hadn't been their best option.

Jack and I approached the grand library entrance, the Tower of the Five Orders, from the Divinity School side.

"Orders of what?" Jack asked, as we slowed, hand-in-hand, to lift our eyes to the top.

"It's the columns." I pointed to the five sets of columns that ascended, one above the other, from the square. "They represent the five orders of classical architecture—Tuscan, Doric, Ionic, Corinthian…" I bit my lip. The last one always escaped me.

"What's this? Sahara Aldridge's knowledge falters?"

I elbowed him and grinned.

We were trying to keep it light. Had been doing so since leaving Highclere a few days ago. Standing on the windswept cliff of Beacon Hill high above the estate, as Lord Carnarvon's casket was lowered into the ground, had been a sad way to say farewell to 1923 and everyone I'd known there.

"To America," I'd told Almina and Eve, hugging them tightly as we said goodbye.

They accepted my new status as the wife of the American reporter without question. Eve begged me to return in October for her wedding to Brograve Beauchamp, and I promised to try, not looking at Jack who would have seen the guilt in my eyes.

And now we were here, entering "the Bod" as we affectionately called the library when I had studied here, ready to navigate to a painted panel in Duke Humfrey's Library, the Bod's oldest reading room.

Ready to navigate to the year 2003.

No amount of joking and avoiding the topic could settle the jumpiness in my veins.

I was about to step into H. G. Wells' *Time Machine*, and travel to a future so advanced I'd ceased to believe Jack's stories.

According to my parents, the painted panel was the location of my entrance into 1894, though I had no memory of it.

And thus, it needed to be the location of my exit.

But first, Jack needed to be unconscious.

Thankfully, we'd thought ahead while still at Highclere, and gotten Dr. Johnnie to give me a sleeping powder, to cure the insomnia I'd claimed since returning from Egypt. I asked careful questions about how much I could safely take.

I led Jack to the first floor reading room, and let him enter ahead of me, to take in the two-story paneled ceiling and massive oak bookcases.

"No way." Jack pulled up short at the entrance.

I laughed. "I didn't take you for someone to be amazed at a library."

"But it's Hogwart's!" He turned to me, a joyful grin plastered across his face.

"Hog-what?"

"It's the library at Hogwart's School of Witchcraft and Wizardry!"

I felt my jaw drop. By 2003, they'd turned the Bod into a... school of *witchcraft*? The idea terrified me.

But Jack was laughing, pulling me into a sideways embrace. "You'll see. I have so much to show you." At my sober expression, he kissed my cheek. "It's a movie. A talking film. Well, really a book and then a movie." He gazed at the walls, the ceiling, as if amazed. "They must have filmed it here. They used this library as the library of the school where a boy is learning to be a wizard."

I thought of the seances, held occasionally at Highclere Castle, in the days when Porchy became fascinated with the Spiritualist Movement.

"Sounds like not much has changed."

"Ready to find out?"

But of course, it was not that simple.

We first had to find places to stay out of sight, as the library closed down and an elderly security guard made his rounds, checking for students asleep at their reading desks or lost in the stacks.

Finally, the last lights flickered off, and the room went silent.

Jack pulled out a small metal flask—water only—and unwrapped a tiny paper package containing the grains of Veronal.

"Don't draw any mustaches on me," he said, then funneled the powder into the flask and downed it with one swig.

"Mustaches... what?"

He shrugged. "It's what my friends always did, when we spent the night at each other's houses. First one to fall asleep had a mustache drawn on his face."

"Ah. Well, no promises. Especially if mustaches are fashionable in 2003. I might like to see that."

We sat, propped against the wall beneath a panel of Humphrey of Lancaster himself, first Duke of Gloucester, and the man for whom Duke Humfrey's Library was named.

Jack noted the plaque and asked about the two different spellings.

"I have no idea."

He smiled. "I just realized. When we get to 2003, I am going to know so much more than you."

"Very funny."

It took far too long for Jack to fall asleep. Though not as long as I'd waited in the tiny room in the Venice *pensione* three months ago.

In the hour before he dropped off, we rehearsed our plan, our backup plan, and our contingency plan if the backup plan failed, at least a half-dozen times.

My stomach was rebelling, and it had nothing to do with my pregnancy, which was now at the halfway point, and hadn't given me trouble for weeks. It was fear, plain and simple. Fear that I would lose Jack, that something would happen to my baby, that nothing would happen to the baby but he or she would grow up without a father, that I would be unable to stay sane, eighty years in the future.

All of this I voiced to Jack, in the dark silence of the library.

He only held me close and whispered assurances, which both of us knew could not be counted upon.

Eventually, his body relaxed against mine, his usual restlessness stilled. "I love you, Sahara," he mumbled against my head. "Whatever happens, I want you to know, you've taught me to accept myself. To know that the person I am is a person worth being."

I said nothing, only snuggled closer, and tried not to cry.

And then finally, he was dozing, his head lolling against my shoulder and his breathing even.

Could I take this risk? Could I trust that someone was watching over us, bringing us back to 2003 together? Was I prepared to live a life without Jack? A life raising our child, believing in my own value and destiny apart from the man I loved?

I didn't have answers. But my parents had given me all the knowledge I needed.

It was time to meet my future.

# CHAPTER THIRTY-THREE

"*J*ack?"

The darkness of the library seemed deeper, more complete, in what I assumed was 2003.

I floundered, hands reaching into empty space around me.

"Jack? Where are you?"

My voice echoed back from the stacks.

"Jack!" A guard might hear. I didn't care.

I stumbled through the library, bumping table corners with my hips, hands skimming leather and oak. The windows at the end of the room beckoned with moonlight, oriented me toward the entrance.

*No. Don't leave yet. Remember Rome.*

When we'd traveled to 68 AD, inside the *Curia Julia* in the Roman Forum, Jack had appeared a few minutes after me. Long enough for me to get in trouble with Decima.

I shuddered at the memory. But perhaps that was all that happened here.

He would follow in a few minutes.

*No, he was your passenger.*

I exhaled, bent at the waist, heart pounding.

Where was he?

*You never came back.* Reuben's insistence, that Jack never made it back to this time.

*Oh, God. Don't let it be true.*

Had we tested fate, and failed?

I spent the night with my back against the wall of the library, knees drawn to my chest for warmth.

When the lights buzzed on the next morning, waking me, I was surprised to find the library unchanged. Was I truly in the year 2003? Or had I stayed in 1923, and Jack had gone... where?

But no, my unfamiliar clothing told the tale.

I fled the library before anyone saw me, out into the square in front of the Tower of the Five Orders.

The first thing that struck me, like an assault on my ears, was the *noise.*

A steady hum surrounded me, like a thousand of Porchy's automobiles, all running at once, somewhere unseen just beyond the buildings.

My second impression was of the people.

All the women walking fast, wearing trousers.

Knitted hats like upside-down bowls and short, puffy coats.

White wires running into men's ears.

People standing in clusters, drinking out of white cups that seemed made of paper.

And then a young man passed me, a black device held to his ear, speaking as though to someone in the same room.

After that, I suppose I fainted.

When the world asserted itself again, I focused on the familiar cerulean sky, the marshmallow clouds, even allowed myself a glance at the Tower, unchanged since my Oxford days.

"Ma'am, are you okay?"

I tried not to look at him. He was one of the ones with the white wires plugged into his ears. Was he a man, or some sort of machine that needed power?

"Ma'am, I think you fainted. Do you want me to call a doctor?"

"No." I shook my head, which felt loose on my neck. "No," I murmured again. "I am fine." I put a hand to my belly, blood suddenly racing.

But the bulge was still there, under the strangest hot-pink blouse, which, like my odd blue trousers, fit as tight as a man's undershirt and left me blushing.

The young man's eyes followed my hand. "You're pregnant? I should call a doctor."

Even more embarrassed by his familiarity, I struggled to stand.

"No." I searched the square. "My husband—my husband is around here somewhere. I'll just sit here." I pointed to a low brick wall, and he guided me there. "He'll be here any moment. Thank you, though. I am fine."

But Jack did not arrive in a moment, nor for the rest of the morning.

It was time for our first backup plan.

Three weeks.

For three weeks I must come here every morning, to the entrance of the Bodleian Library, to see if Jack arrived.

But if he had somehow returned to last November, despite what we knew, why was he not here right now, waiting for me? He had six months to plan our reunion.

While I could try to conjure some delay that kept him from being here with me, there was one thing I could not reconcile. If Jack had returned to last November, he would have erased his time in the past, and I would not remember him at all.

I could think of no other answer, other than the single one too awful to accept. Jack was either lost in the muddy void between centuries, or the trip had killed him.

I would stick to the plan. If he did not come by the end of three weeks, I was to somehow make my way to meet him in 30 BC, on the day of Cleopatra's death.

From London to Alexandria, Egypt, with nothing more than the scandalously tight-fitting clothes on my back.

And if we didn't find each other in Egypt, the contingency plan would be to meet at the time and place we'd chosen with my parents for our next vacation together—the island of Cyprus at the end of the Byzantine era.

How was I to navigate the world with no money, no passport?

The multiple plans had seemed sufficient, when I'd been confident of my Amplified ability to carry Jack with me from 1923.

Now, the hubris of it all struck me.

Did I think I controlled the universe?

Jack was dead, and I had killed him. We thought we would defy the odds and live together here in this century. Instead, he was either lost in a void, or lost in the past, or dead.

And it was my fault.

I had tried to adopt my mother's faith, but what had it gotten me?

I inhaled deep breaths through my nose and exhaled through my mouth. It would do no good to faint again. And the idea of fainting because of anxiety really angered me, anyway.

I didn't move from the brick wall until the Great Tom chimed noon from the bell tower, another familiar and comforting sound.

Finally, hunger drove me across the campus, to a pub where they used to leave out small snacks for the patrons, and thankfully, still did. I nibbled enough to stave off the hunger, cringing at the loud music and averting my eyes from a hanging box like a tiny film screen, with colorful flashing images.

It would fill another journal, to describe those days of waiting. Of discovery and wonder, of panic and grief.

They say "necessity is the mother of invention," and I found that hunger is the mother of creativity as well. I managed to procure some large sheets of paper, and some pens that held ink inside a barreled chamber, and set up on a grassy quad, where I sketched students' portraits for a bit of money. Well, in truth, after the first boy paid me five pounds, I thought I'd found a way to grow rich. But then the five pounds barely paid for my supper.

I drew more portraits.

I spent part of my earnings on more paper and ink, part on food, and hid at night in one of the various reading rooms around the colleges, alternating between snatches of sleep and long hours poring over books that told me the rest of the story that played out in the Valley of the Kings after I left. Enjoying a look at many of the photographs Lord Carnarvon had taken over the years, some of which I'd never seen.

I found no trace of myself in this history.

Six months ago, that fact would have left me bereft and believing myself worthless. But Time had taught me otherwise.

Late the second night, I turned a page in an obscure text about the Carnarvons, and sucked in a shocked breath.

My own face stared back at me. A photograph taken by the Earl, captioned only "Head Shot, 1918."

Before I'd cut my hair, and my expression so serious. I could almost see that suffocating *aloneness* in my eyes.

I turned the page again, willing to leave that girl behind.

The nights were long, but each morning, I waited beside the Tower.

By the third day, when the clock struck noon, I had given up any notion of Jack simply being delayed. He was gone. Truly gone.

I could no longer tolerate the thought of another day drawing students, nor of the noise and strangeness of it all.

Was there no place in this world untouched by the passage of years?

I sat on the pavement outside the library, head braced against the brick wall, as the twelfth gong of the clock tower echoed into oblivion, and placed a hand against my belly.

"It's the two of us now, little one," I whispered. "We will belong to each other. And we will be just fine."

I would finish out my three weeks here. I owed Jack that much and would take no chances.

But it was time to think of the future. To say goodbye to the past.

I asked enough questions to navigate to a train station, paid for a ticket out of my meager earnings, and traveled first to Paddington Station and then south to Putney Station, on a sleek silver train that ran without steam.

From there, it was only a twenty-minute walk to find the Anglican chapel and the Gothic-Victorian cemetery, where the Bod's history texts told me I'd find two people I loved.

Two people to whom I owed a proper goodbye.

I found Eve first.

A simple black granite marker, placed by Eve's only child, her daughter Patricia, now nearly eighty and apparently living somewhere in England.

*EVELYN BEAUCHAMP*
*1901 - 1980*
*Widow of Sir Brograve Beauchamp*
*Daughter of the 5ᵗʰ Earl of Carnarvon*
*IN MEMORY OF MY BELOVED MOTHER*

Beloved mother. And my beloved friend.

I kissed my fingertips, then brushed them against the top of the stone. Prayed she had lived all her seventy-nine years in happiness.

More wandering. And then, finally...

*HOWARD CARTER*
*Egyptologist*
*DISCOVERER OF THE TOMB OF*
*TUTANKHAMUN, 1922*

*BORN, 9 MAY 1874*
*DIED, 2 MARCH 1939*
*"May your spirit live, may you spend*
*millions of years, you who love Thebes,*
*sitting with your face to the north wind,*
*your eyes beholding happiness."*

He'd lived another seventeen years after we found the tomb, until the age of sixty-five. The discovery was the high point of his life, the texts told me, and he faced difficulties after. But the epitaph was fitting—a quote from the translated lip of the beautiful alabaster cup I'd sketched in the tomb one December morning more than eighty years ago.

I pressed my fingertips to the black granite of his marker as well, and whispered my gratitude. "Thank you, Howard. Thank you for allowing me to be part of such a life-changing adventure. For caring for me, in your own way. You were a good man. I hope you also found some measure of happiness."

I criss-crossed through the cemetery markers and gravel-pathed gardens, aimless and barely registering the names on the stones. Thinking of the past, of mortality, of time. There was nothing more for me here, but it seemed too soon, too casual a visit to walk back to the station.

My steps took me into the spired gray stone chapel, where my footsteps echoed down from the arched wood beams of the vaulted ceiling. I slipped into a pew at the back, alone under the sunlight filtering through stained glass above the altar. The building reminded me a bit of St. Michael's, the parish church in Highclere village, and with the remembrance, brought a sense of peace.

But how much had changed since the last time I sat in a pew. The world had opened to me in a way I never thought possible. And yet, instead of growing larger, it seemed to have grown smaller. As though I could now see the entire sweep of human history. Contain all of it between my two hands, like a child's ball. Stand outside of it, even.

And if outside, where did that leave me? An outsider?

I ran my fingers along the top of the smooth wooden pew in front of me, and blinked up toward the high windows and the ruby-red oval of glass with its inset cross.

No. Not an outsider. Perhaps even the opposite.

I had learned that my past did not dictate my worth, and is as unreliable as fragments dug from the sand. Neither did my future give me worth, which could only come from outside myself.

No, I was not an outsider. I was at home in the entire world. At home in myself. A purpose somewhere to discover, and valuable regardless of what I would accomplish.

I thought of St. Michael's again, on the wooded edge of Highclere village, and the grand estate only a twenty-minute walk southward.

It was time for one final goodbye.

Back to the train, to the Newbury Station. I resisted the detour to see if the racecourse still remained, where I'd spent many afternoons beside Eve, cheering on our favorite horses, and instead searched for a taxi.

In the end, I could not pay the taxi's exorbitant rate, and was directed by its somewhat-surly driver to what he called a "bus" which was like a streetcar, I suppose, but without rails. This conveyance deposited me, blessedly, on the bottom edge of the village of Highclere, near the doorstep of The Pheasant—an inn and pub where I'd eaten with my parents many times, which looked from the outside to be largely unchanged.

This close to the estate, I decided to forego the circuitous route of the road, and struck out across well-known fields, with the sun at my back.

For the first time in three days, I was at peace.

And then suddenly, the trees opened and there she was—the estate cast in the warm yellow glow I so loved as a child, with green expanses of grass leading up to its grand walls.

I approached from the back of the castle, saw no one, and circled to the long gravel drive in front, so familiar. I crossed the grass lawn to the entry road, wanting to arrive from the same direction I'd taken each time I came for summers and holidays.

I'd come home.

Should I knock on the iron-studded walnut door far ahead, where I'd freely entered hundreds of times?

Ask to see the house? Meet the family?

Under what pretense? I had no way of explaining my deep-felt connection to the place.

I was just losing my nerve when the front door opened of its own accord.

A figure stood in the shadow of the doorway.

I shielded my eyes against the sun, blinding me from where it sat, low in the sky behind the corner of the building.

And then the figure was running. Running toward me, as though someone in the family still remembered me, still somehow knew me...

But it was not any of the Herbert family.

My heart rose up in recognition, soaring above Highclere into the setting sun.

Running to me was the one person I never dreamed of meeting here.

My husband.

$\sim$

We spent the night at The Pheasant, not leaving each other's side, barely letting go of each other.

In the end, the explanation had been so simple. We tried to laugh that we had not thought of it, but it was still too raw, too terrifying.

Just as I had done from Khufu's pyramid and the Venetian *pensione*, I had brought Jack back as a passenger with me three days ago, with the time he'd been gone passed for him as well, as though he were a Revisionist.

However... unlike our trips back in time to the Great Pyramid and the Venice of 1737, we had not traveled backward from our *own* times in the same location. As a child, I left 1974 from inside the Bodleian Library. And that is where I returned, to 2003, with twenty-eight years elapsed.

But Jack left 2002 from inside the tomb of Seti I in the Valley of the Kings. And that was where he awoke from his drugged sleep, three days ago.

Then ensued the frantic arranging of flights from Luxor to Cairo, from Cairo to Heathrow Airport in London. He tried to find someone to get me a message where I sat outside the Bod and drew portraits on the grassy square, to no avail. The flight from Egypt was delayed by storms, he said. But how glad I was for the speed of travel in this century!

He arrived in London that morning, but it was after twelve o'clock before he could reach the Bod.

And then, as though we were connected in mind and spirit, he asked himself where I was likely to go, then raced to High-clere Castle, praying to find me there.

Unsurprisingly, he'd charmed his way into the estate, spoken with the Countess—wife of the eighth Earl of Carnarvon. But they had not seen me, they said.

And then, there I was.

"Like a dream and a vision," Jack said, his forehead buried against my neck, where we lay in our tiny bed above The Pheasant's dining room, with the smell of baking bread rising up the steps.

He placed a warm hand on my belly, taking in both of us with his love.

I kissed his hair, feeling a peace and a belonging steal over me, like I had never known.

Jack lifted his head to look on me, with those blue eyes I loved so much.

"You can go back to digging in the dirt one day, Sahara. But for me—you are the greatest find of my life. And I am never letting go."

# EPILOGUE

*September 2021*

*Y*ou have asked me for my story, dear daughter. For the story of how I came to live in two places, in two times. And for the story of how *you* came to live.

*Alexandra Giada Moretti.*

Yes, we named you for both your grandfather and your great-aunt, though at times she may have seemed the villain in my story.

Perhaps one day I will write more, of the escapades your father and I have gotten into since those days. But for now, on this—your eighteenth birthday—the beginning of our story is enough.

We returned to the year 2003, to find your father named as sole beneficiary of Giada's fortune. Her wealth had risen and fallen over the years, but was at that time worth more than we could, in good conscious, retain.

We did use a bit of the money to establish a life for me in the States—the necessary papers and numbers, certificates and documents, to make me an official part of the twenty-first century. But then we sold everything, put the money into the

Moretti Foundation, and turned our attention to the good work we could do.

We left ourselves ample time for travel, and you no doubt have many fond memories of family trips with your brother and sister, time spent with your grandparents, and your fearless Aunt Persia and dashing Uncle Pietro, from Athens to Constantinople, from Barcelona to Marseilles.

And what of Howard Carter, the Carnarvon family, and all the furor over the discovery of Tutankhamun? Your history books will tell you all we know, of the battle waged over the artifacts, of Howard's life and legacy. Knowing them all as well as I did, I can sometimes read between the lines, and often feel melancholy over some of those events.

And of course, you have met the eighth Lord Carnarvon and his wife. My work as Director of the Moretti Foundation has opened a few doors, including that aging walnut door familiar to viewers of *Downton Abbey*. Imagine my surprise when Highclere Castle became so beloved to the world!

The present-day Earl and Countess, Geordie and Fiona, have no idea I once thought of Geordie's great-grandfather as a father to me. That I slept in the Mercia Bedroom, wandered the Monks' Garden, devoured books from the Library's shelves and even tended to wounded soldiers there. But they have been as lovely to me as if they *did* know, and they are both devoted to the history and maintenance of that grand estate and to Porchy's legacy—so expertly displayed and honored in the Egyptian Exhibition at Highclere.

Your father's photographs, which we guiltily sold for a few dollars to the Italian newspapers, found their way into the public record. Uncredited, of course. But his much-celebrated work since that time, both artistic and documentary, has taken the sting from any lack of recognition over the Tutankhamun photos.

And the years have not dimmed his devotion to both of us, nor his zest for life and love of adventure. You get that from him.

And what of my relationship to Time itself?

I am fifty-one years old now, nearly the age of your grand-mother Renae, when we were reunited on the steps of Khufu's pyramid. The wisdom she has taught me, I have tried to pass to you. And you have already learned that wisdom which is "old" is precious, for what is Time, really?

I have tried to use my gifts well, though I have come to think we may never know our true destiny until after our years here are finished. The tapestry of history has many hidden and tangled threads. Even stepping outside of time has not allowed me to see what only the weaver can see. But I know we each have a purpose. Some of us must travel through time to understand this, but I would see you awakened to this truth before you begin your own travels. I would ask you, even as you embrace the holy joy of living, to see beyond the distractions and ask your own questions.

And I have discovered something else true, about the search to belong. So many lonely years, wishing to belong to someone. But it has only lately become clear to me... there are only two ways for one person to belong to another. For anything to belong, it must either be *taken*, or else freely *given*. And since no one should ever be taken, it becomes a truth that our highest and best way to belong to others is actually to *give ourselves* to them. An action which begins with selflessness, even as it culminates in what our hearts truly desire.

You are eighteen now, dear daughter, with much to learn of the past, of the story of time and its author. And of your place in the world, beyond the things of time.

Go boldly. For just as each of us, you have a glorious destiny.

And you are fiercely loved.

# AUTHOR'S NOTE

## AND SOME FUN LINKS

Thank you for reading *A Time to Love,* and hopefully all three of Sahara Aldridge's Time Travel Journals!

Writing time travel stories is no easy task. And when I decided, more than two years ago, to create a story in which not only my protagonist, but also her parents and the "bad guy" could travel through time, I had no idea what I was up against. As Sahara and Jack, Renae and Alexander, and Giada all criss-cross in time, sometimes intersecting and sometimes missing each other, the story began to feel like a Sudoku puzzle. Every time I put in a new plot-twist, everything around it didn't fit anymore!

I'm counting on your ability to suspend disbelief and enjoy this story. Those of you who are time travel aficionados will no doubt find a few holes and paradoxes, but (just between us), that's because, sadly, I'm coming to believe, time travel is actually impossible. It just can't be done without undoing cause-and-effect in a way that unravels logic. But that's a bit of the fun of it, I think.

For those who have taken the ride, would you enjoy seeing a list of all the events in this series in chronological order, as they happened? You'll find that list right here.

## An invitation...

Besides the chronological scene list mentioned above, I've also compiled tons of Bonus Material for you on my site — photos, videos, and some amazing "virtual tours" – you'll feel like you've taken your own trip to the Valley of the Kings, I promise!

Please visit my website to encounter all the real history of the ancient characters like Tutankhamun, Seti I, Hatshepsut, Khufu, and Nero, as well as all the colorful but real characters who were part of the discoveries of 1922, like Howard Carter, Lord and Lady Carnarvon and their daughter Evelyn, Harry and Minnie Burton, Herbert and Helen Winlock, and many others.

## A few notes...

You may have noticed the alternate punctuation used in the pharaoh's name: Tutankhamun and Tut-ankh-amun. I chose to use the hyphenated version from Sahara's point of view, as this was the convention at the time the tomb was discovered, and in Howard Carter's writings. In recent years the hyphens have been dropped, and I used the modern usage in the later periods of the book.

Besides scouring the internet for tasty research morsels, I largely relied on two sources:

*Howard Carter: The Path to Tutankhamun*, by T.G.H. James. This biography of Carter remained at my side for most of the writing, providing day-by-day details of all that went on surrounding the momentous discovery. (And a fun side-note: James and other biographers owe a great debt to none other than Minnie Burton, and her extensive journaling of the goings-on surrounding the digsite and the Metropolitan Museum's American House. Thanks, Minnie! I'm sorry I made you seem like such a meddler!)

The other source I relied heavily upon was the current Lady Carnarvon herself, and her two books, *Lady Almina and the Real*

*Downton Abbey,* and *Egypt at Highclere: The Discovery of Tutankhamun,* as well as the official Highclere Castle website (highclerecastle.co.uk). The eighth Earl of Carnarvon and his wife Fiona work tirelessly to preserve history and share the enjoyment of this beautiful estate with the world, and I'm indebted to the Countess for her work!

The discovery of Tutankhamun, the most intact royal Egyptian tomb ever unearthed, captured the imagination of the world. It influenced fashion, artwork, and architecture, and spawned a fascination with ancient Egypt that persists to this day.

I'll not deny it, I've been hooked since I first saw *The* Mummy in theaters, nearly twenty-five years ago.

And if you've joined me for this ride, I'm guessing you feel it, too.

So I'll leave you with Howard Carter's oft-quoted own words, as he related his first moments peering into the tomb...

"As my eyes grew accustomed to the light, details of the room within emerged slowly from the mist, strange animals, statues, and gold – everywhere the glint of gold. For the moment – an eternity it must have seemed to the others standing by – I was struck dumb with amazement, and when Lord Carnarvon, unable to stand the suspense any longer, inquired anxiously, 'Can you see anything?,' it was all I could do to get out the words...
'Yes, wonderful things.'"

# FREE NOVELLA

I'd love to give you a free novella!

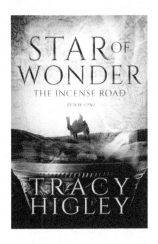

A MAGE, A SOLDIER, AND A PRINCESS,

ON AN EPIC QUEST ACROSS THE SANDS OF ARABIA.

FOLLOWING A STAR, IN SEARCH OF A KING.

Get this FREE ebook when you join "The Caravan" – my affectionate name for those of you traveling through the pages of history and fiction with me.

You'll also receive discounts on books, updates on new releases, and fun history tidbits along the way!

To claim your free book, visit this link:

https://BookHip.com/MCRMCST

ALLURING... FASCINATING... AND MYSTERIOUS.

**The Seven Wonders of the Ancient World** still reach out to us, with stories waiting to be told.

From the **Hanging Gardens of Babylon** to the **Great Pyramid of Egypt**, each of The Seven Wonders Novels takes you into an adventure of history, mystery, and romance.

*NOTE: Each book in The Seven Wonders Novels is a stand-alone story and they can be read in any order.*

Start your adventure through the Seven Wonders of the Ancient World with *Isle of Shadows...*

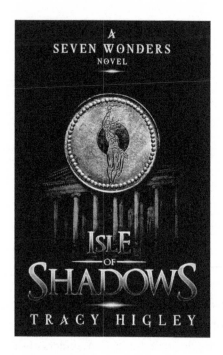

A
SEVEN WONDERS
NOVEL

ISLE
OF
SHADOWS

TRACY HIGLEY

What will freedom cost her?

**Enslaved in an Ancient World of Money and Power, Tessa Dares to be Free.**

**Raised as a courtesan** to wealthy and powerful men, Tessa of Delos serves at the whim of the corrupt politician, Glaucus, on the opulent isle of Rhodes.

**Ten years have passed** since she was forsaken by both the gods and her mother. To survive, Tessa abandons any desire for freedom or love, choosing instead to lock her heart away.

**But when Glaucus meets a violent death,** Tessa grasps at a fragile hope.

**Only she knows of his death.**

**And if she can keep the explosive secret** long enough, she can escape.

**But time is running out.** Another treacherous politician emerges from the shadows, in a bid to seize power over Rhodes.

**And this one is claiming Tessa for himself.**

**What will freedom cost her?**

BUY ISLE OF SHADOWS HERE

# HOW TO HELP THE AUTHOR

I hope you enjoyed *A Time to Love!*

If you're willing to help, I would really appreciate a review on Amazon or Barnes and Noble.

**More than anything else, reviews help authors spread the word about their books.**

It doesn't have to be long or eloquent – just a few lines letting people know how the book made you feel.

Thank so much!

BOOKS BY TRACY HIGLEY

**The Seven Wonders Novels:**
Isle of Shadows
Pyramid of Secrets
Guardian of the Flame
Garden of Madness
So Shines the Night

**The Time Travel Journals of Sahara Aldridge:**
A Time to Seek
A Time to Weep
A Time to Love

**The Books of Babylon:**
Chasing Babylon
Fallen from Babel

**The Lost Cities Novels:**
Petra: City in Stone
Pompeii: City on Fire

**The Coming of the King Saga:**
The Queen's Handmaid
The Incense Road

**Standalone Books and Short Stories:**
Awakening
The Ark Builder's Wife
Dressed to the Nines

Broken Pieces
Rescued: An Allegory

Made in the USA
Coppell, TX
12 May 2022

77712341R00184